THE

FIRST

HUSBAND

BOOKS BY ELISABETH CARPENTER

ELISABETH
CARPENTER

THE

FIRST

HUSBAND

bookouture

Published by Bookouture in 2025

An imprint of Storyfire Ltd.
Carmelite House
50 Victoria Embankment
London EC4Y 0DZ

www.bookouture.com

The authorised representative in the EEA is Hachette Ireland
8 Castlecourt Centre
Dublin 15 D15 XTP3
Ireland
(email: info@hbgi.ie)

ISBN: 978-1-83525-785-2
eBook ISBN: 978-1-83525-784-5

To my beautiful granddaughter, Charlotte.

ONE

NOW

Two days until the wedding

I have visited Lakeside Cottage only twice since that night almost eight years ago. It looks quite different to how it was then. Now, it has a white wooden veranda spanning the front and the oak trees each side are taller than the roof. The edge of Lake Windermere is just fifteen metres away. The place is picture perfect; the light grey stone walls are accented with pretty flowers in the window boxes and yellow and red roses around the doorframe.

But if it were up to me, I'd never step foot in this place again.

'What's this, Mummy?' My son Noah bends to pick up a pebble. 'What's this picture?'

He passes me the cold wet stone.

'It's a fossil. Looks like it was a leaf.' I pass it back to him. 'You're holding history in your hand. It's millions of years old, you know.'

'Wow!' His chubby little fingers sweep gently across the stone's surface. 'Like Grandad.'

'Don't let him hear you say that.'

I laugh, but it's lost on Noah because he's only three years old. Plus, my dad's always going on about how old he feels, so Noah's not far wrong.

We're standing on the bank of the narrowest part of the lake. The water's so still today; there's barely a breeze. My shoulders stiffen and my spine tingles when I think about what might be below it. About *who* might be below it.

Almost eight years ago to the day.

'Noah!' shouts Matt, as our little boy steps a little too close to water's edge. 'Stop!'

I leap to Noah's side.

'Sorry. I was miles away.' I pick up Noah and drop him next to his new football. He doesn't complain, bless him. 'You made it sound as though a crocodile was about to eat him.'

Noah's head shoots up. '*Coccodile?*'

'Leah' – Matt's taking our bags out the car – 'you shouldn't let him get too close. He can't swim.'

'I'm literally right next to him.'

'I know,' he says. 'Sorry. I just worry.'

I didn't think Matt would be as hands-on as a father as he is with Noah and, honestly, it's great.

Matt unlocks the door to the house, dumps the bags in the hallway, and heads towards us.

'Let's get you inside, little man.' He holds out his hand and Noah takes it. 'You're covered in mud.'

'It'll do him good,' I say, though I've no idea if it will. I often find myself coming out with phrases my mother said to my brother and me when we were children. 'I'm just kidding,' I add. 'You don't know what's in mud these days.'

'I'll get him cleaned up,' says Matt, 'if you take up the bags.'

'Deal.' My phone's vibrating in my pocket. 'Ah, it's my brother. I'll just take this in case they've missed the turning.'

'Hey, Jake,' I say. 'What's your ETA?'

'ETA?' he says, laughing. 'Joined the army, now, have you?'

'Yes, very funny.'

'You couldn't join the army anyway. You hate flying.'

'Thanks for the reminder. On my wedding weekend as well. Our honeymoon is on Monday and I'm trying not to think about the plane.'

'Sorry, sis. You'll be fine. Have a pre-flight glass of fizz. That'll help.'

'Turn off the radio,' Katherine says in the background. *'I want to hear Leah, too. Put it on speaker.'*

I *hate* being on speaker.

Jake flicks off his car radio and I hear the rattle as he places his phone on the dash.

'Oh my Godddddd, Leah!' Katherine shrieks. 'Are you excited? I'm so excited! I've got us some nibbles for tonight. I know you just wanted a quiet night tonight to settle in, but seeing as there's two days to go till the wedding, and you've already had your hen weekend, I thought us girls could get a little tipsy tonight instead of Saturday night so you don't feel ropey on the big day.'

My mind takes a few seconds to compute all the information.

'Tipsy? Ropey? Are you all right, Katherine?'

'Oh,' she says. 'I thought your dad or Matt's parents might be listening.'

'I'm the one on speaker, not you. But I would love to get pissed with you tonight, so I don't feel like shit on my wedding day.'

Katherine laughs, and I glance behind guiltily, but Matt has taken Noah upstairs to the shower by the sounds of it.

'Yeah,' she says. 'That's what I meant.'

'I know.'

'Satnav is saying we're about half an hour away, so don't start on the cocktails without me.'

'It's only just gone midday, so you don't have to worry about that.'

'I've had a hell of a week; I'm counting down the minutes. See you soon! Jake says bye.'

'I'm literally right here,' he says. 'See you soon, Leah.'

At least Jake sounds in good spirits. He's been up and down since our mum passed away almost two years ago. Katherine has been doing her best to distract him: they've had at least three once-in-a-lifetime holidays this year alone.

Mum's death has been difficult for me, too, but Noah has been a wonderful distraction. He has her eyes, and her thoughtful and kind nature. It catches me off guard sometimes, and I feel a jolt of pain in my heart that she isn't going to be here for my wedding day. It's why I need to keep busy all the time. It will no doubt catch up with me, the grief.

'Marry in May and rue the day,' is what she used to say. She was overly cautious (and superstitious) about everything.

I head into the house, trying to ignore my sense of dread. It's not as though I haven't been here since it happened. The inside looks so different now, too. It's been totally updated. Once clad in oppressive walnut, the walls are now brilliant white with carefully curated art that hangs on every wall. Matt's parents hired the *best people*, naturally.

While Noah and Matt are upstairs – I can hear Noah's excited footsteps as he tears along the landing – I head into my favourite room: the snug. There's only a small window, so I flick on the two lamps either side of the huge inglenook fireplace to make it feel cosier. I flop down onto the squishy sofa opposite. It's amazing how tiring travelling can be, even as a passenger.

I close my eyes and let my head sink into the soft corduroy.

Eight years ago, almost to the day since it happened under this very roof at Matt's parents' holiday home. And now I'm getting married at the same place where my first husband disappeared.

Callum.

I haven't said his name out loud for a long time.

I can't stop that nagging feeling that my mother's warnings might become a reality.

* * *

Noah's having a nap downstairs on one of the settees in the main living room, snuggled under his favourite blanket, his cheeks rosy. It's a bad time, given it's six p.m. My dad should be here soon, and he's offered to babysit while Katherine and I have drinks on the veranda. He loves spending time with his grandson, but I hope he's not too perturbed that Noah will be awake later than usual. Not that he'd ever show it.

Matt and my brother are heading into the village to the small bar that Matt's parents own. Olivia and Greg don't own the whole town, but it feels that way sometimes, the amount of clout they have around here. It's a bit intimidating. Especially as my own business has taken me almost six years to get to where it is now. It certainly wasn't handed to *me* on a plate. (*Stop it, Leah.*)

I'm almost 'party' ready. Even though we're staying at the house, and even though it's only Katherine and me, I like to have at least some lip gloss on, and concealer to banish the shadows from under my eyes. Noah is usually a great sleeper, but he becomes unsettled when he's out of his usual routine; these past few days have been filled with pre-wedding panic, even though I've not had to organise much. At least I'll be on hand if Noah gets too much for Dad.

Matt's on his phone. I sit next to him to see what's caught his attention this time. He's scrolling through pictures of the lake he took earlier.

'They're lovely,' I say. 'Very good composition on that one.'

I sound like I know what I'm talking about.

'Just picking one for Insta,' he says. 'What's the point of being here if no one knows about it?' He glances at my horrified expression. 'I'm just kidding.' He takes my hand and kisses it. 'As if I'd post anything that might suggest our location.'

I supress the shudder that always washes over me when I think about his ex, Tania. It's been years since they were together, but it feels as though she's always there, lurking in the background. Her actions haven't helped at all with that feeling. Soon after Matt announced my pregnancy to the world (i.e. Facebook), the stalking began. It was a living nightmare. The landline would ring at all hours of the day and night; taxis and takeaways were sent to our house at random hours in the early morning. It left me anxious for months, if not years.

We didn't have proof it was actually her, though. Not enough to get a restraining order. Sometimes, I think she'll never leave us alone. We were in London last year when Matt tagged our arrival on his Facebook page. The next day, he posted a picture of us in the queue at Madame Tussauds. Thirty minutes later, there she was jogging past in her running gear. The surprise on her face was almost believable. What a coincidence. 'Yeah, right,' Matt had said when she jogged away. 'Over two hundred miles from home.' He hasn't posted our whereabouts since. He rarely posts anything on social media, these days. Since Noah was born, Matt's become protective over us, his little family.

'I might put a picture on the family WhatsApp. It'll be nice for the people who can't be here to see the lovely view.'

'We don't want to rub their noses in it, Matt.'

'I know. But you didn't want a big wedding – neither did I, really – and I feel bad some of my aunts and uncles can't be here.'

'When did you last see them, anyway?' I say with a smile.

'Good point.' He opens Instagram and scrolls through, idly.

'Any new followers?' I say. 'Not that Tania would ever use her real name.'

'No new requests. Not that I ever post anything on there. And that's fine by me. I'd rather under-share than over. I've learned from my mistakes.' His gaze has wandered to the window. 'I do feel bad about how I ended things with her...'

Contrary to what he says, Matt *can* sometimes be guilty of oversharing.

I stroke the side of his face.

'That's because you're a nice person. We haven't heard from her for months now. Enjoy the peace.' I hop off the bed. 'I'm meeting Katherine in the kitchen in five minutes.' I bend down to kiss him. 'I'd better get going if I don't want to be late.'

He laughs. 'Have a lovely time. Get as drunk as you want – we have plenty of babysitters on hand tomorrow.'

'God, I daren't.' I smooth my freshly straightened hair that's already showing a slight halo of frizz. 'I can't take hangovers these days. Especially since I had Noah. I'm getting old.'

'Thirty-eight in a few days. Positively ancient. You'd better make the most of it. You'll be drawing your pension before you know it.'

'Ha. At least we'll be on our honeymoon by then.'

'I'll see you before you head out,' he says, and I pause to look at him from the doorway. He's still horizontal, still scrolling on his phone. He's always on that thing. My first husband Callum was constantly on his phone, too, but for totally different reasons.

I hate that I'm thinking about him right now. It's because we're here and the ghosts of what happened still linger. Even though he's dead, he's having an impact on me.

I'm reading too much into things, as usual. There's nothing sinister about this house.

Everything's going to be fine. Isn't it?

TWO

EIGHT YEARS AGO

Thirty-two hours before Callum's disappearance

I slam the boot shut and lug my weekend suitcase towards the front door where Matt and Callum are hugging hello.

'Happy Birthday, Leah!' Matt welcomes me as though we haven't seen each other for years. 'Long time, no see!'

I give him a quick hug, and Tania appears at Matt's side, hands clasped together and a pleasant smile as though she's lady of the manor.

'Thanks, Matt,' I say. 'But it hasn't been that long.'

'It's been months!' he says. 'But I understand you've been busy with your new baby. It's lucky your birthday landed on a bank holiday weekend.'

He means my own business, not an actual child. It's a sore point between Callum and me – the children thing. Surely Matt knows this. I wanted to start trying for a baby three years ago – twelve months after we married – but Callum's been pushing the date further and further away. It's almost like torture.

'Baby?' Tania's positively beaming. 'Congratulations! What a wonderful birthday present!'

She knows full well we don't have a child and nor am I pregnant. The whole world would know if that were the case.

'Hey, Tania,' I add, mirroring the same saccharin smile, ignoring her deliberate confusion. I honestly have no idea why she's being like this. When we saw each other a few months ago, she was quiet, but not unkind. 'You're looking well.'

Her smile drops.

'What do you mean by that?' she asks, throwing daggers at me with her eyes.

Matt glances at her.

'What are you talking about, Tania?' he asks dismissively. 'Leah literally said you looked well.'

'We all know what that means,' she says quietly.

'You're glowing,' I say quickly. 'I mean it. I love your shirt; it really brings out your eyes.' She is stunning. Her almost black eyes are striking against her white-blonde hair that's silky smooth and styled in giant waves; her skin is almost iridescent. How can someone who looks so perfect feel so insecure? It's not a great start. Is it too late to turn around and go home? Tension was high between Callum and me on the drive up here. It's put me on edge, and I fear Tania might think my prickliness is due to her presence.

'Thanks, Leah.' Her smile is small this time and I feel awful for hurting her feelings.

'You look positively ravishing, Tania,' says Callum, stepping in front of me to kiss her cheek. 'And you smell divine too.'

Ravishing? Divine?

If Matt is bothered by Callum's fawning over his girlfriend, he's doing a great job of hiding it.

Tania reaches over to take my case.

'I'll show you to your room, Leah.'

Tania steps inside, and Callum gives me a wink as I follow.

He knows how to make people feel good even if it's not always a hundred per cent genuine; his heart's in the right place.

'Matt wanted you to have the lake view,' Tania says as we head up the stairs, 'seeing as it's your birthday.'

'That's nice of him.'

She places my bag on the bed.

'You're one of his best friends.' She sits on the bed. 'He talks about you *all* the time.' She smiles and I can't tell if it's a mask or if it's sincere. A bit like Callum. 'And before you say anything, I'm not exaggerating.'

'That's nice,' I say again, absently. I daren't say anything that might be perceived as a slight.

'You're lucky.' She examines her glossy nails. 'Callum wants this weekend to be perfect for you, too. You and he are relationship goals. How long have you been together?'

'Ten years.'

I thought she'd have known that. Tania and Matt have been together for two years. But this is the most she's taken an interest in my life in all that time.

'Wow,' she says. 'Callum loves you so much.'

'I know.'

She is the last person I'd confide in. I unzip my bag and take out my outfits for tonight and tomorrow night.

'You won't need both of those,' says Tania. 'It's casual dress tonight.' There's a slight smirk on her lips. 'Didn't Matt tell you?'

'Casual dress on my actual birthday night? I thought there were going to be loads of people coming.'

'Callum said the idea of a room full of people as a surprise party was your worst nightmare.' Her hand goes to her mouth. 'Sorry. I wasn't meant to say anything. Oops!'

I try to hide my disappointment, but I can't. I know my parents aren't able to make it, but I thought Callum would've at least invited *some* of my friends. Perhaps he thought it would be inappropriate, given my mum's diagnosis, and he's probably right. It won't be the same without them and Mum hates missing out on a swanky party.

'Don't worry, Leah,' says Tania. 'Matt has lots lined up for you. A surprise tonight, and board games tomorrow—'

'Board games?'

Holy shit. I've just turned thirty, not thirteen.

'Matt's really into them,' she says, 'isn't he?'

'I guess.'

'I thought he must've got it from you, the time he took curating them.'

'Maybe when we were students.' I hang my red jumpsuit and sparkly black dress in the wardrobe, then flop down onto the bed next to Tania. The image of champagne and canapes and mingling with friends I haven't seen for years vanishes from my mind – the one weekend of putting any worries and problems aside and pretending to be someone glamourous. 'What else is planned?' I can't hide the gloom in my voice this time.

'A hike tomorrow, dinner tomorrow night.' She pauses. 'Oh, poor Leah. Look at your face.' She sticks out her bottom lip and pats my hand. 'I knew you would want a bit more sparkle, but Callum said you wouldn't want a fuss. I insisted on candles tonight, though. And I'm tasked with decorating the table.'

'Thanks, Tania.'

'It must be hard enough as it is, turning thirty.' She tilts her head. 'I can't imagine being that old.'

My mouth drops open, but before I can reply to twenty-five-year-old Tania, the sound of footsteps on the gravel outside triggers her to jump off the bed and head to the window. She takes her phone out of her back pocket as it vibrates.

'Message from Matt. They're just off to get more booze.' She turns and tilts her head again. 'You look like you need it.'

She sits next to me, still with her phone in her hand, and opens an app. A photo of Matt's head is moving along a map.

'It's for safety, really,' she says. 'I'd hate to think of anything bad happening to him.' She touches his face on the screen. 'I wouldn't be able to live without him. He's my world.'

'Does he track you, too?'

'I feel safer knowing he can see where I am.' She looks at me, frowning. 'You should do the same with Callum.'

'Nah,' I say. 'And he doesn't need to know my location all the time, either. It's not as though we go anywhere exciting.'

She narrows her eyes.

'You might regret that,' she says, 'if anything bad were to happen to him.'

I stand and head to the door.

'Come on,' I say. 'Maybe you can show me around.'

She glances at her phone before putting it back in her pocket.

'OK. I suppose they won't get up to anything if they're together. Let's get some prosecco.'

'I think you need it more than I do, Tania,' I say as we head down the stairs. 'You sound like you need to relax.'

Her voice is quiet when she says, 'I think you might be right.'

THREE

NOW

Two days until the wedding

We're sitting outside on the veranda that looks out onto the quiet, still lake. It might be May, but there's a chill in the air. A small chiminea offers us warmth from its metal stand, and we're sipping red wine from beautifully intricate glasses. It's all very decadent for a Friday evening.

'So,' says Katherine, wrapping a blanket around her shoulders, 'who else is yet to arrive?'

Our peaceful set-up is interrupted by Matt and my brother Jake almost falling out of the cottage door. They make so much noise for only two people. They've must've already had a few drinks after Dad took Noah up for his bath.

'Don't get into trouble,' says Katherine. 'Jake, look after Matt. You know what a lightweight he is.'

'Hey,' Matt protests while tripping over a small twig. 'Yeah, Jake. Look after me, mate. Don't want to fall into that lake after —' He glances at me. 'Oh, God. Sorry. I didn't mean to say that – it just came out.'

I hold a hand up. *It's OK.* Callum was Matt's best friend; I know he misses him too. He wouldn't be so flippant as to joke about his death.

I predict that it won't be a long night out for them, judging from Matt's behaviour. It must be nerves combined with the fact he's been *eating clean* for the past year, as well as training for a half-marathon next month. He's almost too healthy to drink alcohol.

'Take care, you two,' I yell as they head off towards the main road, Jake's arm resting on Matt's shoulders to steady him.

I grab my phone, open Life360 to check he has his mobile, which he does, of course. It's not like I'm spying on him or anything. We have it on each other's. If I don't want to be tracked, then I just switch off my location. Simple. It's peace of mind. I don't want to lose anyone again.

Katherine and I watch Matt and Jake disappear from view, heading up into the thick cluster of trees that lead to the precarious footpath at road level. I pray that Matt gets there in one piece. He's usually so sensible but it'll be good for him to let off a bit of steam. He's been so stressed that everything will be perfect this weekend. Though, thankfully, his mum Olivia has taken over—I mean taken *care of* everything. Don't get me wrong, she's lovely. And it's nice to be looked after now my mum isn't here.

I immediately feel a pang of sadness when I think of her. I blink to stop the tears, but it's inevitable that she'll be at the forefront of my mind in the run-up to my wedding.

I grab a blanket from the pile in the wicker basket. Olivia thinks of everything.

'Matt's parents, Olivia and Greg, are arriving in the morning.' I drape the blanket over my lap. 'A couple of Matt's friends are staying at the hotel up the road.'

'Eh?' Katherine is already showing the signs of one glass of wine. 'Did I ask something? Or are you trying to read my mind?'

I laugh. 'You asked before those two came out' – I nod to the distance – 'who else was yet to arrive at the cottage. Matt's parents.'

'You've a better memory than I have. Gosh, I must be a gold-fish. Not a good look for a lawyer.' She takes another sip and holds up an index finger. 'Right. And I was about to say that it's a very intimate wedding.' She grabs a handful of nuts and rests them in her cradled hand before picking out one of the big ones. 'Even compared to ours, and especially compared to...' She pops the nut in her mouth and looks out onto the lake. Perhaps she's imagining Callum's body in some dark unseen place at the bottom. I shiver as the image flashes in my mind. Why the hell am I doing this to myself? 'I couldn't live here,' she says, shiver-ing, too.

I take a sharp intake of breath.

'I...'

'God, sorry, Leah. It's the wine. And I'm so tired from the journey.'

'It's OK.'

Why did Matt and I let Olivia persuade us to have the wedding here? She was relentless about it. *Why would you pay ten thousand pounds for a venue miles away* (we weren't even considering that); *You can relax more at our cottage, I'll take care of everything; you'll be waited on. You won't have to think about boring cooking or cleaning for a whole weekend.*

But anyway. We're here, now. Katherine and I had agreed to not talk about Callum this weekend. I didn't want to dredge it all up, even though we're here at the same place we were for my thirtieth birthday on the night he disappeared. The same cold evening, the same cloudless sky. But two of those people with us that night aren't here today.

I shouldn't have thought the word *dredge*.

But it's not as though we've never talked about him before now. When he first went missing, I expected him to walk through the door at any moment; first at Matt's parents' cottage, then at our home in Manchester. It took several months for me and those around us to accept that he died the night he went missing. I sold our house two years after and bought a small terrace. A place I could call my very own. Until Matt and I bought a place together five years ago. I look fondly on the time I had a year truly in my own space, but I don't yearn for that time again.

I take a sip of wine. Let the warmth wash over me.

'It's like I was a totally different person, back then,' I say, breaking the silence. 'I relied too much on Callum and then' – I wave my hand – 'he was here one minute and gone the next. I just...'

'I still can't forgive him for leaving you.' She reaches over and squeezes my hand. 'What the hell was he thinking, going into the lake like that?'

'I don't know.' The tears begin tumbling out. I shouldn't be crying over Callum three days before my wedding. 'We don't even know that he did... Not for sure.'

'I'm so sorry, Leah. I didn't mean to make you cry. I'm sorry. It should be a happy time, and here I am putting a downer on everything.'

'You're not.' I dab my cheeks with my sleeve. 'It's fine. You won't be the first person to talk about Callum this weekend, I'm sure. Matt's friends were Callum's friends, too. Callum was Jake's brother-in-law. It's all so...'

'It's so sad. And just so awful that someone could just vanish like that. I know he had his troubles and everything...'

A fresh set of tears fall down my face.

'Shit, I'm doing it again. I'm sorry, Leah. Let's change the subject.'

'I never brought up the subject.'

She reaches over, takes my hand in hers, and gives it a gentle squeeze.

'God, do you hate me? I'd hate me if I were you. I've got such a big mouth. There's no filter between my brain and my lips. Jake used to think it was endearing and now he must be sick of it after twelve years of being with me.'

'I'm sure he isn't.' With my free hand, I wipe my face again. 'He loves you so much.'

'Well, I know that.' She lets go and tightens her blanket, pushing it up to her chin. 'But I don't know if he's actually *in* love with me. He wants children, I'm sure of it.'

'He won't have changed his mind without talking to you.'

This is a lie, and I feel terrible for it. He *has* talked to me about it. We talk on the phone every Sunday – we have done since they moved to Kent for Katherine's job. Since Noah was born, Jake's been trying to bury his desire to have a child; but he and Katherine had decided before they got married that being parents wasn't on either of their agendas. It feels like I'm concealing a betrayal, it feels so huge. I hate keeping things from Katherine and I'm an awful liar; she can always tell by my rosy cheeks and downward gaze. I've known her for so long, I'd be devastated if she and my brother were to split up. Even though we don't see each other often, we keep in touch every day via WhatsApp. I talk to her more than I do my own brother.

'I guess.' She sighs and leans back into the wicker chair. If she's seen anything in my expression, then she's ignoring it. 'Anyway, enough of this depressing talk.' She grabs the stem of her glass and lifts it from the table. 'What do you think the chances are of Tania making an appearance this weekend?'

'And *that's* not depressing?' I tilt my head to the side and raise my eyebrows.

'Less depressing than my husband leaving me to have a hundred children.' She smiles with one side of her mouth. 'And this might be the only chance you and I have to talk alone.'

'It's been years since we heard anything from her. I'm hoping that Tania will have moved on. She and Matt were only together for two years. It's not as though they were going to get married, is it?'

She presses her lips together and shrugs.

'What aren't you telling me?'

'That weekend...' She places her glass on the table again and leans forward. 'Tania said she found an engagement ring in Matt's bag before they set off. She was sure he was going to propose that weekend.'

'What?' I jolt back against the chair. 'Propose? On my birthday weekend?'

'You wouldn't have minded that, would you? It was years before you and Matt got together.'

'I wouldn't have minded back then.' I twist the engagement ring on my finger suddenly wondering if he used the same ring. He wouldn't be as thoughtless as to do that, would he? I know he's chilled about most things, but that's a step too far. 'He's never once mentioned he was going to propose to her. When did she tell you about it?'

What else has Matt kept from me? Does he still talk to her – is that why he's always attached to his phone? Has the idea of Tania stalking him been a rouse, a cover-up of their interactions?

God, this place is getting to me. I wouldn't normally entertain such outlandish thoughts.

'The first day we arrived,' says Katherine. 'The Saturday. I think she said she saw it in his weekend bag before they set off. And then everything changed, didn't it? Everything stopped because of Callum disappearing. Matt obviously didn't get the chance to propose. To be honest, I don't think she was telling the truth. She was young and in love and Matt barely paid her any attention that weekend from what I can remember.'

Katherine looks out onto the lake again, and I know what she's thinking.

Is Callum's body still in there? If it is at all...

'I was never that close to Tania.' I run my finger around the rim of my glass. 'She and Matt never seemed suited. She was so...'

'Energetic,' she finishes. 'And Matt's so relaxed, he's practically in a coma.' She raises a palm. 'Just kidding.'

'I like that he's like that. Compared to...'

A breeze lifts the pile of paper napkins and discards them onto the floor. We leap off our chairs to collect them.

'Shall we go inside? It's a bit too chilly out here.' Katherine picks up the bowl of peanuts and the glasses. 'And a little creepy.'

She's right. The darkness, the breeze, and the idea that my dead husband's body might be in that lake has kept me awake at night. Police searched it for over a week, but there was no trace of Callum in that lake, even though some of his belongings were found by the edge. They searched the surrounding area thoroughly, but there are so many inaccessible areas around here: underwater pockets; dense shrubland; craggy mountains if he ventured further. Some people believe he's still alive – his mother being one of them. Jennie clings to the hope that Callum is still out there. Perhaps he's lost his memory and that's why he hasn't been in contact. It's the not knowing that feeds different theories, multiple stories; only a few have happy endings.

I lead the way to the front door, holding it open for Katherine.

Thankfully, in the beautiful cosy snug, the fire is still going. Only just, but it's still alight. I take a log from the hearth and place it on the dying flame, watching as the edges start to catch. I didn't realise how cold I was until now and the heat is delicious.

'I'll just go and check on Dad and Noah,' I say. 'It's suspiciously quiet up there. Usually, Noah can't sleep till late if he's somewhere strange.'

'But it's his grandparents' house.' Katherine flops onto the sofa. 'Aren't you always here?' She blinks, shakes her head. 'Sorry, sorry.'

I turn to smile at her before heading towards the stairs.

Of course she'd think that. Any normal person would assume we'd spend weekends here, summer holidays, taking advantage of such a beautiful house. But, as this place is only one of their holiday homes, Olivia and Greg can distance them-selves from events that went on eight years ago. It's not as though Callum was murdered inside, is it?

I creep along the first-floor landing. It's eerily quiet, even with the unforgiving landing light. I flick on the lamp on the occasional table between rooms and turn off the main light. The click of the switch is so loud in the silence.

I push open the bedroom door. Noah and Dad are fast asleep next to each other. Dad is still wearing his glasses, *The Tiger That Came to Tea* book is open and resting on his chest. I tiptoe around, scoop Noah into my arms and place him on the other bed, pulling the covers around his shoulders. Dad is a miracle worker when it comes to putting Noah to bed. I kiss Noah on the cheek before turning to gently take off Dad's glasses and place them on the bedside cabinet between the two beds. I walk lightly out the room and down the stairs.

In the snug, I sink into the plush charcoal grey sofa cushions next to Katherine. Everything in this house is designed for comfort. Well, except for the state-of-the-art kitchen. Naturally.

'When did you say Matt's parents were coming?' asks Katherine, tucking her feet under herself.

'Tomorrow morning. Hopefully they haven't had one of their arguments. His dad gets really stressed about big occa-sions, but I'm praying they're getting along. Apparently, they've hired a Michelin-starred chef to cook our evening meal tomorrow.'

'What?' Katherine sits straighter.

Katherine earns six figures but is still the same frugal northerner she's been since university.

'That's right. And I told them you're vegetarian, don't worry.'

'So, I'm invited?' Her eyes are even wider now.

I reach over to hug her.

'You're so cute. Of course you're invited.' I put a blanket over both our laps – you can never be too warm on a cold night. 'I'm so glad my brother met you.'

'Me too.'

The newly laid log crackles loudly and we stare into the growing flame in silence.

Katherine and Jake were here the night Callum disappeared. So were Tania and Matt. The two people who aren't here now – Tania and Callum – are the ones I feel most present. It's almost like they're watching over me.

'What are you thinking about?' Katherine asks.

'You sound like a girl,' I say, laughing.

'I *am* a girl.' She nudges me gently. 'You say it as though there's something wrong with it.'

'Just kidding.'

Katherine is a very serious person, sometimes.

'Shall we put some music on?' I say. 'I've created a pre-wedding playlist.'

I select the first, and Katherine groans as a Taylor Swift song plays.

'You're never going to grow up, are you, Leah?'

I stand and take her by the hands to drag her up to dance.

'Now, why would I want to go and do that?'

* * *

Seven songs – we've just put on 'Wannabe' by The Spice Girls – and two glasses of wine later, Katherine stands to pause the stereo.

'Hey.' I laugh. 'Was my singing that bad?'

'What was that?'

'I didn't hear anything.'

'I heard banging. Was it out the front?'

Bang, bang.

Like a fist on a door.

'I hear it, too,' I say. 'At least I *think* I hear it. I'm very suggestible.'

'You're very merry.' She takes the wine glass from my hand. 'Let's go investigate.'

'It could be Matt's parents here early.' I follow her out of the snug.

'They wouldn't knock on their own front door,' says Katherine, 'would they?'

The hall is lit by a small lamp on a large, polished wood table. Our steps are almost silent on the beige stone flooring. Shadows cast by the porch light swinging in the wind flash up and down the walls.

Katherine turns the handle of the front door; it slams open with a strong gust of wind.

'Jesus.' She rests a hand on the door frame, sticks out her head and looks left and right. 'There's no one out there.' She slips on my dad's crocs that he's left by the door. I linger at the door as she heads outside. 'God, it's really creepy out here.' She walks along the side of the house. 'I'm sure this veranda wasn't as creaky in the daytime.' She lets out a gasp. 'Did you see that? It looked like the tail of a coat or maybe a scarf.'

'Where are you going? It was probably a leaf or something.' I wrap my cardigan tighter around me. 'You know this is how horror films start.' I step outside in my socks. 'Katherine, it's not worth it.' I spot an empty tin. 'It was probably that beer can that blew against the door – it must've blown in from...'

She turns to go down the right side of the house, disappearing from view.

The trees rustle, hissing like snakes. I look around; the moonlight's reflecting on the lake that's rippling in the wind. It's like something is shaking the ground from below.

I'm still standing at the door, facing the spot where Katherine disappeared. I should go after her. Make sure she's OK. But what's going to happen at – I glance at my watch – how did it get to almost midnight?

I inch forward. It must be the wine sparking my imagination.

A hand rests on my shoulders, and I scream.

I spin round and, of course, it's Katherine.

'No,' she says. 'I can't see anything unusual.'

My heartrate is still over a hundred at least.

'Jesus, Katherine. You scared the hell out of me.'

She rolls her eyes, steps inside and kicks off the crocs. 'All in a day's work.' She brushes imaginary dust from both shoulders. She's trying to make light of it, but I'm spooked and can't get back inside fast enough.

'All right,' I say. 'Calm down, Lara Croft. All you did was circle the house.'

'Which you were too scared to do.'

'I wasn't at all,' I say with a smirk, trying to ignore my unease. 'It just means I haven't had as much wine as you have.'

'I thought this was meant to be a party. A party of two, but a party nonetheless.'

A thud comes from the back of the house and I almost leap into Katherine's arms.

'I knew there was someone out there,' I say.

'You said it was a can of beer.'

'I didn't know you'd heard me say that. And I was trying to be brave.' I grip hold of her hand. 'But it feels as though there's someone spying on us.'

'Why would someone be spying on us? You haven't heard from Tania in years.' She pauses. 'And it's not as though it's an easy house to get to.' Katherine rolls her eyes. She's gone into practical-lawyer mode to make us both feel better. 'I'd be more worried about someone robbing your own house in Manchester now it's empty.' She still has hold of my hand as she leads me through to the kitchen. 'Sorry. I shouldn't say things like that. You have good security at home, haven't you.' The back door is wide open. She stops and I almost walk into her. 'Did you open that?'

A gust of wind runs through the room. A roll of kitchen towel blows off the counter, a champagne flute teeters off the edge of the table until another breeze sends it crashing to the floor.

'We should've seen that coming,' says Katherine. 'We're going to be finding shards for days.' She goes to the pantry, gets out a dustpan and brush, refusing to give into fear.

I, on the other hand, am gripping the back of a chair.

'What's going on?' I murmur. 'I don't want to stay here anymore.'

Katherine crouches to collect the smashed glass.

'We left the front door ajar, that's what's going on. And someone must've done the same to the back door. There's a rational explanation for everything. You're letting your imagination run away with you, Leah.' She looks up. 'Can you get a paper bag or bin liner so I can wrap this up?'

I open the nearest drawer behind me. Placemats. I open the next. My hands are shaking. 'I don't know where anything is.'

'Try under the sink.'

I'm being pathetic. I take out a roll of black bin liners; it takes me a couple of attempts to tear one off.

'Leah, it's OK. It was just the door slamming in the wind,' she says kindly.

'I know.'

'Is there something else worrying you? Is it the wedding? You don't have to go through with it on Sunday.' She pauses to look up. 'Just because you're in his parents' house and everyone you know is arriving tomorrow, doesn't mean you can't back out. Marriage isn't always the answer.'

'Oh God.'

'Really?' Her eyes widen. 'You've changed your mind?'

'No.' My gaze is fixed on the mat at the back door. 'Didn't you notice that when you closed the door?'

Katherine shakes the glass into the bag and wraps it into a ball.

'It's a card.' I bend to pick up the white envelope. 'It's addressed to me.' I look to Katherine as she puts the bag on top of the bin. 'Who's it from?'

'There's only one way to find out,' she says, leaning against the counter, folding her arms.

I run my finger along my name. 'It looks like *his* writing...'

It's exactly the same. But there's no way it can be.

The envelope is tucked in, not sealed. Is someone trying to avoid leaving their DNA by not licking the glue?

'Your hands are shaking,' says Katherine. 'Do you want me to open it?'

I wordlessly pass it to her, watching her face as she slides out the card.

'Ah, it's a congratulations-on-your-wedding card. They obviously know you. But whoever it was must've heard the music we were playing. Assumed there was a party going on and didn't want to interrupt.' Katherine always tries to find a rational explanation.

'But why leave it round the back? It's pitch dark out there.'

Open it, open it.

'Oh,' she says.

She holds up the card: a large black heart with *On Your Wedding* in white cursive script. I take it from her and open it.

My knees buckle.

I grab hold of the kitchen counter, letting the card drop to the floor.

'What is it?' Katherine picks up the card, flips it open. 'Oh. Shit.'

I cover my face with my hands.

It can't be from him. It just can't. He died in the lake. The police were sure of it. There's been no proof of life since the night he left.

But it's his handwriting.

When I close my eyes, I can still see the words.

My darling Leah,

Two days to go. I can't wait to see you on your wedding day. I've missed you so much.

All my love,

Callum

Katherine darts out the back door.

'Who's there?' she shouts. 'This is not bloody funny.'

I slide to the floor, resting my back against a cupboard door, and bring my knees up to my chest. I wrap my arms around them.

This can't be happening. It can't be real. Callum's body was never found, but I feel it in my heart that he's dead. It's been eight years since he walked out of this cottage and never came back. We've all had to grieve, get on with our lives without him.

My stomach is stirring; the acid from the champagne has

gathered in the back of my throat. I stand quickly, lean over the sink to rid my mouth of the unpleasant liquid.

I flush the sink with the tap and watch the water swirl down the plug. I grab a piece of kitchen towel, wipe my mouth and pull out a chair to sit.

Who would be so cruel as to send this?

Katherine still has the card. Was it really Callum's handwriting or was I just imagining it? It's been years since I saw it but I'd recognise his writing anywhere. I still have cards from him in a keepsake box that Matt doesn't know about.

'There's no one outside.' Katherine walks back inside. The wind has tossed her hair all over. 'I would've seen something when I went out the front before. I did a whole circle of the house. Perhaps whoever it was posted it ages ago and we didn't notice. We were on the veranda for over an hour earlier. There was no one else downstairs to notice it.'

'What if it's him, Katherine?'

She pulls out a chair and sits next to me on the floor. She opens the card again.

'It can't be him, can it?' she says. 'It's impossible.' She brings the card closer to her face. 'My eyesight's getting worse.' She passes the card to me. 'Does it look like his handwriting? Though, why am I asking that?'

'Because it might be from someone who was close to him.'

She looks at me, frowning.

'What?' I say. 'Do you think it's from someone we know?'

'No... I don't know. Do you think we should tell the police?'

'That someone is playing a cruel prank?'

'But they never found the body. What if he's been in hiding all these years? Especially with what came out about...'

'No.' I squeeze my hands together to stop them from shaking. 'He wouldn't have left me to deal with all of that mess alone.'

'No.' Katherine stands. 'You're right. As if he wouldn't have been seen by someone in all this time. Especially with those appeals his mum did.'

'Who would do this to me?' I try to stand, but my legs are still shaking. Katherine takes hold of my hands and yanks me up. 'Whoever it is knows we're here, and that I'm getting married. I know I thought Matt was exaggerating before, but what if it's Tania?'

'Hmm. I doubt it. She's with that guy, now. What's his name? I saw her in town the other week when we were visiting your dad. I'm sure I told you.'

'No, you didn't. She's back in Manchester?'

'I didn't talk to her. I just saw her briefly in the distance. She was all over this man. Proper flash, he was. In a shaved head, boy-band way. Had his sunglasses on even though it was rain-ing. She had a massive diamond on her left hand too.'

'How did you notice all of that, *briefly*?'

'Like, it's literally my job to read people, to be perceptive. She's still disgustingly gorgeous as well.'

'Don't tell me that,' I groan.

'You're beautiful, too, Leah.'

'I need a brandy or something.'

'God, yeah.' She holds up the card. 'What are we going to do with this?'

I take it from her and walk through to the snug, bending to put it into the zipped section of my handbag. I dash upstairs to check on Noah, who's still sleeping soundly, thank God.

Back downstairs, I leave the door to the snug slightly ajar.

'I'm going to try to forget about it for now. Let's put *Dirty Dancing* on.'

She groans but selects it from the ton of DVDs Matt's parents have collected for their Airbnb guests.

'Gosh,' she says, sliding it in the DVD player. 'I haven't used one of these machines since 2010.'

After Katherine has topped up our drinks, we settle next to

each other on the sofa, a thickly knitted blanket over both our laps. But the night has been spoiled. The card seems to be calling me from my bag.

There is no way I'm going to be able to forget about that. And whoever sent it knows this. Whoever sent that card knows me only too well.

FOUR

Katherine and I are half asleep by the time Matt and Jake almost crash through the front door. They're hushing and shushing each other more loudly than if they were talking normally.

'For God's sake.' Katherine stands and her half of the blanket falls to the floor.

I grudgingly stand. I hate seeing Matt drunk, especially now I feel sober after barely touching my wine since we found the card.

I get to the hall to see Matt sitting on the floor trying to pull a trainer off with little success. Jake crawls towards him, already having deposited his shoes and jacket on the bottom of the stairs. He takes hold of Matt's trainer and almost drags him along the floor. Finally, after several metres, Jake yanks it off.

The pair of them are laughing so hard they can barely breathe. If I hadn't just received a message from the dead, I would've found it funny, too. I glance at Katherine, and she seems to be feeling the same way I do, given the way her lips are pressed together, and her arms are folded.

'How much could you two have drunk in three hours?' she asks sternly.

'Three hours?' Jake narrows his eyes as he looks at the over-sized clock on the wall. 'We've been gone for at least five. It's almost one in the morning.'

'Is it?' Katherine and I say it at the same time.

'Oh,' she says. 'We must've fallen asleep.' She looks at me. 'Sorry, Leah. I'm shit at creating memorable parties. Some Matron of Honour I am.'

I stand close to her and link my arm through hers.

'It wasn't *you* who spoiled it,' I say quietly.

There's no way I can tell Matt and Jake about the card given the state they're in. They'll never remember it by morning.

'I need another drink.' Jake stands and holds out his hand for Matt to grab hold of.

'Bloody hell,' says Katherine. 'I'm going to bed. If that's OK with you, Leah?'

'Definitely. Me too. I don't want to be a witness to what happens next with these two. You go on ahead.'

I pop back into the snug for my handbag. I reach in to feel the card and I'm so tempted to throw it onto the embers of the fire.

'Goodnight, then,' I shout into the kitchen where Matt is rooting through his parents' drinks cupboard.

Neither of them have heard me; they're far too busy. To be honest I doubt they even registered mine and Katherine's presence, but she's sure to remind them in the morning. And it's not as though this is a regular occurrence. They're usually quite sensible.

Upstairs, I peek my head around the door to the room Dad and Noah are sharing. Both fast asleep. Dad has moved the beds closer together and now his arm is resting on Noah's bed next to him. I so want to go and kiss my little boy's cheeks. He looks like an angel with his rosy cheeks and long eyelashes.

I pull the door closed. How those two can sleep through all the commotion of tonight, I don't know. In the large guestroom, I take out my phone and place my handbag on the bottom of the large oak wardrobe. I don't want to scrutinise the card, the meaning of the picture on the front, which I barely glanced at before. Or investigate the handwriting. My head is pounding, and I just want to forget all about it.

I close the bedroom door. I'm half-hoping that Matt will fall asleep downstairs or have the wherewithal to use the spare guestroom because I really don't fancy sharing a bed with him in that state, and I didn't bring my earplugs because I like to be able to hear if Noah needs me.

In the bathroom, I change into my pyjamas and remove what make-up remains with a cleansing wipe, not having the energy for my usual routine. A quick slap of moisturiser and a brush of my teeth and I'm done. This is not what I was expecting on my wedding weekend. No lounging in front of the fire with a margarita, reminiscing about how Matt and I met.

I smile when I remember his being the first face I saw when I walked into our halls of residence kitchen. There were meant to be six of us – each with our own room that was equipped with a sink, then a shared kitchen/living area and bathroom. My parents were lingering after I'd deposited my last bag from the car onto my unmade bed.

'Oh, we're so proud of you, Leah,' said Mum. 'We didn't have the same opportunities you have.'

'We don't have the brains Leah has, Marion,' said Dad.

'Speak for yourself,' said Mum.

God, they were sooo embarrassing. It took a full five minutes for me to garner the courage after they'd left to walk into the shared kitchen.

'Hey,' I said, hovering at the door watching this tall, slim, blond guy opening and shutting empty cupboards. The contents of his many carrier bags had spilled out onto the dining table (Pot Noodles, Super Noodles, about three different types of pasta, about seven jars of green and red pesto). 'I'm Leah.'

He turned around and I almost gasped. He was, like, proper good-looking. He had the kind of skin that looked expensive: tanned, smooth, glowing. His family were definitely the type who took several holidays a year. His jeans looked *ironed*. He returned my gaze, and we didn't speak for a whole ten minutes. Well, in reality it was only a few seconds.

'Hey,' he said eventually. 'Er... Hi... I...' He ran a hand through his hair. 'Sorry.' He turned around again. 'We only have one cupboard each,' he said. 'How the hell is that going to work?'

'Uhm.' I had only one carrier bag of food and, to be honest, I was pretty grateful and touched by my dad having bought it for me. 'I don't know.'

He rolled his eyes. 'Sorry, sorry. That was rude of me.' He held out his hand. His soft skin met my sweaty palm. Great. 'My name's Matt. Nice to meet you, Leah.'

Oh my God, he'd listened when I told him my name.

I admit my expectations of males were spectacularly low at this point, given my disastrous relationship history with commitment-phobes.

'At least we have a wok.' He held it in the air. 'Never used a wok before, but there you go.'

'I've used a wok,' I said. 'It was all they had in the caravan we stayed at in Scotland, and we used it to fry steak in.'

He laughed.

'There's a whole lot to unpack in that sentence.'

His pocket started ringing, and he pulled out a flip phone. I didn't have a phone. Weren't they like, a hundred pounds? I doubted that Matt would have to support himself with a part-time job.

'Sorry,' he said, putting the phone to his ear. 'I'll have to take this.'

I lingered in the kitchen as he went into his bedroom, which was next door to mine. He didn't close the door, which made eavesdropping a whole lot easier.

'Yes, got here OK,' he said, not trying to be quiet.

I walked casually to my room, with the intention of unpacking, but found myself sitting on my bed and staring out the window at the sky.

'Yes,' he said. 'One girl so far.'

I braced myself for cruel words to follow – I had a terribly bitchy friend group at school and was often the subject of piss-taking. To my face as well.

'I told you,' he said. 'It's mixed halls. Girls are so much tidier.'

I heard the springs on his bed squeak as he sat heavily.

'I'm not being sexist... No, she seems nice... I'm not rating her out of ten... No, she's not pretty, don't worry... Yes, for the whole year... I'll be back next weekend to see you, and then the weekend after you're coming here, right?... Ditto... Yes, but that's what I usually say in return... I love you... Yes, of course I mean it.'

I flopped back onto the bed, still wearing my shoes, and covered my head with the pillow. I could almost have been invisible.

Until a tap on my open door.

I shot up. *Oh God, he thinks I'm weird.*

'The pillow's good, then?' he said, smiling.

'They could do with freshening up.' I placed it back behind me. 'Was that your girlfriend?'

'Walls are thin, I guess.' A grin took over his face. 'You're not jealous, are you?'

My face burned. Why was he so forward? Mine was a completely normal question. Did he assume everyone fancied him?

He sat on my desk chair, his tall frame making it look like a seat for primary school kids.

'Yeah,' he said. 'Her name's Stephanie. We've been seeing each other for almost a year.' His eyes glanced at my lips. 'I didn't mean what I said to her. About you, I mean. I'm sorry you heard that. I couldn't tell her that you're one of the most beautiful girls I've ever seen.'

My mouth dropped open. He sounded serious, too. No one had ever said that to me before. My cheeks were already red enough. A flush crept up his neck; his gaze flew to the floor.

'Er. Thanks.' I sounded far more nonchalant than I felt – as though I heard those words every day. 'Where are you from?'

'Derbyshire.'

So, a few hours away. *Will his relationship last the distance?* I didn't ask.

Our moment was over when two very noisy girls crashed into the corridor. One of them stood in my doorway, carrying a bottle of Bacardi Breezer, held out her arms and said, 'My new family. I am so happy to meet you all. We're going to have an amazing year; I just know it!'

I smile, now, at the memory of lovely Amy. I wish she could be here this weekend. But she's lived in Canada for almost five years, and it was just too much of an ask to expect her to pay so much to attend the wedding after her visit to England just last year. It could have been a whole different weekend – filled with shared memories and stories.

But someone has put paid to that anyway with that card. I should be used to events being spoiled. Especially with the fallout from Callum's disappearance. It was a nightmare that I don't want to live through again. All of those people he let down. It was beyond mortifying, heartbreaking.

I'm sure the stress of it all had a negative impact on Mum's health. She'd been diagnosed with breast cancer a few days before that weekend. Her first treatment had been successful –

but over a year after Callum's disappearance, Dad finally had to tell her what my husband had done to them.

The thought of her brings fresh tears to my eyes. Tears that have been threatening to leak since a few hours ago.

This should be a happy time. I shouldn't be feeling like this.

I grip the sink and take in a deep breath.

Come on, Leah. You've been through harder times than these.

Two days to go, the card said.

Who the hell is it? Did he or she mean it? Would they actually turn up on my – our – wedding day. What the hell do they want?

I slide down to the floor. The several glasses of wine have added to my anxiety, my exhaustion.

I look up to the bright spotlights; close my eyes for a moment.

You're stronger than this.

But I don't think I am. I'm not the same person I was eight years ago. The strength in me has faded. I'm a mother now; someone depends on me. My lovely, precious Noah. The thought of someone harming him makes my heart race every time. It's a scary thought, knowing I'm going to feel like this for the rest of my life. That someone else's wellbeing is far more important than mine. But at the same time, I need to keep myself safe and healthy in order to look after him, because I know how precarious and precious life is. It's a feeling that overwhelms me sometimes, but when I see Noah, when he's close to me, it makes me realise that any anxious feelings I have are nothing compared to the love I feel for him.

The thought of my little boy sends a surge of strength through my body. I take hold of the top of the bath and pull myself up. I turn to look at my face in the mirror, look myself in the eyes and straighten my shoulders.

You've been through worse. Much worse. You've got this.

The carpet back in the bedroom feels comforting under my

bare feet. I flick on the lamp, turn off the big light, and select a nice relaxing meditation podcast. They've been working a treat in the busy countdown to the wedding. Either that or I've been so exhausted with all the early mornings and running around that my mind and body have had no trouble getting to sleep. But now I'm here, and it's days away, and...

No. Don't think about it.

I turn and reach to close the curtains and pause.

There's a figure near the trees about ten metres from the house. I'm sure it's a woman, but she has a hood covering her head. She's wearing a large dark blue coloured jacket, fluorescent stripes down the arms, hands in pockets. She's staring right at me, I'm sure of it. There's a glimpse of blonde hair that catches the light. Could it be Tania?

I leave the curtains open, dash out the room and down the stairs. The idea that someone might hurt Noah or Matt has triggered something inside me that I didn't know was there.

I open the front door.

'Hello?' I shout. 'Who's there?'

The hiss of the leaves in the trees is the only reply I get.

'I saw you from the window,' I yell. 'Just come out. Is that you, Tania?'

I look left and right, but there's no sign of anyone. Was it simply a shadow?

'Hey!'

Jake's voice startles me; my heart is already thumping as it is.

'You scared the hell out of me. Why are you creeping up behind me?'

'Sorry.' He grips the door surround to steady himself. 'It's cos I'm wearing socks.' He doesn't sound as drunk as he looks. 'Who are you shouting at?'

He peeks his head out, looks left and right.

'I saw someone standing over there by the trees.' I'm still

staring at the patch of ground the figure was standing on. Where the hell have they gone? 'It freaked me out. Especially since the card.'

'What card?'

'A wedding card.'

'Why would a wedding card freak you out like this? You're usually the calmest person I know.'

'I'll tell you in the morning.' I lock the front door and pull across the top and bottom bolts. 'Make sure you lock the back door, won't you? I don't want anything to happen to Noah.'

'Why would anything happen to Noah?' Jake's frowning: it's like someone told him to look confused.

'I'll tell you when you're sober. You enjoy the rest of your night.' I head to the kitchen and lock the back door myself. Matt's sitting at the kitchen table, his attention focussed on his mobile phone; he doesn't even notice me. 'Night, Matt. Did you have a good night?'

'It was all right,' he says, monotone.

'It seems like you did, with all that laughing before in the hallway.'

'It's been up and down.'

He's still scrolling on his phone, though his eyes don't seem to be fixed on anything.

'Are you sure everything's OK?'

'Yeah.' He grabs the crystal tumbler from the table and downs the shot of whisky or brandy, or whatever it is. He gets up, grabs the decanter and pours a large measure. 'You go to bed, Leah. I'm having a night with Jake.'

He sways as he takes another sip.

'Maybe you should sleep in the back bedroom,' I say. 'Then you won't be bothered by me being restless in the night.'

'Good idea.'

He doesn't turn to face me – no attempt at a goodnight kiss.

'Has anything happened?' I say. 'Anything out of the usual?'

He looks up quickly.

'Like what?'

I shrug, trying to look casual. *Like a card signed by my dead husband.*

'I'm tired,' he says. 'It's been a long day and night. I'd give you a kiss, but we got a kebab on the way home.'

'No worries,' I say lightly as I head towards the door. 'Night night.'

Back in the hall, Jake is where I left him, staring at himself in the mirror.

'I'll leave you to it,' I say, though he looks as though he's having an existential crisis, the way he's touching his face. I hope it's only alcohol the two of them have had. I pause at the bottom of the staircase. 'Did anything happen tonight?'

'What do you mean?'

Jake's avoiding my gaze.

'You two didn't take anything, did you?'

He looks straight at me, frowning. 'No, of course not. We're not seventeen!'

'You're both acting weird... out of character.'

I have a feeling they're both hiding something from me. Though, I too, am concealing something from them. Could Matt have received a card or a message as well but he's trying to protect me?

Jake tilts his head to the side, walks over to me.

'Someone has just...' He glances around, winces slightly. 'It doesn't matter. It'll wait till the morning.' He pats me on the shoulder. 'You get some sleep.' He plasters a smile on his face, and watches as I head up the stairs. 'Night night, Leah!'

'Night, Jake.'

What the hell was that all about? Is Matt having second thoughts? Has Jake told Matt that he's desperate for children like Katherine was talking about earlier?

There's no point in me guessing; it could be anything with

those two. Once, Jake was distraught that the last burger was taken at a barbecue last summer. Too much alcohol doesn't suit anyone.

I contemplate knocking on Katherine's door, but it wouldn't be fair to wake her.

Back in our bedroom, I head to the window. If there *was* a person out there, somebody who sent the card and they wanted to harm me, then I'm probably the most alert right now to handle it. It couldn't have come at a worse time, though, when I need to feel and look my best in a day's time. I can't stand by the window all night and I don't want to disturb Noah by moving him into my room.

There's no one out there now. Was I imagining it before – conjuring it to be the woman who tormented us for months? Might it have been a shadow of something inside the house? I turn off the lamp to get a better look. The wind seems to have died down. The lake is calm, and the trees are no longer moving.

I close the curtains. All the doors downstairs are locked, and I can still hear my brother and Matt downstairs. I need to get a few hours' sleep at least. I climb into bed, put my phone on the pillow next to me and pull the covers to my chest.

Matt's parents are arriving later today. My outfits are all planned out, so I don't have to worry about that. The cake is already in the pantry; Sandra the baker will assemble it on Sunday morning. Noah's outfit and my dress are hanging in the wardrobe. All the chairs and tables are stacked in the barn; the fairy lights are in the box ready to be hung.

Yet my mind can't rest.

Who could have written it? Why would anyone want to do that?

Callum's mother, Jennie, still believes he's out there somewhere. Is she upset I'm marrying his best friend? The last time I saw Jennie, it was by coincidence. Noah had just been born and

I was trying to fill the days with different things and ended up in an arts and crafts place in town – the one that sells the best carrot cake around. It was so long since I'd been to the place, I hadn't realised she was working there. 'Just a few days a week,' she said. 'I need to keep busy.'

She wasn't totally shocked that I'd had a baby. I had written her a letter – she loved receiving letters – to tell her that Matt and I were expecting a child. Not that she was especially over the moon about Matt and I getting together, but I couldn't put my life on hold any longer, waiting for someone who wasn't going to come back to me. And after what came out about Callum in the months following his disappearance, I didn't want him to come back.

I turn to face the window. There must be a small gap in the frame for the cold air outside to waft the curtains slightly.

Whoever it is they're coming in two days, they said, and they know where I am. I'm a sitting duck. But what could they possibly do when I'm in a full house, constantly surrounded by people?

FIVE

EIGHT YEARS AGO

Twenty-six hours before Callum's disappearance

Dress code is casual, which Tania wasn't lying about. It's a good job she warned me because the hint Callum gave – *Something you've always wanted* – was so vague it could've been anything. The disappointment of my party not being a glitzy affair has faded, though it was hard to keep up the pretence of not knowing why I was banned from going outside or near the window for an hour while Matt and Callum prepped everything. I didn't expect it to look this good, though.

Cushions are scattered at the front of the house alongside picnic hampers and buckets filled with champagne, tequila and bottles of beer. Ten burning torches have been stuck into the ground and surround us, giving the early evening a lovely glow. We have eaten salmon and burgers cooked on the barbecue, and jacket potatoes heated in the firepit. Now, we are sitting in a circle, around a freshened fire.

'All we're missing is a guitar and a round of "Kumbaya",' says Callum, leaning close to me.

'Shall I get my acoustic?' Matt's keen eyes reflect the flickering flames. 'I think I can still remember a few chords.'

'Don't show us up, Matt.' Callum pours tequila into a shot glass, downs it, then reaches for another beer out the bucket. 'Everyone already thinks you're Superman.'

'Oh, go on, Matt.' I can feel Callum prickle as I say it. 'A song would be nice.'

Matt shrugs, glances at his friend. 'Maybe later.'

'I could sing along with you,' says Tania who, of course, looks even more amazing by torchlight. 'We often duet when we've had a few glasses.' She giggles and leans into Matt.

My brother's girlfriend, Katherine, to my other side rests her head on my shoulder and whispers, 'She can sing as well? She is literally perfect. God, I hate her.'

I press my lips together to stifle a giggle, but Tania doesn't even glance in our direction. Her earlier insecurity was fleeting, thanks to lots of attention (and cocktails) from Matt.

Katherine and Jake have been together for four years. It's his first serious relationship and he's become a little more capable, which is just as well because he couldn't boil an egg without my mother on the other end of the phone. Katherine is the opposite. Highly organised and loves a list and a routine. I don't know how, but it works between them. These days, Katherine is less anxious in social situations. And Jake? Well, he's getting there. He made pizza dough from scratch the other week. God know what it tasted like; I only saw the photo.

'What about some ghost stories?' Jake shines a torch under his chin. 'In a dark, dark wood, by a dark, dark lake.'

Tania covers her face. 'I hate ghost stories. Ever since I went on holiday with my parents in a static caravan in Cornwall and there was a thunderstorm.'

'Were you reading a spooky book?' I say. 'Like *Goosebumps*?'

'No. Well, we'd watched *The Sixth Sense* the night before,

and my mum and dad left me on my own while they went to the clubhouse for a couple of drinks.'

'How old were you?'

'About ten.' The light from the firepit is dancing in her dark eyes.

'Jeez. I'm not surprised you were spooked.'

Her eyes water but I'm unsure if it's the smoke. I feel an urge to embrace her in a hug, but that might be the two martinis I've had.

'I haven't been in a caravan since,' she says.

'I'm not surprised,' I say. 'You poor thing.'

She rewards me with a smile. God, I'm so easily swayed.

'Damn, that's my next surprise out the window.' Matt laughs. 'I was looking at a static in Devon for our next holiday.'

'Yeah, right,' says Tania, leaning into him. 'Like you've ever holidayed in a caravan.'

'I have, actually.'

'Matt's parents liked him to rough it,' says Callum. 'He even had to get a job at university.'

'Two jobs, actually. I worked at the library one summer.'

'What about you, Callum?' Tania asks. 'Did you have to work yourself through university?'

'Didn't bother with uni.' He leans back on a beanbag, resting on one elbow. 'Launched my first business aged seventeen. OK, it was just washing cars, but it got me started. Next was mobile valeting. I still have seven car washes just outside town.'

'Yawn, business, yawn.' Jake's swinging the torch by its cord. 'Did anyone notice that dilapidated hut down the way there?'

'No,' comes a few half-hearted replies.

I clock the brief flicker of hurt on his face.

'Which one?' I offer.

'About a hundred metres away. Saw smoke coming from it last night.'

'No, you didn't,' says Matt. 'No one's been in that cabin for years. It used to belong to a woman called Mrs Culpepper. There were rumours she murdered her husband and buried him under the coal shed.'

'Yeah, right,' I say. 'You're just saying that because Jake started with the ghoulish stories.'

'I haven't actually told my *ghoulish* story yet.'

'Are his remains still there?' asks Tania.

'I'm not going to go digging in order to find out,' says Matt.

'*My* story,' says Jake, 'is that there's been a mysterious presence around the lake for almost twenty years. Over twelve people have gone missing.'

'That's not a story,' says Callum. 'That's just a statement.'

'If people could let me get on with it...'

'Get on with it, then.' Katherine links her arm into Jake's.

'OK, OK,' he says, gazing at each of us in turn. 'In 1982—'

'Have you just made that year up?' asks Callum, before downing the rest of his beer.

'Let him talk,' I say, not looking at him.

'In 1982, that ramshackle shed over there was once home to Mr Culpepper and his brother. Everyone who passed the house could hear the shouting, the arguing. The older brother used to berate the younger one in public, who always looked so sad. One night, there was an almighty scream. Some say that, in revenge, he took an axe to his big brother while he slept. Then he dragged his body into the lake, weighted down with rocks in his pockets. Whenever people asked where his brother was, he said he went travelling and, with it being the eighties, no one could say otherwise. There were no cameras tracking your every move.

'And from then, on the same day every year someone goes missing. Even though the younger brother was a hermit and was rarely seen out in public; everyone was afraid of him. Some say he still lives there to this day.'

'Well, that's a load of bollocks,' says Callum. 'It's not even an interesting story compared with what goes on these days. How would you know all of that, anyway? You don't even live in the North anymore.'

'I like to do my research on the places I'm coming to stay at. Plus, as I told you, I saw smoke coming from the chimney.' Jake scrambles to his feet. 'Come on. Let's go and have a look.'

'I'm not wasting my time on stupid stories,' says Callum, lobbing the empty bottle into the dustbin. He reaches for a fresh one. 'You lot go and give me some peace.'

I stand, so does Katherine.

'It's my birthday wish,' I say. 'Come on, Callum. Don't be a scaredy cat.'

'A scaredy cat? How old are you? Eight?'

I take hold of his hand and try to drag him up with no success.

He holds up his hands and stands begrudgingly.

'OK, OK.' He kisses me on the nose. 'But only because it's you. I'm taking my beer with me, though.'

Jake leads the way, shining the torch into a little opening in the shrubs.

'Oh God,' says Katherine, clinging to him tightly, 'I think I've changed my mind.'

As I step into the entrance, it feels as though the branches and bushes are folding over me. I take out my phone and scan the torch left and right; it only illuminates the first metre or so.

'It's like we've been transported into the depths of the jungle,' I say.

'That's a bit dramatic.'

It's Matt who's behind me; I thought it was Callum. I take a glance behind me, but I can't see behind Tania.

'Callum?' I shout, still walking.

There's no reply. I bet he's not even coming.

'Almost there,' yells Jake.

We arrive at a large clearing; gravel that's covered in moss and grass, in front of a small single-storey wooden building. The black paint on its walls is peeling, the wood looks half-rotten, but the windows and the door look intact.

'I don't know about this, guys,' I say.

Callum pushes his way to the front. So he *is* here.

'You can't change your mind, now,' he says. 'This was your birthday wish.'

Katherine turns around. 'Why didn't you wish for a superyacht, Leah? Or maybe a helicopter to Paris.'

Jake walks slowly towards the rickety staircase and assesses the bottom step.

'They're sound.' He climbs the few steps and tests the door handle. 'It's open. I'm going in.'

'Well, I'm not.' Katherine walks a few metres away, stands and watches.

'I'll stay here with Kath,' says Callum. 'There'll be nothing in there. The place is a wreck.'

'I've found something!' shouts Jake from inside. 'Quick! Come here, Leah.'

'Oh God. Why me?'

'Don't go in there, Leah,' Callum shouts after me.

He's still shouting, but his words fade as I step onto the dusty floorboards of the cabin. The paint on the hallway wall is peeling, too, and there are two pictures hanging. I pause to look at the first: it's a photo of a little boy rowing a paddle boat on the lake. The second is of the same boy, standing in front of a man who has his hands resting on the boy's shoulders. They look so happy. Is one of them the person in the story, or is what Jake said just a bunch of made-up rumours?

'Leah!'

Jake's calling from the room on the right. Inside it is a small fireplace that I head straight towards. I bend to run my fingers through the ash.

'It's fresh, isn't it?' he asks. 'I told you. But look, come here.'

He's crouching next to the boarded-up window.

'Why are you pulling up floorboards, Jake?'

'One of them has a handle.' He points the torch underneath. 'Look.'

I rest my hand on his shoulder as I crouch next to him. Under the boards is what looks like a rucksack; next to it are rectangular parcels wrapped in plastic.

'What do you think it is?' I say.

'Drugs, maybe? Cash? I know Matt goes on about what a nice area it is here, but drugs are everywhere. Especially around water.'

'It's not exactly a large amount, though, is it? How many bags are there? Five?'

'Get you, narco Leah.'

'We can't be messing with someone's stuff,' I say, aware of the constant chatter outside the cabin masking the sound of anyone returning. 'It's obviously someone dodgy.'

I stand as Jake reaches a hand down inside.

'I'm going to unwrap it. See what it is.'

'No, Jake. That's just bravado and alcohol talking.'

We both startle as someone bangs on the outside of the cabin.

'Quick!' yells Katherine. 'Someone's coming. We can see the light from their torch.'

'Put the board back, Jake,' I say, moving his hand and torch out from underneath.

'All right, all right.'

'We're trespassing. This place belongs to someone – we might get arrested.'

'Who's being the scaredy cat, now, Leah?' Jake laughs as he slots the wood back into place. 'Come on, then. I knew I should've got Katherine to investigate with me.'

'No way would she break into a house,' I say as we leave the room. 'She's on the right side of the law, remember.'

Outside, the others are nowhere to be seen. I look to the right. A flickering light beams off the trees.

'They're right,' I say. 'There's someone coming. Which way did we come?'

Jake leaps down over all the steps, shining his torch into a narrow opening.

'Down here,' he shouts over his shoulder, but I'm already following close behind.

I shine my phone torch at the ground; I don't want to trip on any fallen branches.

It feels like we're running forever.

'Have we come the wrong way?' I say breathlessly. 'I can't see any light.'

'Don't worry.' Jake's barely panting. 'We're almost there. I can see the lake.'

He's right. A few seconds later we're out of the dense wood.

'When did it get so dark?' I bend over to catch my breath. 'How long were we in there for?'

'It just feels darker because the fire's almost out.'

I look to the distance and the others are already sitting around the firepit as though nothing happened.

'Come on,' says Jake. 'Let's get a drink.'

'OK,' I say lamely as I match his stride. 'That was so weird.'

We reach the group.

'Where have you two been?' Matt asks, the guitar resting on his lap.

'You know where we've been.' I flop down onto my spot next to Callum. 'How fast did you get that guitar?'

'You've been hours,' says Callum. 'I've had three beers since you've been gone. We were just about to call for help.'

'What?' My heart begins to pound. 'You mean we've been in some sort of time slip?'

'Fuck off.' Jake sits next to Katherine. 'Very good acting, guys. But Katherine couldn't lie if she had a paper bag over her head.'

She bursts into giggles.

'You're so gullible, Leah!' she says.

'I know I am.' I throw a tiny stone at her shoe. 'Which is why you shouldn't play tricks on me.' I stick out my bottom lip. 'Now I feel stupid. On my birthday, as well.'

'Is it your birthday?' says Matt. 'You should've said.'

Callum puts his arm around me.

'Aw, don't feel stupid. It's endearing.'

Katherine pushes herself up from the beanbag.

'Come on.' She holds her hand out to me. 'Let's make you a birthday cocktail.'

* * *

'But what if that man comes and gets us in our sleep?' I say. We're inside the house now, sitting around the kitchen table and two cocktails down. 'I'm leaving all the lights on and I'm keeping on the television downstairs.'

'That'll scare the big bad drug dealer off, won't it?' Callum says sarcastically. It seems the mask has finally dropped due to the sheer volume of beer and whisky he's been drinking, and he couldn't even wait until midnight. 'Could you stop it now, Leah. It's getting boring.'

'Fine, fine.' I hold up a hand. 'Sorry, sorry. I'll stop now. I was only joking. I don't really think someone's going to break in.'

'Hmm.' Callum's swirling whisky and ice in a crystal tumbler.

'Be nice to your wife, Callum,' says Katherine. 'It's still her birthday.' She stands. 'I'm just going to the loo.'

'Me too,' says Jake. 'The other loo.'

'What's that outside?' asks Matt getting up, He almost drags Tania out the room with him.

'Oh,' she says from the hall. 'I wanted to watch to see if they'd have a fight.'

'A fight?' I say to Callum. 'What have you been saying to everyone? Did you tell them that you—?'

'I haven't said anything.' He gently takes hold of my hand. 'I'm sorry, Leah. I really am. I don't know what's gotten into me.' He looks at our hands. 'Actually, I do know what's bugging me.' He takes out his phone and hands it to me. 'Read that.'

I shield the screen from the glare of the bright kitchen lights.

It's an email from JacksonDean452@email.com

Dear Callum,

I have written this email over twenty times, and over a thousand times in my head. I have wanted to talk to you for a long time, but your mother thought it best I didn't approach you. She said it was better to have no contact than sporadic visits, though I don't know if that's true. Only you could have been the judge of that. I know I shouldn't blame your mum. She has always had your best interests at the front of her mind.

But the heart of what I'm trying to say is this: I'm sorry, son, for not being present in your life. I wish I could have done things differently, but we can't change what's already happened. Below is my mobile number. I would love to hear from you, but I totally understand if you don't want to talk. It's far more than I deserve.

With all my love,

Dad.

I reread it three times before handing the phone back to Callum.

'Wow,' I say. 'That's a lot to take in. Have you told your mum about it?'

His head jolts back. 'Is that all you have to say about it?'

'No. It's the first thing I've said about it. I've only just read it.'

'Sorry.' He shoves the phone into his jacket pocket on the back of the chair. 'Sorry, Leah. I...' He pauses. 'I received it last week. I didn't tell you about it because I was in shock. I still am, to be honest.'

He absently looks across the room, narrowing his eyes.

So, *this* is what he's been worried about? Yes, it's a big enough event to take over his mind, but it doesn't explain the past few months. There's something else, I know it. Perhaps he's having a breakdown of sorts, and everything is getting on top of him.

I shuffle my chair closer to his and put an arm around his shoulders.

'I'm here for you,' I say. 'I know I've been busy recently, but—'

'I've been googling his name for years. Not proper searching,' he adds quickly, 'just idly looking.' He takes a drag on his disposable vape before throwing it in the sink behind us. 'What am I going to say to my mum?'

'You've done nothing wrong, Callum.' I slide my hand from his shoulder, take his hand and squeeze it gently. 'I know you'll feel disloyal meeting him—'

'I feel disloyal *thinking* about him, let alone replying to him and meeting him.'

'You don't have to say anything just yet.' I let go of his hand. 'Just take your time to digest it. I can't imagine if that happened to me. You don't have to do anything about it now.'

'I know. He might think it's gone to junk mail. He'll not know for sure that I've read it.'

I pause, letting everything sink in, replaying the words Jennie told me just before our wedding. She worried Callum's father might turn up to spoil the event. That worry, however, was unfounded.

'Your dad might not stop at an email,' I say pensively. 'From what your mum said about him, he's used to getting his own way. She said he could get quite nasty if he didn't.'

His head jerks up.

'My mum told you that? She hasn't said anything bad about him to me.'

'Maybe that's the problem. If you think of him as some sort of absent hero...'

'I've never said he's a hero.'

'But you might have thought that?'

He shrugs. 'Perhaps. More when I was younger, I guess. You can make up all sorts of things when you're eight and you have an imagination. That my father was a spy, a drug baron in Costa Rica, or a billionaire sheik who lives on the other side of the world. Or in prison for murder. That was one of the less glamorous images.' He smiles.

'Why didn't your mum just tell you the truth?'

'That my dad didn't give a shit about me? What good would telling a kid that do?'

'I know. Sorry, I was just trying to...'

He leans close to me, rests his head on my shoulder.

'You're so lovely, Leah. I'm sorry for being a dick earlier. I guess I could feel something was coming. An impending sense of doom or something.' He swipes his whisky glass off the table. 'Right. It's your birthday. We will have no more maudlin talk. Wait there one second.' He stands. 'I've got another present for you in the car.'

He stands and walks out the room and I hear the beep of the car unlocking, the sound of the boot popping open.

A sound and a flash of light catches my eye. Callum's mobile phone is on the floor; it must've fallen out of his jacket pocket. It vibrates again and curiosity wins, and I lean over, glancing at the screen.

Why the hell is he getting messages from 'Trader Simon' at this time of night? Callum sometimes negotiates international deals late at night with his stockbroker, but it's never on a weekend and I'm sure he's not called Simon.

Another glance at the screen.

I love you with all my heart. I'd do anything for you.

What the hell?

Another one appears in front of it.

You've become a shell of a person.

What? How does this person know this? It's so familiar; someone knows what's going on in Callum's life more than I do. Yes, he's become distant these past few months, but I thought it was due to the stress of one of his businesses failing. It's not like it's never happened before; he's had several businesses go under. He's simply started another.

The car boot slams shut; I sit up straight, my mind racing. 'Trader Simon' seems like such an odd way of saving a contact. And why didn't Callum tell me about the email from his father as soon as he received it?

He walks into the house, lingering in the doorway. He's frowning; his hand rakes through his hair.

'I was sure it was in the boot. I'm sorry, Leah. I can't find it.'

I stand and stride to the front door, noting that Matt and Tania are no longer loitering in the hallway.

'I'll have a look,' I say, shoving on a pair of crocs. 'Is the boot still unlocked?'

I open the front door, but Callum grabs my arm.

'Ouch, Callum!' I whip my arm out of his grasp. 'What are you doing?'

'Sorry,' he says. 'I'm sorry. I wanted it to be a surprise, that's all. I don't want you to go rooting out your own present. You're worth more than that.'

I rub the top of my arm. It's not that it still hurts; it's that I'm shocked that he would ever touch me like that again. I take a few steps back.

'You're not afraid of me, are you, Leah?' he asks.

'Why did you grab her like that?'

Callum and I turn around and Jake is standing at the bottom of the stairs.

'Jake,' I say. 'It's fine. Just a misunderstanding.'

'I'm sorry, Jake, Leah.' Tears flood Callum's eyes. 'I'm sorry.' He glances at me. 'I've had an email from my father. I've been all up and down ever since.' He holds up both palms. 'I'm sorry again.' He walks towards my brother, pats him on the right shoulder. 'I've never done anything like that before. I'll never do it again.' He staggers into the kitchen.

'Can we forget what you saw?' I say quietly to Jake. 'Just for tonight. I've still got ten minutes of my birthday left.'

Jake's expression takes a few seconds to soften; his shoulders relax. He's swaying a little. He might not remember this in the morning.

'Right you are, sis. Let's get another drink.' He takes me gently by the hand as Callum reaches the selection of drinks on the kitchen counter. 'If he ever touches you like that again, though,' Jake whispers, 'I'll fucking kill him.'

SIX

NOW

One day until the wedding

The bedroom door slams open, and I sit up quickly, my hair half-covering my face.

Noah climbs onto the bed and crawls towards me.

'Sorry, love,' says Dad, hovering at the door. 'He was so excited to see you, he couldn't wait.'

'Missed you, Mummy,' Noah says, sliding himself under the covers next to me.

'What time is it, Dad?'

'It's just after eight. I tried to keep him in the room as long as I could. He woke at half past five, but we only had three books to read. We spotted four magpies out the window, though, didn't we, Noah? It's meant to be good luck, isn't it?'

'Four for a boy,' I say, putting my arm around Noah's little shoulders. 'Sorry about him waking you so early, Dad.'

I feel awful that Dad felt he couldn't leave that small bedroom for over two hours. He's not comfortable staying at other people's houses. He takes politeness to a whole new level where he almost becomes invisible, bless him.

'Ah, it's no bother,' he says. 'I didn't want to get in anyone's way. You said that Matt's parents are arriving this morning,' he says. 'I can't sleep when there's daylight. Don't want to miss a minute when I don't know how many I've got left.'

He winks, but it's not funny. It's like he's constantly got his eye on an indeterminate countdown. Since he turned sixty-five, he's turned into a proper grandad. This has been especially obvious since Mum died. But he hides his loneliness better than I ever could. It helps that his next-door neighbour is always dragging him here and there to random clubs and societies.

I was two when I first met Dad. I know it sounds strange when I say it like that, but I don't remember meeting him, nor did I realise it until I was sixteen years old. I was greeted on the last day of school – the start of the summer holidays – to a sombre-looking Mum and Dad sitting at the dining table, which *never* happened on a weekday at four in the afternoon. They were usually both working – Dad at the Post Office and Mum at the council offices.

'What's wrong?' I asked, terrified that they were about to tell me they were splitting up or that something had happened to my brother.

'Come and sit down, love,' said Mum, tapping the back of the dining chair next to her, and opposite Dad.

She turned to face me and took hold of both my hands.

'Leah. OK. Gosh, I've prepared the words for years and I can't seem to recall them.' She squeezed my hands. 'When you were two years old, I met Bill.' She glanced across at Dad.

'You mean my dad?'

'Yes. I often wondered if you remembered that it was just you and me for a while, but obviously you were far too young and—'

'Wait.' I shifted around to face her. I looked at Dad, back at Mum again. 'What are you talking about? I was two when you met?' My eyes welled up and I couldn't stop my knees from shaking. 'You mean...'

She nodded slowly. Squeezed my hands again; wiped the tear from my cheek. 'You were the most beautiful baby.' A single tear ran down her face. 'Your biological father only stayed for two months,' she said. 'He was barely around as it was, love. And then one day, he just didn't come home. Neither of his parents knew where he was. Well, that's what they said. I doubt they'd have told me if they did. They were all as bad as each other. Bunch of loser layabouts!'

I had never heard my mum say the word loser before.

'So it was just you and me. We had a lovely little flat above the launderette. It always smelled beautiful.'

'Mum?'

'Sorry, love. Anyway. I met Bill – your dad – when I was working at the library Monday, Wednesday, and Friday mornings while you were at the playschool. You loved it there, you did, so I didn't feel as guilty getting a little part-time job. Bill used to come in every shift, and we'd talk about books and art and—'

'You and Dad used to talk about art?'

'And then we...'

'I fell in love with your mum the moment I saw her, but it took her a little while longer.'

My mind was whirling. I had a father out there who didn't care about me. A whole other family that didn't know where I was – who didn't give a shit about where I was. I didn't have my dad's eyes after all. They're someone else's. I always used to say I took after my dad in so many ways: we're both left-handed, we have the same sandy brown hair and skin that freckles in the sun.

Another tear ran down my face.

'I thought...'

Dad stood and walked around the table, crouching down next to me.

'You'll always be my Leah,' he said. 'You had my heart as soon as I met you. You're my little girl and that will never change. Never in a million eternities.'

I leant into him and wrapped my arms around his neck.

'Do you promise?' I could feel him nodding. 'You won't leave me like he did?'

'Never. Never ever.'

I pulled away from him gently, and he wiped away my tears.

Mum took out a folded piece of paper.

'This is your birth certificate, love,' she said. 'A copy of your original one before your dad adopted you. It has the name of your biological father on it, should you wish to find him.'

I glanced at Dad. If he felt any hurt at the thought of me searching for another man, then he did a great job of disguising it.

'I never will,' I said. 'He didn't want me then; he's not going to want me now. And I don't want him. He can get lost.'

Dad ruffled my hair, like I was ten.

'You might change your mind, but anything you want, love.'

'Does Jake know?'

'No,' said Mum. 'We wanted to discuss it with you first. Do you want us to tell him, or do you want to?'

'I don't know.'

'You don't have to rush into anything. Everything is up to you.'

I told Jake that night and, at first, he was scared that I was going to leave because he was three years younger than me and didn't really understand. He was young for a thirteen-year-old. Still so innocent and loving. After that day, we didn't really talk about it again. We slipped into the routine of occasional bickering and teasing. The usual.

Now, Dad is holding his hand out to Noah. 'Shall we go downstairs and get you some breakfast, young man?'

Noah scrambles off the bed. 'Cheese toast,' he says.

'Ah yes,' says Dad. 'I promised you that last night, didn't I?'

'Dad, I don't know what state the kitchen's going to be in.' I grab my dressing gown that's fallen to the floor. 'Jake and Matt were up late and I don't think they had the capacity to clean up after themselves.'

I follow Dad and Noah down the stairs and into the kitchen.

I stop at the door.

The room is immaculate. Even the wrapped smashed glass that broke after the gust of wind has been tidied away.

'Did the fairies come in the night?' Dad asks, switching on the grill.

Not fairies, I think. A stranger who left a card on the mat of the back door.

I supress a shudder.

'Fairies,' echoes Noah. He grabs a dining chair, scrapes it back, and climbs on to it.

'This is very strange.' I lean on the doorframe. 'Matt never tidies up before bed if he's been out the night before. And it can't have been Jake. You know what he's like. It must've been Katherine.'

Dad opens the fridge and takes out a block of cheese.

'I know what Jake was like as a teenager. He won't still be like that, Leah.'

'Hmm.' I wander into the snug. 'Where are they? Matt didn't come to bed. They were behaving quite oddly last night.'

They're not in the main living room, either. I'd have heard them go into any of the bedrooms. Since having Noah, I get woken by the smallest of sounds.

I dash back up the stairs. There are five bedrooms altogether. I check the two along the corridor from mine before heading up to the second storey. The stairs are narrow, and curve to the right. The ceiling's lower in this part of the house and, to be honest, I hardly ever come up here. It has a different atmosphere to the rest of the place.

One of the bedroom doors is closed – it must be where Jake and Katherine are sleeping. Matt's not in the small room at the front.

Where the hell is he?

I listen at Katherine's door, hearing the quiet sound of what sounds like a YouTube video playing. I knock quietly.

'Hello?' says Katherine. 'Come in.'

I push open the door. Katherine is sitting up on the bed, still in her pyjamas. Alone.

'Did Jake not come up?' I say. 'I can't find them anywhere.'

'No idea. Jake's not answering his phone. They've probably passed out somewhere.'

'But it was freezing last night. Aren't you worried?'

'Nah. He's a grown-up, Leah. I refuse to mother him. Always have. Remember how he was when I met him?' She flings her phone onto the bed. 'God, I'm starving. Let's go and get some breakfast. We brought some smoked salmon, cream cheese and bagels with us. Not the whole way here, don't worry. We stopped off at the Co-op down the road.'

'I wasn't worried. I don't really eat raw fish, though.'

'It's actually...' She slides off the bed. 'Never mind. One more sleep to go before the wedding! Are you excited?'

She pulls on a giant fleece cardigan and leads the way out.

'I guess.' I pause at the top of the stairs, on the one creaky step. 'Matt and Jake were acting weird last night. And then I thought I saw someone watching the house. By that cluster of trees by the lake.'

I expect her to stop, but she doesn't until she reaches the bottom.

'We had two bottles of champagne last night, Leah,' she calls up.

'We did?'

'And you'd just woken from an hour-long nap. I was convinced I was at home when I woke up this morning. It's probably the stress of the wedding and staying here.'

'I suppose.'

'And Matt and Jake were acting like kids when they got home. I wouldn't take that as something out of the ordinary after a night out.'

I reach the bottom. Perhaps she's right. In the sensibility of daylight, things don't seem so strange and frightening. It is unsettling, being in this house; it's in the middle of nowhere, surrounded by trees that cast shadows of all shapes and magnitudes.

'Did you take a photo of whatever you saw?' she asks.

'I didn't think to.'

'There you go.' Katherine shrugs: she doesn't scare easily. 'You weren't thinking straight. Anyone worried enough would've videoed it or taken a picture at least.'

'I went downstairs to have a look.'

'Really?'

'There was nothing there.'

'There you go. A trick of the light.'

'But what if it's the same person who left that card?'

She stops at the doorway to the kitchen.

'Shit. I'd forgotten about that.'

I reckon it was Katherine who drank most of that champagne. She folds her arms.

'You might not be imagining things after all.'

'Don't say that! I preferred it when you were being positive.'

'To be honest, Leah, I'm probably still a bit pissed.'

'Sit yourself down, girls,' says Dad in the kitchen. 'I've put on a bit of a spread. I've no idea where the lads are. I'll go out and see if they're in the garden room.'

'Oh. I thought they might've taken a walk to clear their heads.' A sudden need for coffee has usurped my worry for my husband-to-be. I pull out a chair and sit at the table, which is laden with steaming coffee in a pot, fresh orange juice, a ready-prepared M&S fruit salad, triangles of toast, a large sharing bowl of scrambled eggs and a plate of crispy bacon. 'How have you prepared all of this in fifteen minutes, Dad?'

'You've been upstairs for over half an hour, love.'

'Really?'

My sense of time is totally warped in this house and being out of my usual routine.

Dad slides on the crocs that he specifically bought for this very need of popping outside. It's a novelty to him as he lives in a second-floor flat.

'Right,' he says. 'I'll go and see what mischief these boys have been up to.'

'Boys?' Noah says with a mouthful of buttered toast, while swinging his legs in bliss. He always does that when he's enjoying his food. 'Samson and Charlie and Eli?'

'No,' I say. 'Not your friends from playschool. Grandad is talking about your dad and your uncle.'

Katherine and I share a look as though to say Dad's not wrong. They are behaving like children.

'It'll be freezing out there,' she says. 'They'll have not thought to put any heating on in that shed. Have you seen inside it?'

'No.'

The garden room, which is just a large shed with windows and a door, was only constructed last year. Matt's meant to be sleeping in there tonight in keeping with the tradition of us not seeing each other before the wedding, which I know is silly considering we have a child together. It was also what Callum and I did the night before our wedding, but considering how that ended up it's not an especially meaningful and blessed tradition.

I really should stop thinking about it – it feels as though I'm being unfaithful. But it's like someone wants me to think of Callum. And there's no harm to Matt if the person I'm having thoughts about is dead. He'd understand. He's probably thinking about Callum, too, given the significance of the location and the time of the year. Same time, same place.

I know what people will be saying about it all; the reason why we kept the wedding small. But Matt wants to make our own memories here – it's his parents' house after all. He doesn't want memories of that night to tarnish what future we might have here.

Katherine has loaded her plate and has already eaten three rashers of bacon – it's been two years since she started eating meat again. My stomach is churning at the thought of it, even though I stopped being vegetarian while pregnant with Noah before he was born.

'Get something down you,' she says, before taking a giant glug of orange juice.

'I don't think I'll keep it down.'

'God, you're not pregnant again, are you?' she whispers.

'You say that as though I've had ten children!' I say quietly, glancing at Noah. 'And no, of course not. I'd never have drunk alcohol last night if I was.'

I get up after Noah polishes off his last bit of toast.

'Do you want to watch some cartoons for a bit, love?'

'Hmm.' He swallows and downs the rest of his milk, slides off the chair. '*Paw Patrol!*'

I lead him to the living room, and he scrambles onto the sofa as I select his favourite show on Netflix.

'I'll be in the kitchen if you need me,' I say, ruffling his hair.

He's already grabbed a blanket and placed it over his lap, bless him.

In the kitchen, I take a small sip of coffee.

'Sorry,' I say. 'I'm just a bit on edge about Matt's parents arriving, plus the wedding obviously.'

'Not surprised. Greg and Olivia are a bit...'

'Formal.'

'I was going to say uptight, but I suppose formal covers it.'

Dad opens the back door.

'Well, aren't they slumbering like a couple of sleeping beauties? I suppose it's only early. We should let them sleep for another couple of hours.'

'At least we know where they are,' I say.

'At least we do.' Dad takes his jacket off. 'I doubt *they* know where they are. Wish I could be a fly on the wall when they see the state of the place. God knows what they were doing. Bits of paper everywhere.'

'Paper?' I sit up straighter. 'What was written on the paper?'

'I didn't look too closely, love. They were in their boxer shorts. Only Jake had managed to navigate one of the camping beds.'

'Oh God,' says Katherine. 'I don't want to know.' She wipes her mouth with a paper napkin and pushes her half-full plate away. 'Why on earth did they get themselves into such a state? It's like they're teenagers again.'

'They were having a pretty serious heart-to-heart last night,' says Dad. 'You two had gone to bed and I popped down for a glass of water.'

'What about?' I say.

'I didn't like to pry.'

'Come on, Dad. I know you do.'

Dad pours a tiny measure of coffee into a cup, ladles in two sugars and fills it to the top with milk.

'Oh. All right.' He sits on the chair Noah was sitting on. 'They were talking about Matt's parents.'

I was expecting him to say either Callum or Tania – the usual suspects of the weekend.

'Seems there's trouble in paradise,' says Dad, raising his eyebrows.

Now it's not that Dad doesn't like Olivia and Greg; it's just that he doesn't feel a hundred per cent comfortable in their company. So much so that he often says little to nothing. He says it's because they have different backgrounds, and he feels they won't be interested in his *insignificant life*. It upset me when he said it – to hear he thinks so little of himself when he means the world to me.

'What kind of trouble?' asks Katherine, reaching over to grab a strawberry.

'I heard the words "photos" and "messages", but that's all I could make out before I went back up to watch Noah.'

'Get you, Inspector Bill,' says Katherine.

'I don't think they realised I could hear them.'

'How odd.'

'Do you think?'

Dad busies himself, buttering a slice of now-cold toast. The butter sits on the top like icing.

'One sec.' I leave the table and head upstairs to fetch the card from my bag at the bottom of the wardrobe. Back downstairs, I pull it out the envelope, and I notice my name printed on the front of the card. 'Look at this, Dad.'

He takes it and puts on his glasses that are on a chain around his neck.

'Ah, that's strange isn't it, love?' he says. 'A black heart for a wedding card. They got it personalised, though, which is nice. I did one for Terry next door last year. Put his face under the headline *Old Not Dead*.' He chuckles. His face straightens when he opens it and reads the words inside. 'Holy...' He glances at Katherine. 'Moly. What the heck?'

'They left it on the mat near the back door,' says Katherine. 'No letterbox, obviously, so they actually opened the door.'

'It's freaking me out a bit, Dad. I barely slept last night.'

'I thought you were a bit quiet this morning,' he says.

'"Two days to go," it says. But that was yesterday. Someone's going to turn up tomorrow.'

'But why?' Dad asks. 'What's the point of all that?'

'Someone wants to ruin Leah and Matt's wedding.' Katherine's staring into the distance.

'But who? Leah wouldn't harm anyone.'

Katherine shrugs, stands and fills a glass with water from the tap. She downs it and wipes her mouth on the sleeve of her cardigan. She rinses the glass and places it on the drainer before turning round.

'It might not have anything to do with Leah.' She wiggles her fingers. 'What if it's a message from the dead?'

I frown. 'That's not funny, Katherine.'

Her mouth drops.

'I'm sorry.' She flops onto her chair. 'Sorry, I was trying to keep the tone light. Everyone knows it was an accident that night. Bravado. Thinking he could...'

She didn't used to say that. In fact, just last night she hinted that Callum was troubled – suggested that he might have gone out with the intention of...

'I don't want to think about that,' I mutter, turning to Dad. 'Do you think Matt's been getting similar messages to mine? From what you said about him and Jake chatting last night?'

Dad takes his phone from his shirt pocket and takes a picture of the handwriting inside the card before putting it back in the envelope.

One day to go, now. Not two.

'I don't know,' he says. 'But it didn't sound anything like

that. It sounded as if they were talking about some woman sending messages.'

'Who was getting the messages?' Katherine leans forward, elbows on the table. 'Was it Olivia or Greg?'

'I don't know, love,' Dad adds quickly, panic in his eyes.

'Or maybe it wasn't his parents who received them. Perhaps it was Matt.' My mind goes to Tania again. 'If it were Jake, he'd have said.'

Katherine slides her arms off the table, flops her hands onto her lap.

'Who knows.' She glances at the clock. 'I'm going to have a shower and get dressed.' She kisses the top of my head. 'Today and tomorrow are all about you, my darling sister-in-law. We won't let anything spoil it.'

When she's gone, I say, 'Dad. Did you read the bit in the card about—'

'About seeing you tomorrow? Yes.'

'Who would do something like that?'

'Someone who wants to spoil your day. What about that man who came after you for money when Callum disappeared?'

'But why would they bother with something as subtle as a card? And he got most of his money back. We left it on... not amicable terms, but respectful.'

'Do you think it could be Callum?' Dad stands and paces the floor. 'I know they never found his body, but do you think he read about the announcement in the paper – that one that Matt's mum and dad insisted on putting in the bloody *Telegraph*. Do you think he saw it and is going to come in when they say, "If anyone here knows of any reason why these two should not be joined in holy matrimony"?'

He pauses, and the air around us feels heavy, stifling.

'He's not alive, though, Dad. I can sense it. There's no way he could've stayed away so long.'

'I know. He would never leave you if he could've helped it. He loved you so much.' He looks out into the back garden. 'He loved you a little too much, sometimes.' He's silent for a moment, his eyes fixed on a branch that's gently tapping the kitchen window. He turns, back in the moment. 'It's such a mystery, isn't it?'

'He's never used his debit and credit cards or touched his bank accounts,' I say. 'He hasn't contacted his own mother. Those two were so close – especially with him being an only child.'

I push the coffee cup away; my heart is beating so hard already without adding more caffeine into the mix.

'Can you watch Noah while I take a walk?' I say. 'I need some fresh air. I need to think.'

'Do you want me to call the police?' asks Dad. 'I know that, legally, Callum's dead, but maybe they've got some handwriting experts they could use?'

'Do you think they'd do that over a card?'

'Does it look like his handwriting?'

I take the card out again.

'If I'd looked at it, not believing he was dead, then yes, I'd think it was from him. But *anyone* who knew him would know what his writing was like.'

'So it's from someone close to him. Someone who's in this area.'

Dad narrows his eyes as he looks at me. There's something he isn't saying. It's like that look he had years ago when he confessed about what Callum had done to him. Or maybe it's something else.

'If you're not totally over Callum, I'd understand if you wanted to get out of marrying again. You don't have to get wed anyway. As a teenager you used to think marriage was an old-fashioned institution.'

It takes me a moment to process his words.

'What?' I say, my voice high. 'You don't think I sent this to myself, do you?'

'I didn't say that at all.'

'No, but you were thinking it.'

'I was just taking everything into consideration. That, say, just because everything's arranged and you have a child together, doesn't mean you can't back out.'

I stand, shove the chair under the table.

'I wouldn't do something like that. That's so strange to think that about your very own daughter.'

'I know. I'm sorry, love.'

I feel a pang of remorse looking at his unhappy face. He was just thinking aloud. Katherine and I have done the same thing. Dad's always been an open book, and that's why I love him so much. He truly wears his heart on his sleeve, and I've never doubted for a moment that he loved me or that he wants the best for Noah and me.

'I'm sorry I snapped, Dad. I know you're just looking out for us.'

'That's all right, love.' He gestures to the door. 'You get some fresh air. I'll sort out the washing up. I'll save the cold eggs and burnt bacon for the lads. Breakfast of kings, that is.' He laughs.

'You're doing so much for me this weekend, Dad.' I walk round the table and kiss him on the cheek. 'See, you've still got it in you. You're not as old as you think you are.'

'I'll need to sleep for a week when I get home to get over it.' He winks. 'I'm just kidding. I exaggerate a bit sometimes, so you'll keep visiting me.'

'I'll always visit you, Dad! What are you like? As if I'd ever abandon you.'

A shadow crosses his face.

'There was a time – when Callum went missing and then all that trouble came out – when I thought you might leave. To join him, somewhere at the other side of the world. That he was in hiding. You two loved each other so much.'

I jolt back.

'What? You thought...?'

'I know. It was silly of me. I've been watching too many dramas about canoeists.'

'I don't think he's hiding somewhere at the other side of the world, or Mexico, or Blackpool, or wherever people go to disappear. He wouldn't have it in him to have stayed quiet for so long. The police are convinced he's dead. They said it happens more than we think. If there was the slightest chance they thought he was out there, he wouldn't have been declared legally dead.'

'I suppose we'll find out soon enough who's behind it.' Dad stands and carries two empty cups to the sink. 'Because tomorrow, whoever it is that sent that card, is going to turn up. I can feel it in my bones.'

* * *

I pull my coat zip up to my chin. It's chilly this morning, and a light breeze makes the lake shimmer. It's really beautiful, despite the secrets it hides.

I look to the house before heading towards the spot I thought I saw someone last night. Perhaps they left something behind: footprints, cigarette butts.

It was here – at the opening of a small cluster of trees and shrubs. I think I can make out the edge of a footprint. I crouch down and take a picture with my phone camera. I can't tell what size the shoe is, but I can see the heavy treads. Perhaps a trainer or a walking boot.

There's a narrow path that leads through dense shrubbery, but the embankment is muddy. If I were to slip while walking, I'd end up in the lake and I'm not the strongest swimmer at the best of times, these days, let alone in freezing cold water in a heavy coat.

I look across the water. Most of the lake's edges are lined with trees and hedges. Hundreds of places to hide if a person wanted to escape. I have pictured hundreds of scenarios about what happened to Callum that night. Police were convinced that he had gone in the water. A man walking his dog around that time said he saw Callum standing at the lake's edge, taking off his boots. But the man reported it over a week later, after it was mentioned on the news.

The night before Callum disappeared, Jake said he'd read a story on some obscure subreddit about a man who hid in a dilapidated shed off Lake Windermere a hundred metres from this house. We'd all gone there, giggling after a few beers around the campfire.

I don't know why I'm thinking like this – it's not as though I haven't been here since.

But someone wants me to think of that weekend, eight years ago. Someone wants to bring up the past when all I want to do is look to the future.

SEVEN

EIGHT YEARS AGO

Six hours before Callum's disappearance

At last, for the first time today, it's not raining, and we're almost back at the house. I must have had a lot to drink last night because the end of the evening is a bit of a blur, and I certainly don't feel my best today. Especially after walking almost three miles in the drizzle. One thing I *do* remember though, is the contact 'Trader Simon'. I can't recall the messages in detail, though. They said something like he or she will always love Callum. I haven't had a chance yet to ask him about it; he wasn't in bed when I woke.

'Jeez,' says a red-faced Katherine as she and I finally reach the cottage grounds. 'I don't think I've walked that far since... Well, I'm not really a hiker. Which won't surprise you considering I've been out of breath for about three hundred and seventy-three minutes. How long have we been? It feels as though we've been out all day. Am I sunburnt?'

'We've been walking for two hours,' I say. 'And your skin looks fine. There's so much cloud and rain.'

'I can burn when there's full cloud cover in a thunderstorm, Leah.'

She turns around to look at Jake and Matt deep in conversation a few hundred yards away. This is the first time they've spent meaningful time together. My brother gets on with Matt so much better than he does with Callum. A flash of a memory from last night: did my brother really threaten to kill my husband? I shake my head. I must be remembering things wrongly.

'It's nice those two are getting along, isn't it?' says Katherine. 'How long have you known Matt, now? Ten years?'

I'm sure she asked that question on mine and Callum's wedding day when Matt was best man, but that was years ago. Katherine's a very busy woman, and she and Jake haven't lived up North for years.

'Since my first day at our university halls when we were eighteen,' I say, anyway. Katherine has just started at another law firm in Brighton; her mind is full of more interesting things than my friendship history. 'We shared accommodation for the full three years we were there. He was the first person I met. I was homesick before my parents even left me there. I was almost in tears.'

'You nearly cried?'

I nudge her gently. 'I was living away from home for the first time. I was petrified. Luckily, I'm hardened and cynical, now.'

'Ha!'

We get to the cottage and scrape the mud off our boots using the metal contraption next to the front door.

'One day,' Katherine sits on the step, 'I'm going to have a boot scraper outside my front door.'

'I don't think they're that expensive.'

'Yeah, but it'd look ridiculous outside our third-floor apartment.'

'Fair point.'

I stand on the highest step to look into the distance.

'Where's Callum?' I say. 'I can't see Tania either.'

'God, poor Callum, being lumbered with her,' she says, laughing. 'Sorry. Yes, she's beautiful, but there's not much else about her, is there?'

'That's not like you, Katherine. To be unkind like that. She's probably shy, being in a group of such close friends. It can't be easy for her.'

'What's got into you, Mother Teresa?' she asks. 'She said her favourite film's *Meet Joe Black*. I mean, come on.'

'That's one of my favourite films, too.'

'I'll pretend you didn't just say that. Anyway, you were slagging Tania right off last night.'

'Was I? I don't remember that. I didn't say anything *really* mean, though, did I?'

'Only that she's insecure and that she's gone full *Fatal Attraction* by tracking Matt on her phone. That she barely leaves his side and it's really weird.'

Heat rises to my face. It's certainly something I'd thought. I didn't think I said it out loud. I'm a terrible person.

'Shit,' I say. 'I hope she didn't overhear me.'

'I wouldn't worry about it,' says Katherine. 'Yes, she was sitting next to Matt all the time, but she was on her phone for most of it.'

'Did I talk to you about Callum last night?'

She takes of her boots and rubs the bottom of her left foot.

'About the email from his dad and those weird messages from his colleague?'

I squint as a beam of sunlight appears from behind a cloud: the spotlight is well and truly on my life.

'I don't remember telling you all of that,' I say. 'You won't tell anyone, will you? Callum doesn't like anyone knowing his business.'

'Of course not,' she says bluntly. 'You can sign something if you like.' She sounds only half-joking.

'I don't want him to realise I've been talking behind his back.'

'Totally get it.' She clocks me looking into the distance. 'You're not scared of him, are you?'

'I...' A flash of him grabbing my arm. I touch it, now, and it feels tender. I didn't think to check if it left a bruise this morning in the shower. 'No, I'm not scared of him.'

Perhaps Jake has told her what happened.

'Why don't you call Callum,' she says, 'to see where he is?'

'I don't want it to look like I'm keeping tabs on him.'

'Hmm.' She clasps her hands tightly on her lap. 'Doesn't work with being married, really, does it? If you two get the chance to become parents, he'll have a shock when he can't do what the hell he wants.'

'I don't know if that will ever be on the cards for us.'

I feel the emotion, the heartbreak of never becoming a mother rise up my chest, creep up my throat until tears fill my eyes.

Katherine reaches over, squeezes my hand. 'I'm sorry, Leah. Jake told me how much you want children. But I suppose given Callum's childhood with his absent father...'

'He said the opposite would happen – that he'd want to be there for his kid because he knows what it's like to deal with abandonment. Especially with the way his mother couldn't get over it. But I don't know. I just can't picture him and I having a family.'

'I suppose,' she says. 'Have you talked about having children with him recently?'

'No,' I say quietly. 'Not since my last birthday.' And now he's receiving text messages from someone declaring love to him. I picture someone young, independent, carefree with no desire to settle down with a family. I rub my temples, banishing the image, and the one that replaces it is me with a man – God knows who – and a child sitting on my lap. 'What about you and Jake?' I say. 'Do you think you'll ever have children? I asked Jake once when you two first got together and I wish I hadn't.'

'I know. The idea of being tied down and not being able to go on holiday at a moment's notice is his worst nightmare. You two couldn't be more different, which I'm glad about, to be honest. I want to become partner at my firm and that will probably take me about ten more years. And even then... I'm just not a maternal person, Leah.'

'I wish I didn't have that yearning,' I say. 'It'd be a lot simpler to get on with my life without thinking there's more to life than work and holidays. No offence.'

'None taken. I'm living my own dream.' She laughs, then rubs her forehead, staring out at the lake in silence for a moment. 'He's been acting strangely, this weekend. Jake, I mean. Has he said anything to you?'

'No. Have you tried talking to him about it?'

'It's never the right time.' She sighs. 'I tried to talk in the car yesterday, but he didn't entertain it. Shall we get a drink while we wait for the rest of them? Hair of the dog and all that. We'll bagsie the seats over there to make the most of the view.'

I head to the white metal table that's seen better days. The chairs don't wobble so that's a bonus. Katherine comes out shortly after with two glasses of I-don't-know-what. She places them on the table and sits.

'I made us a mimosa, but they had carton juice at the shop. No freshly squeezed, I'm afraid.'

'I've never had freshly squeezed orange juice,' I say and take a sip. 'So I don't know if I'm missing out.'

'You've never lived, Leah.' She winks and gives me a warm smile.

Sometimes our different upbringings are so stark. Katherine went to private school and was an only child to parents who both worked in very stressful jobs. She still rings her nanny every week, which is more than she does her own mother. That's what she says, anyway. I'm never sure if she's joking or not. Katherine might be my brother's fiancée, but she and Jake live so far away we don't spend that much time together.

'Weren't Jake and Matt right behind us just then?' I say, craning to look.

'They're probably hiding and are pissed off we haven't noticed.'

I see movement from the boathouse. I say boathouse, it's basically a large battered old shed. There's a canoe and a kayak and an inflatable dinghy inside.

'They're over there.' I point with my glass. 'Probably smoking a joint.'

'For God's sake. Jake will never grow up.'

'Oh.' I shift back slightly.

'Shit, sorry. Sometimes I forget you're his sister.'

'Go easy on him, Katherine. Our mum's going through a lot.'

She reaches over and touches my arm.

'Sorry. I know. Jake doesn't talk about it. Your mum will get through it. She's a fighter.'

'That's what people say, isn't it. "Fighting cancer". It's unfair. A battle people don't sign up for. As if it's on them to combat it.'

The tears well in my eyes like they do every time I think about my mum. I feel guilty enough just being here, celebrating my birthday. I worry that it's the last birthday I'm going to have with her. And now I'm a hundred miles away.

'Everything will be OK,' says Katherine. 'They spotted it early enough.'

'We'll learn more next week. My mum keeps her troubles to herself most of the time. So...'

I don't want to think about it. Even when she's in great pain, Mum will say she's fine.

I take a sip of the mimosa that's more fizz than orange juice. I tilt my head up to the tiny bit of sun that's leaked through the clouds.

She'll be fine; she'll be fine.

Everything else is just noise.

'What are you thinking about?' Katherine asks. 'You're miles away.'

'Nothing, really. A bit of everything. I'm so tired from last night.'

'Yeah, me too. Don't usually drink that much. Callum was quiet towards the end. Wonder if it's a guilty conscience from those messages.'

'Think he had too much to drink like the rest of us.'

I don't want to get into text declarations of love sent from a strange contact, and the way he stopped me from looking in our car boot when he said he had another present for me.

'God, I can smell that shit from here.' Katherine gets up and walks towards the boathouse. 'And don't dwell on Tania and Callum,' she hollers over her shoulder. 'Don't let it spoil your birthday weekend.'

'What do you mean by that?' I shout after her, but she hasn't heard me.

I glance at my phone. Callum and Tania have been almost half an hour. But Callum can talk to anyone about anything. It's why I fell in love with him. The way he puts people at ease – the way I don't have to talk in company if I don't want to. I can sit and observe. But do I want to spend my life being an outsider next to my own husband?

I slide my phone into my pocket, stand and head to the car. Why wouldn't Callum let me look inside the boot last night?

The car doors are locked, but there's another key on my set. I press to pop the boot open and it's completely empty. Not even spare carrier bags or empty bottles of water. Why did he spend so long looking in an empty car? A quick glance in the distance – Callum's still not in sight – before I lift the lining. There doesn't seem to be anything... I hoist up the spare tyre. There's an A4 brown envelope. I peek inside, expecting to find the car's manual or service documents, but it's not. It's bank statements from an account I don't recognise, in Callum's name only.

There are a few photographs, too. I pluck one out.

What the hell? Why has Callum got pictures of my brother and... Who the hell is that? And what the heck are they doing? It must've been before he and Katherine got together.

Voices in the distance. Should I leave the envelope here, or take it?

What's the worst Callum could do to me? We're married. We shouldn't have secrets. I stuff the envelope inside my jacket, replace the tyre and the lining, slam the boot shut and dash inside the house. Upstairs, in our bedroom, I shove the envelope to the bottom of my suitcase under the bed before heading back outside.

Matt and Jake are following Katherine to the table, hands in their pockets and eyes to the ground.

'I think I've just been told off,' says Jake, pulling out the chair next to me as I sit.

'Katherine didn't believe me when I said I'd found the weed in there,' says Matt. 'It's probably my dad's. He was a bit of a hippy back in the day, apparently.'

I hold up a hand.

'I don't want to be party to your criminal activities. It's all a bit high school, if you ask me.'

'Get you,' says Matt, sliding down in the chair. 'All grown up.'

'Thirty years old,' I say. 'And I'm feeling every year of them.'

'I don't know,' says Jake, taking a swig of my drink. 'You oldies.'

'Did Tania say where she and Callum were going?' Katherine asks Matt.

'I don't like to keep tabs on my girlfriend,' he says. 'She's more than capable of looking after herself.'

'Really?' I say. 'I thought you and she tracked—'

'How long have you and Tania been together, now?' asks my brother.

'Just over two years.'

'Serious then?'

'I don't know. Maybe. She can be a little...' Matt looks at me for several seconds too long.

'What's wrong?' I say.

'You're not her biggest fan,' he says, 'are you?'

'I don't mind her. I think it's the other way round. She seems to have taken a dislike to me. Plus, you shouldn't care about what I think.'

'Of course I care. I've known you since you were that high.' He holds up a hand just a foot higher than the table.

'Very funny. I'm not that short.'

'I always wondered why you two didn't get together,' says Katherine with a cheeky smirk. 'Why is that?'

'You've never wondered that,' I say, heat rising from my neck to my cheeks. 'You're just stirring the pot. A man and a woman can have a long-lasting platonic friendship, you know. I only fancied him briefly, before I actually got to know him and his lothario ways.'

'Ha,' says Jake, scrolling his phone. 'Yeah, right.' He looks up and notices me giving him an evil look. 'Sorry. I wasn't listening properly.'

'How did the intelligent, beautiful, ambitious Katherine end up with someone like you?' I say.

Jake drops his phone onto the table and places a hand on his heart.

'You hurt me deeply, sister. You of all people know I'm equally as intelligent, beautiful and ambitious.'

There's a moment's silence until everyone else can't contain their laughter.

'Jeez, guys,' Jakes says, smirking. 'You lot really know how to raise a person's self-esteem.'

'She was only joking.' Katherine reaches over to rub his leg. 'You're very pretty and kind.'

'Oh my God.' Jake stands, suddenly serious. 'You're so condescending.'

Katherine's cheeks flush. He usually enjoys being teased by her. Jake glances at me.

'Sorry, Leah. But I've had enough of Katherine putting me down all the time. None of the other wives and girlfriends talk to their other halves like that!'

'Jake!' Katherine's blushes have vanished – the colour's drained from her face. She watches as my brother storms into the house. 'I'm so sorry. I don't know what's gotten into him.' She stands. 'I'll just go and check.'

'Trouble in paradise,' says Matt, after Katherine's inside the house. 'Do you think they'll last?'

'They're getting married next year, so I hope so.'

'Callum doesn't seem his usual self. Though he seems to be getting along with Tania.'

'I've not really seen that myself. Well, not until now. Where have they got to?'

First Katherine telling me not to worry about Tania, and now Matt's picking up on it. Have I missed something? I haven't noticed them talking; Katherine said Tania was always on her phone.

Trader Simon.

TS

'What's Tania's surname?' I say lightly. 'I don't think you've ever told me.'

'Probably because you've never asked. It's Stephenson.'

Oh no. It's her who's been messaging Callum. It must be. Why would they have sneaked off this afternoon – what the hell would they have to talk about if they hadn't already been communicating?

'I see movement in the distance,' I say. 'Finally.'

Matt turns his chair round to face them as they walk slowly arm in arm towards us. They haven't noticed us, though. They're deep in conversation.

'I wonder if she got a word in,' says Matt.

'You don't think that something's going on between them, do you?' I slide my hands under my legs to disguise their trembling.

'What?' He looks genuinely surprised. 'Of course not. Don't tell me you're jealous of them talking?'

'Of course I'm not jealous.'

'Tania's not his biggest fan, to be honest. She says he's full of himself.' Matt shrugs. 'Says there's a dangerous side to him.'

Tania's more perceptive than I'd given her credit for.

'How would she know that?' I say.

Matt takes a swig of Katherine's drink.

'Something in his eyes, apparently. She asked me last night how much I really knew him. She said she saw something from the top of the stairs, but she didn't say what. Did she mention anything to you?'

Tania bends over, laughing at something Callum has said to her. They're about twenty metres away, now.

'No, she didn't,' I say levelly. 'She might've made that up. She doesn't exactly seem afraid of him, now, does she?'

'I guess not,' says Matt. 'What do *you* think they're talking about?'

'Maybe they're plotting to kill us all.'

Matt bursts out laughing. 'That's priceless. You've always been anxious and maudlin when you're hungover.'

'No, I've not. I have perfectly rational thoughts.'

'You're so funny, Leah.' Matt stands. 'Ah, the wanderers return.'

'Were we that long?' Tania asks. 'Time has just flown.'

I supress an eyeroll. Callum bends down to kiss me on the cheek.

'Don't be mad at me, Leah,' he says.

I jolt back. 'I'm not mad at all.' I hate it when he does this – acting like I'm having some sort of hysterical outburst in reaction to his behaviour. 'Not at all. In fact, it's been nice for Matt and me to catch up, hasn't it, Matt? Anyway.' I stand and brush the creases from my trousers. 'I'll head inside. Need a rest before I get ready for dinner.'

'Ah yes,' says Tania, leaning her shoulder into Callum's arm, 'it's your turn to cook, isn't it?'

'Yes,' he says. 'It's a surprise.'

'Don't forget I'm vegan.'

'No, no. I've something special for you, Tania. Don't worry.'

I allow myself the eyeroll as I turn and head to the house. Callum is certainly putting on a performance for Tania. Unless it's real. Who knows?

He's making coq au vin. It's as though it's a lot of effort but he just bungs it in a pot with minimal chopping. We have it every other week, and he's bought ready-made mashed potato. He'll pass it off as his own – he's hiding it in a taped-up plastic bag in the fridge.

Jake and Katherine are standing at the bottom of the stairs; Katherine's hair is wet and she's in a robe. They're so deep in their conversation they don't notice I'm here.

'Have you two made up yet?' I say and they almost jump at the sound of my voice.

Jake rubs his forehead.

'Not now, Leah.'

He pushes past Katherine and stomps up the stairs.

'Jake hasn't forgiven you?' I say. 'It's not like him to take a joke so seriously.'

Katherine sighs loudly and walks into the kitchen. I follow and sit at the breakfast bar as I watch her open and close the cupboards.

'What are you looking for?'

'The fucking cups.'

I slide off the stool to open the one door she hasn't tried.

'In here,' I say. 'Where they've been all weekend.'

She pauses, rests her hands on the kitchen counter and lowers her head.

'Deep breaths,' she whispers. 'Deep breaths.'

'What is it, Katherine? You're scaring me. Has something else happened?'

She stands straight, brushes the hair away from her face.

'Don't worry about it.' She reaches past me and takes out two mugs. 'I don't want to taint your birthday weekend.'

'My birthday was yesterday. You can tell me.'

'It's nothing. Jake's blown things out of proportion. There's something he's not telling me, and it's not just about your mum.'

'Do you want me to talk to him?'

'I don't know. Maybe. If it continues. We usually tell each other everything, you know?' She turns to face me, her eyebrows raised. 'Has something happened between him and Callum? Not just about last night.'

'Like what?' The image of my brother and the barely dressed woman in the photograph burns into my mind. I cannot mention that. I must not mention that.

'I don't know,' she says. 'For weeks Jake has been slagging Callum off, saying why did his sister marry such a scumbag.'

'What?' I slide off the stool again. 'A scumbag? Why?'

'I've no idea, Leah. That's why I'm at a loss as to what's wrong with Jake.'

'He hasn't said anything to me.'

'That's what I gather from the look on your face. But I think it's serious. Whatever Callum has done has made your brother despise him.'

EIGHT

NOW

One day until the wedding

I make my way to the boathouse down the side of the house. It looks totally different to how it did back then. Now, it's bright blue and the wooden door has been replaced by a steel one. The boulder is still there, though I doubt they still keep a key underneath. I don't try the door. I haven't been inside it since that night.

Everyone was saying Callum would turn up any minute. But he didn't, obviously. Matt said it was so unlike him – and Matt was the one who had known him the longest. They'd met at the start of high school and had been in each other's lives ever since.

I first met Callum at a dinner party that Matt hosted several months into our first year at university. Matt was no longer seeing the girl he was with from home. He was enjoying his new freedom, and it seemed as though he was with a new girl every month. He was obviously trying to impress the one he'd invited that night with his hosting skills. He'd moved the dining table into the middle of the kitchen and lit several tealights around the place, which melted to nothing after an hour. He'd cooked pasta and pesto (one of the two things he could make), and then there were M&S profiteroles for afters. He called it dessert and, seriously, what student could afford to buy the ingredients for fresh pesto *and* a dessert from Marks & Spencer? (Matt).

Matt had prepared me for the type of person Callum was without actually slagging him off. What was that phrase? *If you want to know what a person is really like, praise them to their best friend.*

I was expecting someone quite flash: designer clothes, at least two mobile phones and his own car. When he walked in (on time) I was surprised to find he was almost a foot shorter than Matt. He had dark red hair and a smattering of freckles on his nose. He wore a simple black T-shirt and generic jeans that looked like they were from Ethel Austen (it was my mum's favourite shop for years). He didn't brag about his new business like Matt said he would. He barely looked me in the eye.

A week or so later, he was at one of my lectures – I only noticed him halfway through. It was a psychology one, if I remember rightly. He was sitting at the end of the row, chin resting on an upturned palm. He was the only one in the theatre not taking notes.

Had he just enrolled? What the hell was he doing there?

I was mortified when he caught me staring at him, and after that I had to pretend I didn't notice as he kept looking at me, his eyes burning into the side of my face. When the lecture ended, he was waiting for me, sitting cross-legged on the floor among the busy throng of people wanting to leave. I thought it was kind of quirky, but then I was only nineteen. Anything 'different' impressed me.

He stood when he spotted me, then bowed grandiosely, and I felt my cheeks burn because I always blushed at any inkling of attention.

'I feel as though I've known you forever,' he said.

I turned round, thinking he was talking to someone else. Matt had probably introduced him to loads of girls in the past few months.

'Very funny,' I said, realising his gaze was on me. 'Sorry.' I don't know why I said sorry, either.

I looked to the floor and pushed the heavy glass door open. I normally went to lectures without talking to anyone. Psychology was my second subject, and I had to take it for my criminology degree. I didn't know many people on my course. They always wanted to talk about feelings and that wasn't me at all. They wanted to talk about the troubles they had growing up and I couldn't really join in. No one else saw an interested but protective mother as an issue. They said at least she was bothered about me. Cue tales of having to cook their own meals, get a job at the age of eleven or whatever. The competitive race to the bottom I didn't want to take part in. It seemed that the seventy people studying psychology needed some sort of psychological help themselves.

'Wait, wait!' Callum called behind me, but I carried on walking. I was meeting Matt at the Union for lunch, and I didn't want him to think I was standing him up like last time. 'Leah!'

I stopped and turned around slowly. It was only then that I noticed he was wearing Doc Martens and rolled-up jeans and was jogging towards me. He took a drag on a barely smoked cigarette then lobbed it into a plant pot.

'What are you doing here?' I said, hoiking my heaving rucksack up. 'I have to get going. I'm meeting someone.'

'You're meeting Matt, aren't you?' he said, slipping sunglasses from his head to his eyes. 'Sorry I was so quiet the other night. You're quite intimidating, you know.'

I took a step back. Just because someone has a nice face, doesn't mean they don't have nefarious intentions. The lecture had literally been about social psychological face perception. Yeah, not falling for your flattery, mate.

Thank God I hadn't said that out loud.

'Don't look so worried,' he said. 'I'm not stalking you, really.'

I started walking again.

'I'll come with you,' he said. 'The Union, yeah? Twelve o'clock?'

I glanced at him.

'See,' he said. 'I'm not so weird. Matt asked me to join.'

'When did you start here?' I said. 'At Manchester. Have you started late? I thought you still lived in Derby.'

'Oh, I'm not a student.' He took a black flat cap out of his pocket and put it expertly on his head. 'God, no.' He doffed the peak. 'No offence.'

'None taken.'

'I wanted to start earning my own money.'

I glanced at him again. His coat looked expensive; so different to how he was dressed the week before.

'Why did you just take that lecture if you're not a student?'

'To see you, of course.'

Well, now he was just winding me up.

'Right.'

I was always an easy target because I was so gullible.

'I started my own business two years ago,' he said.

'OK.'

Almost at the Union and I couldn't shift the feeling that he was making up a story.

I reached for the door, but he intercepted, holding it open for me.

'Thanks,' I mumbled.

If he thought I was going to fawn over him for such a simple gesture, then he didn't know me. Actually, he didn't know me at all, did he?

'Up the stairs, I gather?' he said.

'Uh huh.'

It was like heading up to a nightclub, the staircase was that dark, and my heart was hammering. My shaking and heightened adrenaline – why was I so nervous around him? – eased a bit when I saw Matt through the glass doors. I almost ran to the table.

'Hey,' I said. 'Did you know he was coming today?'

Matt looked confused until he looked over my shoulder. His face dropped for a second before he stood.

Callum held out his arms.

'Surprise!'

'Callum!' Matt shuffled out of the booth to give this strange, red-haired man a hug. 'What the hell are you doing here? You said you couldn't get time off this week.'

'I managed to get the afternoon off.' He shook off his trench coat. I'd not seen a man under fifty wear one before. He sat on one of the stools and patted for me to sit next to him. 'So that's two weekends in a row that you have my delightful company. I'll have a JD and Coke please, mate.'

Matt's eye widened, and he reached into his pocket and pulled out a note. I was sure it was his last tenner, and a whisky and Coke would eat into most of that, even at the Union. It turned out that Matt did indeed have to support himself while he was at uni. No handouts for poor Matt.

'Err,' he said. 'OK.'

Callum pulled out his wallet and handed Matt two twenties.

'That should keep us going for a while.'

Matt's cheeks flushed and he spun round on his heels.

'You know Matt's parents are loaded,' said Callum. 'And now here he is acting the poor student like something out of a Pulp video.'

'Loaded?' I obviously had an inkling.

'Yeah.' He picked up a beer mat and tapped it on the table

by its corner. 'But because he wanted to do Film Studies – I mean, come on. What's the point of doing a degree in Film Studies? – then they wouldn't support him.'

'Oh.'

'His mum wanted him to study Law. Said she'd pay for his accommodation and give him an allowance if he did. She wanted him to follow in her mother's footsteps, but that was so far from what Matt saw himself doing. I mean, it's not as though he hasn't got the brain for it. Sometimes I think he'd have been better coming into partnership with me.' He looked up as Matt approached. 'Ah, there he is.'

'What have you been saying about me?'

'Nothing much,' said Callum.

Matt sat back in his place and pulled his drink towards him.

'On the lemonade?'

'There's vodka in it.' Matt put the two notes back on the table. 'I got this round in. I'm not a charity case.'

'Don't I know it.' He glanced at me. 'He was the loaded one growing up. Got to go on all the fancy school trips. Skiing, Easter in the south of France.'

Callum swiped the cash and placed it under his glass.

Forty pounds would have bought me at least two weeks of groceries.

Callum rested his chin on his hand again.

'I'm sorry I was so quiet the other night,' he said again. 'I was on strict instructions from this one to behave. He was really trying to impress that girl. What was her name? Lindsey? Elsie? Can't remember.' He sighed and gave the place a once-over. 'Matt has talked about you non-stop for as long as he's known you, Leah.'

'No, I haven't.'

'Why haven't you two ever hooked up?'

'What?' God, this was mortifying.

Matt wrinkled his nose. 'As if.' He nudged me with his elbow. 'You wanna see her in the mornings. Frightening.'

'Yeah, you wish. You wanna smell the bathroom after he's been in it.'

Matt slapped his hand on his heart. 'Low blow, Leah. Low blow.' He leant his head on my shoulder. 'You love me really, though, right?'

I picked up my drink, my little finger out, and took a delicate sip.

I shrugged. 'Someone's got to.'

Callum cleared his throat. 'Right. Anyway.' He downed almost half his drink. 'Before I met you last week, I saw your picture on Matt's Facebook.' Callum was looking at me, now. 'I hadn't seen it before – can't believe I've never been curious enough to seek it out after the way he's been going on about you. You're very striking.'

'Callum, don't, mate. You're making her feel uncomfortable. Leah doesn't do compliments.'

He wasn't, actually. No one had ever called me striking before.

'That's why I came here today,' he said. 'So I could meet you properly. I had to leave early the other night.' He says it as though I wasn't actually there. He tilted his head to the side. 'I hope you don't mind. I'm not always this impulsive.'

'OK,' I said. 'I thought you'd enrolled for a minute, earlier.'

Where was my usual banter, my usual taking the piss, my actual thought process?

'Why?' asked Matt.

'Because he was in my lecture.'

'Really?'

'Yes.' Callum raised his glass before taking a swig. 'Social Psychological Face Perception.'

'You remembered the title?'

I have to say I was impressed. Matt barely knew what

time it was most of the time, let alone knowing what course I was taking. Not that there had ever been anything between us. We'd not so much as even shared a drunken kiss.

'It was quite interesting,' said Callum. 'What do you think you'll do with your degree once you finish?'

'You actually went to Leah's lecture?' said Matt, shaking his head slowly.

'I didn't think it was a big deal. I thought anyone could just turn up.'

'How did you know when it was, mate?'

I shifted in my seat. It was such a weird feeling, having people talk about me when I was right there.

'Look,' I said, finally finding my voice. 'Yes, it was weird, you turning up like that, given that I hardly know you.'

'But you liked it, right?' Callum was smiling, totally unfazed by my stern tone of voice.

'I...'

'Did Matt tell you I've bought my own house?'

'He did.'

'At the ripe old age of twenty?'

'Yes.'

Matt leant back in the booth and threw his eyes to the ceiling.

'And I bet you checked out my Facebook profile.'

'Erm.' Was he psychic as well?

Callum put down his drink and raised both palms.

'It's OK,' he said. 'I won't embarrass you. I'm flattered, I really am.'

'I've had enough of this.' Matt got out of his seat again. 'What's going on, Callum?' He didn't wait for an answer. 'I'm going to the gents'.'

Callum watched as Matt strode off.

'Oh dear,' he said. 'I think I've hurt his feelings. Mentioning money... the fact that he talks about you all the time. Matt's more sensitive than he looks, you know.'

'I know what he's like. Matt doesn't pretend to be someone he's not,' I added pointedly.

Callum held up his hands again.

'Fair point. I'm sorry. I know I'm acting like a bit of a dick. Usually it impresses people, but I can see it's having the opposite effect on you. It's hard trying to big up my game. I'm totally faking it until I'm making it.'

'So you were lying about buying the house?'

'No, no. I have bought a house. I meant faking the confidence. Inside I'm shaking.'

'I don't believe that for a second.'

'It's true. Matt will tell you. I had the lot. Big teeth, cow's lick, a forty-inch waist. I'm telling you. Hot, I was not. Unlike our friend, Matt.'

'You shouldn't put yourself down. I was quiet in school. Observing more than joining in, but it made me who I am now. It's why I'm interested in human behaviour.'

'Listen to us,' he said. 'Talking as though we're old before our time.' He glanced at Matt who was coming out of the loos. 'Hey, do you fancy coming out to dinner with me tonight?'

'Dinner?'

'I'm bigging it up again, aren't I? I mean, maybe a Wetherspoons. You don't have to. I won't be offended.'

'You're very contrary, aren't you, Callum?'

And that was our second encounter. I always remember calling him contrary because that was what he was. Sure of himself one minute, the next crippled with anxiety.

That night I wore my black flowery dress, DMs, and my favourite leather jacket. I sat on the edge of my bed waiting for the doorbell. At five minutes to eight I had convinced myself he wasn't coming, and he wasn't even late.

'You're wearing your favourite dress.' Matt leant against my bedroom doorway, holding a bottle of beer. 'I didn't think you actually liked him.'

'What do you care?' I said, a little too huffily. 'Why are you two so competitive?'

He shrugged. 'Just the way it is. The way it's always been. He's like my brother, I suppose.'

'Aren't you going out tonight?' I said. 'With Annalise?'

'I called in sick.'

He laughed.

I didn't.

'You shouldn't treat people like that. Annalise is a really nice person.'

He sat on the other end of my bed, causing me to bounce slightly.

'I knew this would happen if you two got together.' He started picking the label off the lager bottle. 'That's why I've kept you two apart so long.'

'What are you talking about?'

'That you and Callum would gang up against me. Then you'd realise that I'm a shithead after all.'

'I like you, Matt. You're like family to me. I don't mind you being a shithead. I just don't want you to treat women like shit.'

He stood as the doorbell chimed.

'Sorry, Leah. Just ignore me. I'm just feeling sorry for myself.' He paused at the door. 'Do you want me to get it?'

I stood, checked my hair in the mirror.

'I'll get it.'

Matt walked towards his room, head down. 'Tell him I said hi,' he said before shutting his door.

I took several deep breaths in and out, checked my hair and lip gloss in the hall mirror before I opened the door.

'I like that,' he said. 'That you wanted to look nice.'

'How did you...?' I closed the door behind me. 'Ah, yes. The frosted glass in the door.' I glanced at the sky. 'How embarrassing.'

'It's not.' He took hold of my hand, and my heart gave a jolt. 'It's lovely. I knew you'd be lovely. I really feel like I've known you for a long time.'

'I...'

'It's OK. You don't have to say the same. I know Matt has barely talked about me. I get it.'

He held open the door to a small Italian off the high street.

'I thought you said Wetherspoons,' I tried to say without moving my lips. 'I didn't dress posh.'

He laughed.

'You know it doesn't matter what you wear.' He pulled out the chair for me after we were shown to our table. 'Class is good manners – how you behave and how you treat people. You can't buy it.' He was still standing as he took my jacket from the back of my chair and handed it along with his and a fiver to the waiter. 'Though money does help.'

* * *

Standing by the lake, now, I realise I've not thought about that day and that night for so long.

Where have the tears come from? I wipe them away with my sleeve. The memory, and the tears.

Callum really was quite lovely.

For over a decade he was quite lovely.

Until he wasn't.

I get up from the rickety seat outside the boathouse and head towards the garden room, finally hearing some signs of life from inside. The blinds are down but I can definitely hear movement.

I knock on the glass door.

'Good morning,' I say. 'Is anyone alive in there?'

'Is that you, Leah?' asks Jake.

I hope it's Leah, I think he whispers.

'Yes,' I say. 'Why are you acting so weird?'

The key turns in the lock and Jake opens the door. He's wearing cut-off denim shorts.

'Oh my God, Jake! Weren't they jeans last night?'

'Yeah.' He runs a hand through his hair. 'I have no idea.' He bends down and holds up the two legs of his jeans. 'I found these next to a pair of scissors. I think it was because it was so hot in here, and I think this place is sometimes used as an office. Didn't realise we'd had the heating on full blast. Thought it was summer. At least, I think that's how it happened.'

I peek over his shoulder; Matt is lying on a camp bed, still fully dressed. Didn't Dad say they were in their boxers?

'I'm sure our drinks must've been spiked last night,' says Matt, his eyes still closed.

'Right. OK,' I say. 'Well, it's almost eleven. Isn't your mum supposed to be here soon?'

'Yes, yes.' He's staring at the ceiling. 'I'll just wake up a bit.'

'Come on, Matt. In case you've forgotten, it's Saturday and we're getting married tomorrow. Come inside the house and get some coffee. I think you're in dire need of some. And it's not often we have our family under one roof.'

'Listen.' Jake steps out the garden room and pulls the door to. 'Has there been something going on with you and Matt's parents?'

'Like what?'

I admit, Matt's parents and I are not close. I always feel as though I'm a disappointment to them – especially Olivia. Even after all I've achieved with my recruitment business. I guess it's just a fraction of what Matt has felt like for most of his life.

'Like, er...' He rakes a hand through his hair, squints in the sunlight. 'Erm.'

'Spit it out, Jacob!'

He looks over my head at a granite-coloured SUV that pulls onto the gravel drive at the side of the house.

Olivia is the only one in the car.

She gets out and starts walking towards me. She was so excited when she saw me last weekend because she loves an event. She even took me out for lunch to that gorgeous Italian restaurant in Alderley Edge. Today, she's wearing a striped navy and white long-sleeved top with a gilet over the top, paired with dark blue jeans. It's her weekend uniform.

'Morning, Olivia,' I say lightly. 'The boys are a little worse for wear this morning.'

She doesn't meet my gaze. She opens the glass door. 'Come on, Matt. Wake up. You need to be up and ready. I need to talk to you before your dad gets here.'

'What's going on?' I say. 'Is everything all right with Greg?'

'Huh.'

She finally casts a glance in my direction. I've never seen her look so enraged. She puts on a pair of sunglasses and stomps towards the house. She pauses at the corner.

'Leah,' she shouts. 'Noah is wandering on the veranda. You'd better come and see to him.'

'What?' I walk quickly. 'My dad won't be far behind him.'

By the time I get to the veranda, Olivia has disappeared into the house.

Noah is indeed alone on the veranda.

'Dad?'

'Boo!' Dad pops his head around the other side of the house, causing Noah to jump and then run towards him in a fit of giggles.

''gain, 'gain!'

'Noah's fine,' I say, walking in the house. 'Dad's just playing hide and seek with him.'

Olivia's not in the kitchen, the living room, or the snug.

But Katherine is sitting on a bar stool at the breakfast bar, nursing another cup of coffee.

She looks up from a magazine when I enter the kitchen.

'I don't know what's wrong with Olivia,' she says, 'but she just stormed through the house looking like fury personified. She didn't even look at me when I shouted hello. What's happened?'

'I have no idea. Did she go upstairs?'

'I'd say. Surprised you couldn't hear her stomping up from outside.' Katherine gets up to rinse out the coffee cup. 'Is Jake awake? Did you manage to get any sense out of them?'

I try to listen to where Olivia is upstairs.

'Jake cut the legs off his trousers,' I say.

I hear a creak from the floorboard upstairs. It's the room Matt and I are staying in. Is Olivia rooting through my things?

Jake comes through the front door in bare feet.

'Leah,' he whispers, and I hear it even though I'm several metres away. 'Come upstairs. I need to have a word.'

'Olivia's upstairs,' I whisper, too. 'I think she's in my room.'

He stands at the door to the snug and beckons me to join him.

Inside, I stand near the fireplace; he closes the door gently behind him.

He takes out his phone.

'Matt was sent these screenshots last night from an unknown number.' He passes me his mobile. 'He forwarded them to mine.'

It's a photo of a WhatsApp exchange with the initials 'GT' at the top.

> Hey, Greg. I've been thinking about you all night.

I think we should stop with the messaging. I don't feel comfortable with it.

Party pooper. I was going to send you another picture as well.

I'm going to delete these messages. I think you should do the same.

Boohoo you're no fun. I thought you liked me like that. I've seen you looking at me, Greg. I was rather flattered.

I'm going to block you now.

You haven't though, have you?

I know you want it as much as I do.

I've taken a picture just for you. Do you want to see it?

I know you're reading these messages.

Here you go.

'Why are you showing me these?' I say to Jake. 'It's not Matt's dad Greg, is it?'

'Really, Leah?' His eyes are narrowed, examining my face. 'Are you sure you don't recognise them?'

'Stop being so weird! Of course I don't recognise them. You've only just shown them to me.'

'Yeah, I thought as much. Swipe to the left.'

I do as he says.

'Oh, my God.'

On the screen is a photograph of me from the waist up. I'm only wearing a bra and a grey silk dressing gown off the shoulders.

What the hell is this doing on my brother's phone?

'Who would send this?'

'I've no idea. Some weirdo pretending to be you.'

'God, that's so embarrassing. And to Greg.' I bend, groaning with mortification. 'What number has it been sent from?'

'I'm not sure. Matt was sent the picture from a number he doesn't recognise.'

I crumple onto the sofa.

'This is terrible. And Olivia... She must know all about it. Oh, Jesus. This is so embarrassing. I can't believe anyone could do something like this. Why?'

'Maybe we need to ask Greg to ring the number – if he still has it.'

I look at the image again. The photo of me isn't that reveal-ing, but the implication of me sending it to my father-in-law-to-be is so shameful.

I take a calming deep breath.

'I can't remember when this was taken. My hair is shoulder length and it's cherry red. God, it must be years old.'

'That's what Matt said when we talked about it last night.

'Oh. What did he say? He doesn't think it was actually me who sent them, does he?'

'Not from what he said last night. I told him it would be so out of character for you to do something like this, and he seemed to agree with me.'

'Seemed to?'

'I can't presume to know what's going on in his head, Leah.'

'This would explain why he was acting so strangely with me last night.'

'It's just so weird that someone would do this. How would they have got Greg's number?'

'On his company website, I guess.'

I'm shaking all over.

'Who would you have sent the photo to?' Jake asks gently.

'It's so old – why would I send it to anyone?'

'Are you sure? Not even when Callum was alive?'

'I... I don't know. We might've exchanged pictures when he was away, but they were always tongue-in-cheek. It was so long ago. And the police took his phone. How would someone get hold of this?'

'It's really strange.'

'It's really creepy.'

There are footsteps down the stairs.

God, I can't face Olivia right now. Even though it wasn't me – she still *thinks* it's me who's been sending messages to her husband.

'No wonder Olivia's been in a mood with me. What's the date on those messages?'

'They're dated yesterday, but Matt only saw them after you'd gone to bed.'

My mind goes to the card signed with Callum's name.

'I think it's linked to something else,' I say. 'Someone's trying to ruin – or even put a halt to – our wedding.'

'Who would do this, though? Tania perhaps? Or someone from your past?'

'I don't know. But I'm going to get that number off Greg – as humiliating as that's going to be – and ring the number. No one is going to spoil tomorrow. I won't let them.'

Fury builds in my chest with every breath.

'Do you think it's to do with you getting Callum declared legally dead?' Jake asks. 'Or someone pissed off that you're marrying Matt? And at the house that Callum disappeared from?'

'But the legal stuff was finalised months ago. And it was Olivia's idea to have the wedding here. I don't think Matt thought too deeply about agreeing to it.'

'Really? Callum was only declared dead a few months ago. Why is Matt rushing it?'

'I don't think we're rushing it. We've been together for over five years; we have a child together. And I've known him all my adult life. I think he wanted to change the memories of this place to happier ones. I think it's quite sweet, really.'

'I guess.'

'No. It's nothing to do with Matt. We have a child together.'

Could it be someone I've not thought of? Something related to Callum's past. Could his biological father be trying to ruin my life in some kind of sick game of revenge at missing out on a chance to get to know his son? I don't even know what he looks like, so it's not as though I can be on the lookout for him.

A wave of lightheadedness overwhelms me; I lean against the settee.

The idea that it might be a stranger doing all of this makes my skin prickle. The person responsible is coming tomorrow. And, without knowing who it is, I can do nothing to stop them.

NINE

First the card signed from Callum and now inappropriate messages to Matt's dad from someone pretending to be me. And there's still over twenty-four hours until the wedding. A part of me thinks it can't get much worse than this; another part believes this is just the beginning.

I feel sick. When I close my eyes, I see the pictures of me in my underwear that Greg has seen. It's just so mortifying. And from Olivia's behaviour towards me, it's clear that she knows something's amiss. They were pictures I sent to Callum almost ten years ago judging from my hairstyle, but I wasn't going to say so explicitly to my brother.

I haven't got the same phone now, but the pictures will be stored on my iCloud. I need to check on my laptop. Thankfully I bring it with me everywhere.

I haven't sent any pictures of that nature to Matt or anyone else. Someone could've hacked my account. That sort of thing happens all the time. It could be someone I've unknowingly upset at work, but I try to get along with everyone. It's all just so creepy thinking that someone out there is trying to ruin my life.

'Mummy!' Noah runs into the snug and dives onto the sofa. 'I'm hungry.'

'Right, right.' *Come on. Pull yourself together, Leah.* 'Let's go and see what's in the fridge.'

He slides off and takes hold of my hand.

'I brought some of those Dairylea Dunkers you like with us. It'll keep you going till lunch time.'

My voice falters and my stomach drops. Olivia's in the kitchen, scrolling through her phone. She doesn't look up, but I know she knows that I'm here.

'Hey, Olivia,' I say. I've got nothing to be ashamed about. I reach into the fridge for Noah's snack, then settle him at the table. 'Can I have a word? My brother told me that Greg's been getting messages from someone pretending to be me.'

Might as well just come out and say it.

She looks up, narrows her eyes.

'*Pretending* to be you?' She cocks her head to the side.

'Honestly, I wouldn't do that. Why would you think that of me? We're family.'

She places her phone on the table.

'I thought I knew my husband, but he was replying right back to you, wasn't he? For weeks!'

'Weeks?' I steady myself, grabbing the edge of the table. 'But Jake showed me the messages. There were only a couple.'

'How did Jake get the messages?'

Why does she believe they could actually be from me? Greg and I get on well, but at a respectful distance. Like an uncle, I guess. Though I don't have an uncle to compare our relationship to.

'From Matt's phone. Someone sent screenshots to him from an unknown number. I thought you or Greg might've sent them to him.' My hands tremble. 'I don't know, Olivia. I've just found out about this myself. I am mortified.' A surge of adrenaline seems to flood my chest. 'I need to find out who did this. I... I can't believe...'

A tear runs down her face.

'I promise you,' I say. 'It wasn't me. Why would I do such a thing? I love Matt.' I step closer to her. 'Someone left a wedding card on the back doormat last night. It had a black heart on the front and inside it was signed from Callum.'

She wipes her face with her sleeve. 'What?'

'I know. It's awful. But I believe the same person who sent that is behind the messages sent to Greg.'

'Oh, gosh. That is very strange.' She looks around the kitchen. 'Where are the caterers I hired? Have they not been in this morning? The place is a mess.'

I was expecting more of a reaction about the card. And I don't know what she's seeing; the kitchen looks perfectly fine to me. Bless Dad, he's done a great job of cleaning up after breakfast. I shouldn't have left it to him. I'm a terrible daughter.

'I don't know. What time were they meant to be arriving?' I ask.

She glares at me – a look of loathing in her eyes. She's never looked at me like that before and it hurts more than it should.

'Yesterday morning, just before you all arrived.' She walks over to the fridge and opens it. 'They didn't touch the lamb I told them to cook last night. And there's still potatoes, carrots... What did you all eat last night?'

'Matt organised a curry to be delivered. It was lovely.'

She picks up her phone.

'They texted me yesterday morning to say they were on their way. They were meant to cook, keep on top of the cleaning.' She looks up at me. 'Are you sure you haven't seen them? You've probably been quite busy on your phone.' She raises an eyebrow.

'I haven't seen them, Olivia. No one else has arrived since yesterday evening.'

Olivia goes into the hall, and shouts, 'Matt!'

I have never seen this side to Olivia before. She's always been lovely to me. But this ambivalence seems to come from her so easily, it's like she's thought ill of me all this time. Did *she* think Matt and I shouldn't have gotten together, too?

Noah slides off the chair and follows his grandmother.

'Nana!'

Olivia's face softens as she bends to pick him up, and my skin prickles as she strokes his face. I want to grab my son out of her arms.

Why won't she believe me? Does she really think I'm that type of person? I feel like running or screaming to release the rage that's inside me.

I need to prove to her that it wasn't me. Right now, it's more important than preparing for my wedding. Because if Matt's family think I'm a liar and a cheat, then I'm not sure I even want to marry into it.

TEN

I'm heading up to Katherine's room; the voice of reason. I'm hoping so, anyway. I try to make my way there quietly – Dad's having a well-deserved nap in the next bedroom – and tap on her door.

'Who is it?' she yells.

'It's me.'

'Why are you whispering?' she says, flinging open the door.

'You look lovely!' She's curled her beautiful long red hair into big waves, and her eye make-up is stunning. 'How did you manage that in half an hour?'

She shrugs, trying to look casual.

'Well, you know. Years of practice.' She beckons me into the room. 'Your eyes look red. Have you been crying?'

I sit on the bed. 'Not yet.'

The release of the tears that have threatened to spill over for this past hour is almost a relief.

'Oh no, Leah.' Katherine sits next to me and puts an arm around my shoulder.

'Did Jake tell you what happened?' I say, dabbing my face.

'Which bit?'

I look up, eyes wide. 'How many bits are there?'

'Well, the card,' she says, 'the messages, the disappearance of the housekeepers...'

'You know about them?'

'Didn't want to pile more on top of your shoulders. I doubt they're anything to worry about. You've enough on your plate.' She sits next to me. 'Sorry for mixing the metaphors.'

'You don't believe I've been sending messages to Matt's dad, do you?'

'Of course not! Not for a moment. God, he's about seventy, isn't he?'

She hands me a tissue; I wipe my eyes and nose.

'He's sixty-five.'

'Looks pretty good for his age.'

'You just said he looks seventy.'

'I wasn't far wrong.'

'So you're saying if he was, like, Matt's stepdad, and in his forties or fifties, then there'd be a chance of me messaging him?'

Katherine rubs her forehead between the eyes.

'God, it's too early and I feel too headachy to be over-analysing what I meant.'

'Olivia thinks they're from me. She probably thinks we've been having an affair.'

'If we get the number they were sent from, we could solve this pretty quickly.'

'If whoever it is answers us.'

She stands; I follow her out the bedroom.

'The number wasn't on the screenshots.'

'Let's go and ask Jake,' she says, heading downstairs. 'If I can find him. This house is so big, isn't it? I've no idea why they call it a cottage.'

Olivia's standing near the front door helping Noah put his wellies on.

'Not big enough,' I say quietly.

'We'll go into the snug,' whispers Katherine. 'You all right, Noah?' she says more loudly.

'Me and Nana feed ducks.'

Olivia doesn't look up.

'Rightio.'

I've never heard Katherine say that word before. *Jolly, jolly. Everything's perfectly fine.* Just my life going to shit. Once again.

'Thanks for that, Olivia,' I say, using the same tone as Katherine. 'Have a lovely time, Noah!'

He runs over to me and hugs my legs.

'Bye, Mumma.'

Olivia still hasn't looked at me, though I can't say I blame her, really. I watch as they leave the house hand in hand.

'Come on,' says Katherine, pushing open the door to the snug, 'let's light a fire and get cosy. We need to figure this out.'

'I don't think we're going to sort anything just sitting around in front of the fire, tempting as it sounds.' I sit on the edge of the sofa as Katherine scrunches sheets of newspaper into balls. 'I need to find out the phone number that sent the messages. The same person might be the one who sent the card. And they've already let us know that they're in the area.'

'Unless they asked someone else to post the card.' Katherine places kindling onto the newspaper and lights it. 'It's all a bit weird, don't you think? Whoever it is has had plenty of time to split you and Matt up.'

'Someone who wants to humiliate me in public, Katherine.'

'That's a bit scary.'

'And whoever it is, is going to turn up tomorrow.' I stand. 'I can't sit and wait for something else. I'm meant to be excited for my wedding, not sitting here a nervous wreck. I'm going to talk to Matt. Have you seen him?'

'We passed on the landing about half an hour ago.' She prods the igniting flames with a poker. 'He didn't reply when I said, "Good morning". Maybe he thinks I knew about the messages to his dad.'

'Eh?'

'I don't mean that I believe you sent them. It's just that nothing fazes me. I've heard a lot of things at work. People seldom surprise me.'

'Thank you, Katherine.' I almost want to drop to the floor and kiss her feet. Tears come to my eyes like they always do when someone throws me a glimmer of kindness. 'I think you're the only one who believes me.'

'No, not at all.' She places the poker on the stone fireplace. 'Your dad and your brother believe it wasn't you.' She swivels to face me. 'Jake mentioned it to your dad and me last night, but we didn't want to worry you. And now, after the card...'

'Does Matt know about the card?'

'Not that I know of.'

'OK. Right. I'll go and speak to him. We'll get this sorted. I'm not having some psycho trying to spoil our weekend.' Could it actually be Callum? Has he been in hiding in the area for almost a decade? With no trace, no bank accounts touched, no passport used, and no relatives or friends contacted, it's a ridiculous notion. It's wishful thinking, but at the same time what would happen if it was him? My wedding couldn't go ahead for sure. I feel awful that I'm thinking such things when I should be wanting him to be alive more than anything. It can't be him, I know that. 'If whoever it is is doing these things to me, they might be messing with Matt, too.'

I head out the room, upstairs and into our bedroom. Matt's clothes from last night are draped on the chair in the corner and, in the bathroom, the shower is running. I know him well enough to know he wouldn't appreciate me knocking on the bathroom door no matter how overwhelming my sense of urgency is.

I stand at the window and in my mind's eye, I see the woman that was there last night. Dressed in black, staring straight at me. In the darkness I was convinced it was Tania, but would she really humiliate herself like that?

Now, Olivia and Noah are standing at the lake's edge. Noah, in his wellies, squealing as he splashes in the water. He bends to pick up a pebble and lobs it into the water; it lands just a metre from him, bless his heart.

Olivia's head turns to the right. It looks as though she's talking to someone but they're out of my eyeline. Even when I stand on the bed and press my head against the window, I can't see who it is.

'What the hell are you doing?'

Matt has opened the bathroom door and is standing at the door wearing only a towel.

I jump off the bed, and wipe the window clean of condensation I made with my breath.

'Your mum's talking to someone – I can't make out who it is.' I sit on the bed. 'Never mind.' I don't recognise the person I'm becoming. I wasn't this bad after Callum went missing. Perhaps it's some sort of delayed reaction – PTSD, perhaps.

Matt grabs his clothes out the wardrobe – he doesn't like to live out of a case – and takes them to the bathroom. This cannot be a good sign – he normally doesn't mind about getting dressed in front of me.

My heart, and mind, are racing. If Matt doesn't believe me, then effectively our relationship is over. I know that's a strange way of thinking. A form of self-preservation, probably.

He opens the door, now fully dressed, still holding the towel. He rubs his hair with it before putting it in the laundry basket.

'Why didn't you tell me about the screenshots?' I say. 'Do you think it was me who sent them?'

'Of course I don't think it's you.'

I want to collapse in relief. Thank God he trusts me. I

shouldn't have doubted that. I want to hug and kiss him right now, but he looks pensive.

He sighs loudly. 'I'm just upset about my dad. I didn't think he was that type of person. I mean, we've *all* got those message requests in our DMs – usually scammers wanting money. I can't believe my dad would...'

'Sorry. I don't mean to brush off your feelings about your dad, but' – I head to the wardrobe to retrieve the card from my bag – 'I got this last night. I was going to tell you when you and Jake got back from the pub, but you were a bit wasted.'

'Sorry about that.' He moves the clothes from the chair and sits. 'Let's have a look.'

I watch his face as he opens the card and takes in the words.

'Holy shit. When did this arrive?'

'I'm not sure, but it was on the doormat near the back door last night. After you and Jake left for the pub.'

'Hand delivered, then?'

'Yes. And then, this morning, Jake showed me the messages that someone sent to your dad, saying they're from me. It's so weird. Who would think to do something like that? What the hell is going on?'

His expression is so hard to read. Is he going to think I'm making all of this up – trying to save my own skin? Or is he wondering if his ex-girlfriend is the person behind it all?

'Do you recognise the handwriting?' he asks after an excruciating wait.

'It looks like Callum's handwriting to me.'

'That's what I think, too. Whoever wrote this knows him. Well, *knew* him.' He sits next to me on the bed. 'What if...?'

'So you really do believe me?' I say, reaching over to touch his hand, scared that he'll swipe it away. 'About the messages to your dad, I mean. That they weren't from me.'

'You wouldn't write anything as graphic as that. I mean, I'm not suggesting you're a prude or anything...' He laughs, and it quells some of my paranoia that everyone is out to get me. 'You can't bear people typing in text speak. And as if you'd send a picture like that of yourself.' He reaches to the bedside cabinet for his phone and opens the photo app. He zooms into the one with the selfie, and I can't even look at it, my face burns. 'When is this actually from? Are you wearing a wig?'

I want to flop onto the bed and cover my face with a pillow.

'It was over ten years ago.' I reach under the bed to get my laptop, flip it open and go into my iCloud account. I scroll through the years until I come to 2014. 'Look. It's time stamped. Halloween ten years ago. And yes, it's a wig. I must've taken it for a laugh. But there's no way I would've sent it to anyone.'

'Not even Callum?'

'Not that I remember. He was right there – why would I send him the picture if he was right next to me? But I might've done. I can't recall.'

'This is really weird, Leah. Who has access to your laptop?'

'Everyone in this house. People at work. But I have a PIN.'

'Have you noticed logins from unknown devices?'

'No.'

'Saying that, if they have your passwords, they'd delete any alerts. Change your iCloud password. Right now. You don't know what else they've been up to with your account.'

I navigate to the settings and set up the convoluted password my laptop suggests.

'Change it every few days until this is sorted,' he says. 'And don't let anyone know what it is.'

'I don't anyway.'

'I know. But just to make sure.' He pauses. 'Do you think...?'

'What?'

'Well, it can't have come from Callum's phone because I found it that night.'

'I know.'

'But still. I have got the strangest feeling. These

things... They are totally something Callum would do. He'd find it hilarious. Did he have another phone?'

'Not that I know of. But it can't be from him. It's impossible. The police found no proof of life. They think he died the night he disappeared. And why would he have waited so long?'

'Until we find his body, Leah, nothing's impossible.'

'If he is alive,' I say solemnly, 'then we can't get married.'

I watch his face as that realisation sinks in.

'But he's been declared legally dead. It won't make a difference, will it?'

'If he's alive,' I say, 'it will cancel all of that out.' I glance at the ceiling, tears threatening to fall. 'Why can't anything ever be straightforward.'

'Well, we'll make it straightforward.' He strokes my cheek. 'You know how long I've waited to be married to you. Especially as I watched him treat you like shit.'

'I don't tend to dwell on all of that.' I can't tell him that I was planning on leaving Callum. I've never told anyone. How would that have looked? Katherine certainly knew about it, but she kept her word and has never told a soul.

'He used to go out all the time,' says Matt, 'leaving you wondering where he was.'

'I guess I had my own life, too, so it didn't sting so much. I was in denial for a long time. I enjoyed my freedom, too.'

'Not in the way *he* enjoyed his freedom. He didn't take care of you like you deserved to be taken care of.'

'I'm not made of glass, Matt. I don't need looking after.'

'You know that's not what I mean. I'm not trying to patronise you, Leah. You know I love you so much. I'd do anything for you.'

'Are you still drunk?' I nudge him gently with my shoulder and smile.

He grins and nudges me back. 'No.'

'It's not like you to get absolutely wasted. Last night was the first time in years since I've seen you like that.'

'I know. I'm sorry. Your brother sold it to me as a stag do, which is a bit sad considering there were only two of us. He's a very bad influence.'

'He's not that bad.'

'I know. He had quite a lot to drink last night, though, and was slagging off Callum. I didn't know Jake disliked him so much.'

'He wasn't his biggest fan.' I don't go into the details. My brother wouldn't like reminding of the trouble Callum stirred up for him.

At the same time, Matt's phone and mine beep with a message.

As he clicks on it, his mouth drops open.

'Check your messages, Leah.'

'What? Why?'

'To see if you got the same one I did.'

I reach into my pocket and pull out my phone, tapping open the message:

> One of you killed me that night. I know who.
> Tick tock, tick tock. Not long till the truth
> comes out.

ELEVEN

I take Matt's phone from his hands; the messages are identical.

'What the hell are they talking about?' I say. 'Killed him?'

'Well, now they're really grasping at straws.' He strides to the window. 'I can't see anyone watching. Though it's not like they're going to hang around here, is it?' His phone camera sounds as he screenshots the message. 'The whole thing's ridiculous. It must be a kid behind this. It's just—'

There are footsteps up the stairs.

Katherine barges in, the colour drained from her face.

She's holding her phone in trembling hands.

'Did you get the message, too?' I ask.

She nods slowly.

'Someone thinks one of us killed Callum,' she says. 'But the police took our statements years ago. We weren't persons of interest. There was a witness who saw Callum alone at the lakeside. They were convinced he'd taken his own life.'

A floorboard on the landing creaks.

Jake stands at the doorway, holding his phone. Katherine ushers him inside and closes the door.

'What are we going to do?' he asks.

'I don't understand,' I say. 'Why would we have to do anything? This whole thing is made up, you know it is. Like the messages to Matt's dad.'

That Matt, Jake, and Katherine received the same text message is a little comfort to me. I know I shouldn't be thinking this way, but now I'm not going through this alone.

'Why would someone say this?' Matt asks. 'It's not as though there's any evidence that he was murdered. The police couldn't find his body. They've got nothing to go on.'

Katherine and Jake exchange a glance.

'What is it?' asks Matt. 'What are you two not telling us?'

'It's not that.' Jake slides his phone into his jeans pocket. 'But some of us weren't exactly honest in our statements, were we? As long as we keep it all between ourselves, then nothing can happen to us.'

'What the hell are you talking about?' I stand, but the room isn't big enough for four adults. I move closer to the head of the bed near the window. 'Keep what between us?'

I look to Matt; he's frowning, staring at Jake.

'Can someone tell me what's going on!' Even if I jumped up and down on the bed, it feels as though they won't see me. 'Matt. What is it?'

'Jake seems to think I lied to the police.' He's still staring at my brother. 'Don't you, Jake?'

'I didn't mean it like that.' Jake runs a hand through his hair. 'Sorry. Sorry. This message has shaken me.'

'Why has it shaken you,' I ask, 'if you've done nothing wrong?'

'I could say the same to you, Leah.' He holds out his hand. 'Why the hell am I shaking so much.' He sits at the edge of the bed, swivels to face Matt. 'What I meant was, we kept certain things from the police. Like the beef each of us had with him.

You, Matt, because he was trying to convince Tania you were having an affair with Leah—'

'What?' Matt and I say it at the same time.

'—and me, because he was blackmailing me. Didn't each of us go out after Callum left?' He stands to face the room, looking at Katherine, then to Matt.

'I didn't.' The three of them turn to face me. 'I went upstairs. Tania was there. Katherine was crying in her bedroom.'

'What?' Jakes shoots a look to his wife. 'I don't remember you crying that night.'

'It's nothing. I was pissed, that's all.'

'But you didn't know Callum was blackmailing me at that point, did you?'

Katherine strides into the ensuite, pulls several sheets of toilet paper to blow her nose.

'You told her?' I say, shocked. 'When did you tell her?'

'It doesn't matter,' Jake says dismissively.

'This whole thing's ridiculous,' says Katherine. 'Letting some coward, some weirdo stranger disrupt our lives like this.' She throws the tissue in the bin. 'God, I must be hormonal or something.'

'We won't need to wait for long to see who's behind all of this,' I say quietly. 'They're coming tomorrow.'

'I don't believe that for a second,' says Katherine. 'What we're going to do, is have a lovely weekend, have a lovely wedding, and push this whole thing to the back of our minds. I for one' – she takes out her phone – 'am switching mine off.' She throws it onto the bed. 'See, I feel better already.' She walks towards door, opens it. 'I'm going to get changed. I need a very stiff drink.'

She closes the door gently.

'What the hell was all that about?' I say to Matt, to Jake. 'I've never seen Katherine like that before.'

Jake sticks his hands in his pocket. 'No idea.'

There's a tap on the bedroom door.

'Hello, Leah?' Dad pushes it open. He looks as though he's seen a ghost. 'Hey, love. There's someone at the door for you. And it's someone I don't think you're expecting.'

TWELVE

Matt and I glance at each other before dashing from the room, leaving Jake in the bedroom alone. We thud down the stairs, me on pure adrenaline.

This might be it. The person who has been taunting me – us – has made their appearance early. Maybe they couldn't wait.

The front door's ajar; I can't see who's behind it.

I pause and Matt almost runs into the back of me.

'I can't open it,' I say, breathless. 'What if it's someone dangerous? I know it *can't* be Callum, but... The card said they'd show up tomorrow, not today.'

He squeezes my hand, then strides to the door.

I'm fixed to the spot.

'Oh,' he says, opening the door wider. 'Jennie.'

Jennie? Callum's mother, Jennie?

I haven't seen her for almost three years.

'Jennie,' I repeat. 'What... Why are you here?' I walk slowly towards her. 'Sorry. I mean, hello! It's just I wasn't expecting you. Is everything all right?'

She looks as though she's aged twenty years since I saw her

last. Her hair is almost totally grey. Her skin is pale, and she isn't wearing make-up. She used to always wear a full face of make-up.

Matt bends to kiss her on the cheek. He's almost twice the height of her.

'Come in, Jennie,' he says. 'Did you say hi to Mum?'

I peek over Matt's shoulder, but Olivia and Noah must've walked further along the lake's edge.

'Yes, yes,' Jennie says, distracted.

She steps inside. Matt helps her take off her coat and she's wearing a huge scarf and two cardigans underneath. She's even smaller than she first appeared.

'Why don't you show Jennie through to the main living room,' says Matt. 'I'll make us some tea.'

'Thank you, Matt,' she says. 'That's very kind of you.'

How old must she be now? When she gave birth to Callum, she was in her mid-forties, after believing she could never have children. Eight-five, eighty-six? I sit on the sofa opposite her.

'How did you get here?' I say. 'Did you drive? I mean, sorry, I didn't mean for it to come out like that. It's just you never liked driving for longer than thirty minutes. I can't say I do either to be honest.'

'It's OK, Leah.'

She pulls one of the cardigans tighter around her middle. I want to offer a blanket, but I don't want her to get the wrong idea.

'I know I look old to you,' she says. 'But I certainly don't feel it. These past eight years have been so tough for me. I know they're showing on my face. That's what grief does to you: turns you into a person you don't recognise. I'm sure you understand. Having gone through it yourself.'

'I do understand, Jennie. I think about you all the time.'

'I'm sure you do.' Her tone is clipped. She looks around the room. 'It still looks the same, doesn't it? I know it's been decorated and updated since, but the bare bones of the place are still the same. I almost didn't come.'

I want to ask her why she did, but my lips won't work; I can't find the right words.

'I remember the first day,' she says. 'After the night he went missing. The hours we spent in here, constantly looking out the window. The others going out searching but you and I stayed together here, waiting. Because we didn't want him returning to an empty house. Because what if he'd been freezing cold out there? What if he'd got lost. And I know that's a silly thing to have thought because he'd been here so many times with Matt and his family.'

'I know.'

'And I remember, the second night – because Olivia and Greg kindly let me stay for as long as I wanted – I remember listening to you from the room next door. You cried yourself to sleep. I'm sorry, I shouldn't have invaded your privacy by listening and I'm only mentioning it now. But hearing you crying... I knew I wasn't alone in wanting him back. Hearing you cry made me feel that there was hope.' She glances at the ceiling. 'I don't know what I'm trying to say.'

I slide off the sofa and walk on my knees towards her. I don't know how she's done this for all these years. Stayed strong, stayed hopeful. Stayed alive. If it were Noah and he'd gone out one night and never came back, I don't know if I'd have ever gotten out of bed with grief.

I place a hand on hers, and she clings to it tightly. The gesture makes a tear fall from my eye. Kindness always touches me.

'It's all right,' she says. 'I knew you had to make a fresh start.'

The tears won't stop, and I feel awful; this is her grief and not mine. I've always cried more about other people's sadness than my own.

'I know, love.' She pats my head. 'It's OK.'

She takes a packet of tissues out of her handbag. 'I always carry a packet with me.' She shakes out a rectangle and passes it to me. 'You never know when it might hit you.'

I sit up and dab my face.

'I'm so sorry,' I say. 'This weekend has been so overwhelming.'

'I dare say it has. To be honest I was quite surprised when I heard you were having the wedding at this house.'

'It wasn't my decision.'

'Come on, Leah. You're not a wallflower.'

'It was important to Matt and his parents. This place means a lot to them – they wanted to host a happy occasion, to rid the place of any bad memories. That's what they said. It seemed like a good idea when it was sold to me.'

'I suppose I see the reasoning in that.'

The door slams open and Noah runs in, still wearing his wellies.

Jennie stands and places her hands on her knees, bending slightly to match his height.

'Who do we have here, then?' she says. 'Don't tell me, you're little Noah?'

Noah puts his little finger in the corner of his mouth and nods shyly.

'Last time I saw you' – she puts her hand to his knees – 'you were this high. Do you remember?'

He nods seriously.

'So, that means you must be about twenty-one, now. Is that right?'

He shakes his head, giggling. 'Noooo.'

'Thirteen? You look very grown up.'

'Three!' He jumps up and down. 'I'm three!'

'Well, you are very grown up indeed.' She sits back down, pats the spot next to her. 'Do you want to come and sit next to me and tell me all about it? It must be challenging being three.'

Noah goes to leap onto the sofa.

'Noah!' Olivia's standing at the door. 'Not with those muddy feet! Come here. Let's get those wellies off.' She gives a small wave to Jennie. 'Let Leah know if you need anything. Sorry I'm not able to talk longer. So much to do. Come on, Noah.'

Jennie's mouth drops open, but she quickly replaces it with a small smile. 'Not a problem. I can see you've got your hands full.' She waits until the door is closed.

'That was short and sweet,' she says. 'I've known Olivia for years – I was expecting more of a warm welcome, to be honest.'

'Don't take it personally, Jennie. She's having a bad time of it at the moment.'

I think Olivia was as surprised as I was to see Jennie.

'Ah, I see,' she says. 'Money issues, is it?' She shrugs. 'Happens to the best of us.'

'It's lovely to see you, Jennie,' I say. 'Really, it is. But...' Heat rushes to my face. 'What are you doing here?'

'Didn't you get my RSVP? I thought I'd sent it to the right email address. I think I need new glasses, and I haven't the patience for that old laptop.'

'No, I didn't get the RSVP.' The blood seems to have rushed from my head; I rest a hand on the settee. 'Do you have the invitation handy, so I can check the email address I put on it?'

I can't admit it wasn't from me – it would mortify her.

She delves into her handbag.

What is going on? Matt wouldn't have gone behind my back and invited Jennie, would he? I have nothing at all against her being here, but I wouldn't have wanted to rub her face in the fact that I'm moving on. Perhaps, if it were up to her, I'd spend the rest of my life either searching or grieving for him. Misery loves company, after all.

There I go, being mean again. Sometimes I can't help it, but at least I keep it in my head. Not like some people. I can't believe Olivia was so rude to Jennie after everything she's been through. It's something I'm feeling terribly guilty about, but I can't think about that. Not with Jennie right in front of me.

'Here it is.' She hands me the card. It's a generic one, not personalised like the ones we had made. 'It's so lovely that you invited me. I've booked into a B&B up the road. I didn't know whether I should have popped in today. I was expecting the house to be buzzing with preparations, but it's so quiet in here. Have you managed to get everything done?'

'I... I don't know. Olivia is meant to be sorting the food and the flowers, but there seems to have been a mix up with the staff she hired for the house. They haven't turned up.'

'Really? How strange. And yet you seem so calm about it.'

'I have a lot on my mind, plus Olivia said she'd take care of everything. I should be worrying more about it, shouldn't I?'

'I don't want to tell you to stress yourself out, dear. Is there anything I can do to help?'

I take my phone out.

'I've a list here somewhere. It's not very long.' My hands shake as I navigate to my Notes app. 'Matt and I are meant to be putting the lights up in the barn this morning. Well, it's not a proper barn, it's a huge outbuilding that looks like a barn and—'

Jennie places a hand on my shoulder.

'Take a breath. It's OK. Shall we have a walk outside and see what's what?'

'Yes. Yes, let's.' Anything to get out of this room. The last room Callum was sitting in before he stormed out and disappeared into the night. The room where the rest of us spent countless hours waiting by the window for his return.

I stand and reach out a hand to Jennie.

'Thanks, dear,' she says, taking it and standing. 'If you were a man, I wouldn't have let you help me. I'll be stubborn to the end. Since Callum's dad walked out on us, I've had nothing to do with them since. Life has been so much more interesting without them.'

A woman loves to hear such words on the eve of her wedding...

I lead her into the hallway – thankfully Olivia's not lurking – and out the front door. Dad and Noah are kicking a football to and from each other by the lake. Matt's taking chairs out of a white transit van that must've only just arrived. Matt's dad, Greg, appears from the other side of it, carrying a box of lights.

My stomach and my heart drop at the same time.

Oh lord.

Do I ignore him, or just pretend everything is peachy?

This is turning out to be one hell of a day. Someone somewhere is having a great laugh at my expense. I'd laugh myself if I wasn't the target.

'Hello there, Greg!' Jennie wanders over to him with her arms wide. 'How the devil are you? Looking as handsome as ever.'

Awkward.

'Jennie!' He places the box on the floor. 'It's so lovely to see you. I'm so glad you're here!'

Did everyone else know Jennie was coming?

They exchange kisses on the cheek.

I can't bear to look at him. All I can think about is his replies on the other screenshot my brother showed me: *We shouldn't be talking like this; You look amazing in that photo; Sorry I shouldn't have said that, but you do.*

Maybe Jennie was right about men. Maybe they're all like that if you peel enough layers off.

But it's not my fault. I've done nothing wrong.

'Hey, Greg,' I say.

'Er, yes. Hi, Leah.' It seems he's finding looking me in the eye difficult. He bends to pick up the box. 'I'll just get these to the barn.'

'Excuse me for a second, Jennie.' I match Greg's speed as he strides towards the outbuilding. 'You know those messages weren't actually from me, don't you?'

'That's fine. I'll say whatever you want.'

'They weren't, Greg. Someone was pretending to be me. Do you think I'm the type of person who would do such a thing?'

'No. I was quite surprised, actually.'

'Why did you reply? Why didn't you tell me?'

'Eh?'

'You have my real phone number from the family What-sApp group. Didn't you think it was odd that I'd get a whole new number with the sole intention of sending pictures to my soon-to-be father-in-law?'

He places the box on a trestle table.

'Look, Leah. I know you're trying to cover it up because we got found out—'

'We?'

'Yes, *we*.'

'Can I see your phone?'

'I've deleted the messages.'

'Greg, please. I need to see who's been sending them. I need to know if they've contacted anyone else.'

'How will you find that out by looking at my phone?'

'Hmm.' I cross my arms. 'Perhaps those weren't the only messages you were sending. Is that the real reason you won't let me see it?'

'Who do you think you're talking to, Leah? You can't tell me what to do.'

'I'm not.' I drop my arms. 'I just need you to help me.'

He takes in a deep breath, reaches into his pocket and pulls out his phone. I stand at his side as he brings up WhatsApp even though I don't feel comfortable being this close to him. Our relationship has been tainted and I can't see it ever going back to how it was.

'I archived the messages,' he says. 'I didn't actually delete them.' He passes me the phone. 'Here.'

I feel nauseous that he's kept them, but also slightly relieved.

There are hundreds of messages. Some of them are just mildly flirtatious, some just chit chat.

'Oh no.' There are three other pictures of me. 'I would never send these to you, Greg. This is awful. It's so embarrassing. Why did you reply?'

I look across at him. His neck and face have turned deeply red.

'I'm sorry, Leah. I thought...' He loosens the collar of his T-shirt. 'I don't know what I thought.'

I tap the contact icon at the top.

'You saved me as *Lee*. Nice.'

'This is so uncomfortable.'

'Tell me about it. But we're not going to get anywhere by being awkward about it.'

I click on the phone symbol, and it begins to ring.

'Leah, what are you doing?'

'It's obvious what I'm doing.'

It rings out. I press it again.

'I'm not going to stop trying until someone answers.'

'But we could be here all day. What if Olivia sees us? It's bad enough as it is.'

'Who's fault is that, Greg?'

I look over to the house and Jennie is talking to Dad. Someone has got a camping chair out for her to sit on as she watches Noah kick his ball about.

I almost drop the phone when the ringing stops. Someone's accepted the call.

I hold it up to Greg.

'Hello?' he says. 'Is that Leah?'

The background is busy, like a pub beer garden.

'Hey, Greg.' It's a woman's voice. *'Aren't you at the house yet?'*

'What?'

'You're being very daring calling me, aren't you?'

Is that Tania's voice?

I want to grab the phone off him and tell her to stop taunting us like this.

'I know you're not really Leah,' says Greg. 'Why have you been pretending to be her?'

'You're a very naughty boy, aren't you, Greg?'

Beep, beep, beep. The call has ended.

I didn't recognise the voice, unless the woman – it was definitely a woman – affected her speech in some way. Tania's voice could've changed over the years. Olivia's in the kitchen but her back's to the window, and Katherine's somewhere in the house. I'd have known if it were either of them, wouldn't I?

'Now you believe me,' I say to Greg. 'Don't you?'

'Yes, yes. Obviously. And now I'm the one who looks like... Oh God.'

I walk past him to grab the ladder leaning against the side of the barn.

'I'd better get on with putting up these lights,' I say. 'They're not going to put themselves up. And I think you and Olivia need to have a chat, don't you?'

Greg's still looking at his phone as a message pops up.

'What does it say?' I shout as I reach the top of the ladder.

'It says, *There's no fool like an old fool.*'

'Well' – I screw the first hook into the almost-rotten wood – 'quite.'

THIRTEEN

After I've put the lights up and I'm still at the top of the ladder, I turn, gripping the top handle, to face the lake. The ever-present body of water that has the capacity to be deadly, is now eerily still. Would Callum's body have deteriorated into just bones, or would it have been preserved? We will never know until we find it. No one can understand what happened to him. Some think he's out there somewhere with a new life, new identity, but how can someone vanish like that so easily? No amount of planning could account for the lack of CCTV of him – and the police were thorough in their search for footage because Olivia and Greg pressed them, because Jennie was so inconsolable, she was unable to push them herself.

I can see Matt's parents through the kitchen window, talking. I'm thankful that Katherine's playing football with Noah in the back garden because I hope Greg's explaining things to Olivia, though I wouldn't put it past him to brush things under the carpet.

The temptation is too much. I hastily climb down the ladder and rush to the house, kicking off my shoes by the door as quietly as I can. I tiptoe to the kitchen door.

'I know it wasn't Leah,' Olivia's saying. 'She couldn't lie if her life depended on it.' The warm glow I feel doesn't last. 'Though I did actually think it was her to begin with. I've never totally trusted her – especially after she got together with Matt so quickly after Callum disappeared. But that's by the by, now. She's given me what I thought I would never have, and that's a lovely grandchild. I've more to lose falling out with Leah than I have with you.'

'Ouch.'

Greg's voice is small, and I imagine he's making himself a lot smaller right now.

'Oh, drop the self-pity. Stop playing the victim...'

I don't need to hear any more. After shoving my shoes back on, I run back to the barn to find Jake loitering.

'Isn't Matt helping with the decorations?' he asks.

'Where were you ten minutes ago?' I reply, smiling. Olivia believes it wasn't me. That's one less thing I need to worry about.

'I've been putting wedding favours into organza pouches.' Jake collapses the ladder and leans it against the wall. 'I'd never heard of wedding favours and organza pouches before today.'

'Didn't you have them at your own wedding?'

'God knows.' We walk slowly towards the house. 'Probably. Katherine loves things like that.'

He's frowning, looking at the ground.

'What is it, Jake? Is Katherine all right?'

He shrugs. 'I don't know. I assume so. She's playing with Noah at the moment.'

I take hold of the top of his arm, and we stop.

'You know that's not what I meant. Something's wrong. I can tell. And not just with what's happening with the text message. When did you tell Katherine about Callum black-mailing you?'

'The night he disappeared. She took it better than I thought she would. To me, at least. I don't know if she said anything to Callum.' He glances at the sky before rubbing his right temple. 'You shouldn't be having this wedding here.'

'You know I tried to put Matt off the idea, but he was having none of it. He said it would cost a fortune if we hired somewhere.'

'What's wrong with the local pub?'

'Could you see Olivia in a posh frock in the local pub?'

'Maybe not.'

'Matt's her only child. She's always dreamed of hosting the wedding here. I didn't think it was such a bad idea, but now I realise...'

My words disappear into silence.

'So who do you think's behind all of this?' he asks, looking out onto the lake.

'Have you had anything else strange happen?' I step a little closer to him, trying to read his expression.

'I've had nothing since. It's getting more sinister now he or she is involving all of us, isn't it? Saying that one of us killed Callum that night. Katherine and I have been talking about it. You know she likes to dissect things. Who'd send an invitation to his mother when you've barely seen her for years? It's really weird.' He scans the area. 'And didn't you say you saw someone outside the window the other night?'

'By the lake. You thought I was seeing things.'

'It's not so hilarious anymore. Do you have any theories as to who it was?'

'I was thinking Tania, but she surely wouldn't be bothered about Matt getting married.' I'm trying to convince Jake as well as myself. 'She'll have known through the grapevine we already have a child together. I can't think who else...'

'What about Greg? What if he made the messages up? I haven't thought about why he'd do that. He's just one of the people I'm suspicious of.' He pauses. 'I have a horrible feeling it's someone you know. A member of Matt's family. Why else isn't he worried about your safety, and the safety of his son?'

'Of course Matt's worried. He might not show it in front of you. It can't be him.'

'I didn't say it was him specifically...'

'It can't be either of his parents. It's not as though they were especially close to Callum, at least not during the time we were married.'

'Someone knows what happened that night. What if that text message was right; that Callum was killed by someone he knows? And that someone is either here now or will be coming very soon. And we need to be prepared for that. There will be no secrets anymore. I can feel it.'

FOURTEEN

In the kitchen, Noah is sitting on Jennie's lap as he scribbles on the front cover of a magazine with a biro. It's a scene that shakes me slightly. It should be my mother with her grandchild on her lap, but I shouldn't overthink it. Jennie was family to me for almost ten years. Now, she has nothing. This peek into a bustling family life is something she's never had. Even when Callum was growing up, it was only her and him. I feel awful for not inviting her, but I thought it would be awkward and uncomfortable for her. A glimpse into a life that Callum could've had.

On the kitchen counter is a box piled high with the bags of party favours. I smile at the thought of my brother putting tiny things into the little delicate pouches.

'Hey.' Matt's hands rest on my shoulders, and he kisses the top of my head from behind. 'I've got the rings, and the flowers are in the boot of the car. Shall we leave the latter there safe until tomorrow? Don't want this little one doing some gardening again.' He ruffles Noah's hair. He's referring to the time Noah decided to be helpful and dig up the freshly planted sweet peas in Dad's window box last week, thinking they were actual peas.

'Good plan.'

He takes Noah by the hand.

'Come on, little man. Let's go and have a look at the forest. We might see some birds' nests.'

'Birdies!' Noah excitedly leaps from the chair.

I look gratefully to Matt. He still looks tired, but there's an excited glow behind his eyes.

'I can't wait to marry you tomorrow,' I say as he walks a jumping Noah out of the room.

Saying those words sounds strange after all the anxiety I've been feeling this weekend. Perhaps I could suggest to him that we could run off to the nearest register office right now and not tell anyone. But he'd only counter that there are legal implications or permits we'd need, and it was not at all possible.

The last text message and my brother's words are still ringing in my ears. That someone who murdered Callum is here or will be here. Four out of the five people who saw Callum stomp out that night are already here. It was at least three hours after that when Matt went out to search, and he came back within an hour. There would've been no time to have done... No, I can't think like that. Matt's not some hardened criminal that would be able to hide a body – one that police dogs, and trained volunteers were unable to find.

Olivia appears at the doorway – I can see her from the corner of my eye, but I can't bring myself to look at her.

She clears her throat.

'Could I have a quiet word with you, Leah?' she asks. 'Please.'

'It's all right,' I say. 'We can talk here in front of Jennie. I've got nothing to hide.'

I say it so defiantly I almost believe it myself.

'Erm.' Her cheeks are flushed. 'Right. Well, I wanted to apologise for the misunderstanding about the messages Greg's been getting. He told me about the phone call.'

Jennie turns around to face the action.

'What's happened?' she asks. 'Has Greg been getting spammed? I tell you, the only people who telephone me these days don't even know me. You should tell him to contact his service provider, that's what the people on *Scam Interceptors* suggest.'

'Oh dear God.' Olivia strides to the fridge and takes out a can of pre-mixed gin and tonic. She flicks it open and almost downs the whole thing in one. I have never seen her drink out of a can before. She places the tin gently on the counter and dabs her mouth with a tea towel. 'I don't want to talk about it.'

'Fair enough. I hope they didn't steal too much of his money.'

'It's not about money.' Olivia swipes the empty can from the counter and lobs it into the recycling. She looks around the kitchen. 'I can't possibly manage to tidy all of this mess on my own. Where the hell are the caterers?'

'The kitchen is perfectly fine,' I say. 'No one expects you to do everything, Olivia.'

Olivia grabs her phone from the counter.

'There's been nothing at all from them,' she says. 'I don't understand it. They're usually so reliable. They know how important this weekend is to me.'

Greg walks into the room carrying a bucket that looks like it had flowers in; he places it near the back door.

'Shall I give them a ring?' he asks.

Obviously, he's been listening to the conversation and only entered when the heat was off him.

Olivia sighs loudly. 'You think I haven't already tried that? There's no answer. The agency has their answer machine on. No one who's any good will be available at this short notice. We can't have me or the bride and groom running around after everyone in front of all the other guests arriving tomorrow. I just don't need this stress right now, not the morning before our big day.'

I supress a reaction. Normally it would've been a sarcastic or good-natured quip, but mine and Olivia's relationship has been tainted in the last twenty-four hours. More than a day, probably, given that the messages started over two weeks ago.

A knock at the door provides a welcome reprieve. The atmosphere in this kitchen is so tense, though Jennie is doing a great job of being absorbed in the television magazine.

Olivia flusters out the room; her hair is looking wilder by the second.

Everyone is silent as we listen to who has arrived; I half want to warn them to escape while they still can.

'Who is it?' Jennie asks, looking up. 'I can't hear what they're saying.'

'I can't either.' The front door opens a little wider. 'It's two women from the sounds of it. The caterers might finally have arrived.'

'Thank fuck for that,' says Greg. 'This weekend is turning out to be a fucking nightmare.'

Charming, Greg. Say what you really feel, why don't you?

'Come, come,' says Olivia with the pair in tow. She really does play the part of lady of the manor very well. Much like Tania all those years ago. I would never speak to anyone like that. 'This is the kitchen, obviously.'

'Hello, everyone. I'm Teresa.' Teresa's a short woman, rosy-cheeked with her hair in a sleek bun. I can't tell how old she is – mid-sixties perhaps? She's wearing black trousers and a black shirt, as is the younger woman standing next to her. 'This is my business partner, Sandra. We've come to your rescue!'

'Do you know what happened to the original duo?' Greg asks. The two women shake their heads. 'Well, anyway. I think you might have saved the weekend.'

I so wish Matt and I had eloped. I'm seeing a new side to

Greg. It's like he's dropped his pretence of caring about anything.

'That's right,' says Teresa. 'So sorry we couldn't come until this morning, but the agency only contacted us late last night. We'll get to work straight away so you can relax. We've brought the food for tomorrow's menu, and I believe you have the rest here. Was that the agreement, Olivia?'

'Yes. That's right.'

'What happened to the original caterers?' I say. 'Are they OK?'

'I don't know,' says Teresa with a frown. 'Rhiannon at the agency said she hasn't heard from them since yesterday morning.'

'I hope they're all right.'

Olivia takes me by the hand and tugs me out of the kitchen.

'Just leave them to me, love,' she says, and for the first time since yesterday there's no edge in her voice when she speaks to me. 'I'm just thankful someone is here to help.' She stops me at the bottom of the stairs and rests her hands on my shoulders. 'I know this weekend must be so hard when your own mother can't be here for your precious day. I so want to be here for you – not to replace her by any means – because I have no daughters of my own and I'm so sorry that I believed that you could ever have it in you to send such messages. I mean, it's not as though Greg's such a catch. Well, he used to be good-looking twenty years ago, but now, well, not so much.'

A laugh escapes me. 'Isn't that a bit mean?'

'We have to be realistic. Plus, I dare say he deserves it after some of his responses. Anyway. Let's not talk about all of that ever again. From right now, everything will be about you and Matt, and making everything as perfect as it can be. Why don't you go upstairs and have a lie down?'

'I don't need a lie down. I've only been up a couple of hours. And I've barely spent any time with Noah.'

'He's having a great time with Katherine, his dad and his grandad. It'll be like a holiday for your dad, won't it? That's why he's here, isn't it?'

'He's here because he's my dad, and he likes spending time with his grandson.'

Olivia closes her eyes for several moments.

'I'm so sorry, Leah.' She runs a hand through her hair, smoothing down the crown of frizz. 'I've been terrible, haven't I? I didn't mean that about your dad. He's welcome here any time. I'm just finding everything so stressful.'

'I'm sorry, Olivia. I am grateful for you hosting the wedding and—'

'You don't have to be grateful. I insisted. I know I can be hard work sometimes. I feel better now the caterers are here. I can relax a little, now.' She walks backwards, heading back to the kitchen. 'I might see if there's another can of gin in the fridge.' She gives me a mischievous grin. 'I think the last one helped. See you in a bit.'

I don't think there's enough gin in the entire house that will help me.

FIFTEEN

Noah's sitting on the bed with my iPad while I'm attempting a smoky eye at the small vanity table that Olivia set up in our bedroom. Matt's in the shower, singing away. Apparently, he hasn't a care in the world, which makes one of us, but I will try to put everything at the back of my mind in order to enjoy this pre-wedding three-course dinner that the new caterers have managed to create with less than a day's notice.

This afternoon was filled with more wedding prep: Matt going over his speech in the garden room, pacing; me, making sure Noah's outfit is pressed and double checking it still fits him because it's been two months since he tried it on in the store, and the finished pieces only arrived yesterday. Nothing particularly taxing compared with the stress of my first lavish wedding where we had a hundred and fifty guests. There are only twenty-three attending tomorrow.

I glance in the mirror at Noah lying on the bed; the iPad is resting on his chest.

'Noah, love!'

He sits up quickly, looking confused.

'Don't go to sleep yet. It's only half past five. We've still got to have dinner.'

He crawls to the end, slides off the bed and I pick him up to sit on my lap.

'Don't like chicken,' he says, rubbing his eyes.

'Since when? You've always loved chicken.'

'They're two real chicks in oven.'

'It'll be fine.' I smooth down a piece of his hair that's sticking up, but it just pings back. 'I'm sure there'll be plenty of other things to choose from.'

Dad sticks his head around the door.

'Hi, love,' he says. 'If Noah's tired, I can look after him up here while you have dinner, if you like?'

'Don't like chicken, Grandad.'

Noah slides off my lap and hugs Dad's legs.

'I wanted him there, Dad. I'm sure it'll be fine. There's bound to be something he can eat. I've hardly seen Noah this weekend.'

'But I wanted you to have a relaxing time. I've seen the place settings and Noah is sitting in between you and Olivia. I don't think that's a good idea. She's been really snappy, and I don't want her to be stressed, either. Not after she's hosting us all here.'

'Are you making excuses, Dad?' I smile at him. 'Are you sure it's not *you* who doesn't want to sit at the table?'

'I'm not great at small talk, love. You know that.'

What can I say? He's been doing me a huge favour all weekend – and I didn't want to invite him just so he could look after Noah.

'What is it you want to do, Dad? I can have Noah tonight – you can chill upstairs, if you like? I could bring you a plate up. Tell everyone you're not feeling too well and want to be at your best for tomorrow?'

He rolls his eyes.

'I'm not having Jennie talking about me again.'

'What do you mean?'

'I overheard her before, telling someone that I'm getting on a bit. The cheek of it! I'm at least fifteen years younger than she is. And I can walk a lot faster and can still kick a ball around.'

I stand and pick up Noah.

'I'm sorry, Dad. I'll have a word with her. She wasn't even meant to be here. Someone invited her without clearing it with Matt and me.'

'Really?'

'Dad, please don't saying anything about that to her.'

'Of course I won't.' He chuckles. 'But it's good to know she's crashing the party, and she doesn't even realise it.'

'I don't want to upset her. She's been—'

'Yes, yes. I get it.' He holds his arms out to Noah. 'Shall we go and have a kick about, lad? I think we both need waking up before the dinner.'

'Thanks, Dad. I really appreciate it.'

'I can't promise to stay for dessert. I mean, if Noah gets tired, I'll take him up.' He gives me a wink.

'Thanks, Dad.'

As the bedroom door closes, the ensuite opens.

'Did I hear talking?' Matt rubs his wet hair with a towel. I wish my hair was so easy to manage I could wash it twice in one day. 'Where's Noah?'

'Dad's taken him to play with the football.'

'We've hardly seen him all weekend.'

'That's what I said.'

He drops to his knees and kisses my neck.

'Does that mean we have time for...?'

'No.' I shove him away jokingly. 'We have ten minutes, and I need to wipe this eye make-up off and start it again.'

He stands and pouts.

'I really can't wait to go away. I'm sure this house is cursed.'

My gaze lingers on his face; he's totally serious.

'Why would you say something like that? I knew we shouldn't have had the wedding here.'

I pluck out a wet wipe and swipe across my face as tears gather in my eyes. I'm left looking like a zombie with black eyes and smudged red lips.

I grimace at myself in the mirror. Matt might have a point.

'Do you think anything else will happen today?' I ask. 'I feel constantly on edge thinking about what they're going to do next.'

'I don't know,' he says, selecting a pale blue shirt from the wardrobe. 'The last message was pretty ominous, but at least we know they don't actually know anything.'

'What do you mean?'

'As if any one of us would've killed Callum.'

My hand is shaking as I reapply my mascara.

My thoughts go to Jake, to Katherine. She would know how to cover a crime.

I stare at my reflection.

'I guess you never really know someone,' I say. 'Not deep down.'

The formal dining room looks stunning with white candles along the table, glasses gleaming, gold napkins and bright white plates. I'm carrying a very unenthusiastic Noah and sit him on my knee when we reach my name on the place holder.

'We're the first ones here, Noah.'

He looks at me as if to say, *Yes, obviously*, before resting his head on my chest. His hair is still a little damp and smells of Johnson's Baby Shampoo. I will never tire of that smell.

'Are you hungry, love?' I say.

He nods.

Matt saunters into the room and his eyes light up when he sees us sitting here. He pulls out the chair next to me, noting the name on the place card. He switches for the one next to him.

'Why the hell haven't they put us together?' he asks.

'Perhaps they thought we should mingle with our guests. As few as they are.'

He shrugs and pours water from one of the glass jugs into three glasses. 'I thought they'd check with us first.'

He offers a glass to Noah, who takes it with both hands, taking several gulps before passing it to me. I place it on the table then wipe the spillage from his face and top.

'Maybe it was the caterers who brought the card addressed to me. I mean, they could literally be anyone.'

Matt kisses my shoulder.

'Your imagination is running away with you.'

'Do you blame me? I'm suspicious of everyone right now.'

'Even me?' He displays an expression of mock horror. 'How very dare you!'

'No, of course not you. You're the most sensible one in the house. Apart from my dad.'

'Don't let my mum hear you say that.' He looks to the door. 'Talk of the devil.' He stands and greets his mother like he hasn't spent all day fetching and carrying various items for her. 'Thank you so much for this, Mum. I've never seen the room look more beautiful.'

She sits at the head of the table and wafts a hand.

'To be honest, I just suggested the colour and the caterers did the rest. Totally exceeded my expectations.' She leans towards me. 'To be honest, it might've been for the best that my usuals didn't turn up. They certainly wouldn't have laid a table so elegantly as this.'

'Don't let the caterers hear you say that, Mum. They might be friends with your *usuals*.'

'I suppose. But it's not very professional of them to cancel last minute after talking for months in preparation.'

'Leah thinks the replacements might have been the ones who left the card.' Matt's tone is serious, now.

'I don't actually think it was them,' I say. 'I don't know what to think. The thought of it being someone I know...'

Am I being unreasonable in thinking such things? Or should I keep my suspicions to myself?

'Sorry,' he says. 'I didn't mean to make light of everything that's happened, the card and the...'

He glances at his mum, not finishing the sentence. I think the text messages are now a forbidden topic, although Greg is still acting as though he's been convicted of indecent behaviour and is being extra nice to everyone. Talk of the devil.

'How the hell is this our dining room?' He bends to kiss Olivia's cheek, and she reacts by turning statue still with a wild look in her eyes. He sits next to her on the opposite side to Matt and me. 'They've done a wonderful job, haven't they, darling?'

'Hmm,' says Olivia, the subtext being: Don't *darling* me.

Olivia does a great job of masking bubbling resentment beneath a calm and capable façade. Greg will be reminded of his replies to the messages for a long time, no doubt. But not in front of the children.

I lean towards Matt.

'How are you feeling about all of that now?' I nod towards his parents who are deep in hushed conversation. 'Are you all right?'

He shrugs again.

'Well, how should I feel about my dad thinking he was talking to my fiancée, looking at pictures of her in her under-wear?' He takes the bottle of white wine and pours a little into the glass in front of him. He takes a small sip. 'I'm trying not to think about it too deeply until we get home. I don't want it to spoil our wedding, and I don't want to think about it on every anniversary. Which is why I'm pretending it never happened.' He takes hold of my hand and squeezes it gently. 'I'm actually fuming with him, and he can tell. But he's not once said he's sorry. It's really weird, isn't it?'

Tears come to my eyes. Again.

'It's very upsetting. I feel violated, Matt. If it weren't the day before the wedding, I'd have gone to the police.'

'We still can, you know. It's a crime, isn't it?'

'Don't they have to be nudes to be a crime?'

'I'll have a word with Katherine.'

'Not yet. Not until we get home from our honeymoon.'

He gives my hand another squeeze before letting go.

'This is what some people rely on,' he says, glancing at his father. 'People's silence, the embarrassment.' He takes another sip of wine. 'Anyway. Game face on.'

I can see Dad lingering outside, seemingly having a breath of fresh air, hands in pockets, staring out across the water. I hadn't realised before now how anxious he can be in social situations. When Mum was alive, the fact she could talk to anyone about anything disguised Dad's shyness as he nodded along. I'm about to get up and head outside, when he turns on his heels and walks back inside the house.

He follows Jake into the room and walks quickly to the seat next to Noah's. Jake sits in the chair opposite me and pours himself a large glass of red. Jennie follows, stopping to give thanks to Olivia for having her.

'Sorry about the delay,' says Dad. 'I didn't want all eyes on me when I walked in. Waited till the conversations were flowing.' He pats the seat between us. 'Are you going to be a big boy and sit in your own chair, Noah?'

Noah nods his head enthusiastically. Seeing his grandad has given him a second wind.

'Remember what we said about us both trying new things, tonight?' Dad says to him. 'I'm so excited.'

Noah grabs his fork and eats some invisible food.

'That's right, lad.'

By the time I glance at Jake again, he's already reaching to refill his glass.

'Steady on, Jake.'

I laugh, but I can see from his eyes that that wasn't his first drink.

'Hey,' he bellows. 'I was telling Olivia before about what I read the other day. Well. Saw it on telly. Some random channel about the unexplained or unsolved or something. It reminded me of that story I tried to tell this lot.' He raises his glass to Matt and me. 'Not that they believed it.'

'What did you see?' Matt swirls the wine in his glass.

'About that serial killer on the loose in the Lake District.'

'There are probably loads of killers on the loose,' pipes up Greg from nowhere.

Olivia gives him a withering look, and he seems to shrink in size.

'This one in particular, Greg,' counters Jake with a confidence supplied by the booze, 'has been roaming the Lakes for twenty years.' He looks us each in the eye, and the flame from the candle nearest to me flickers. 'They say that a wanderer has made a dwelling on the banks of Windermere. No one knows where he lives. Seven men have gone missing in the past two decades. All were last seen along the banks of the lake.'

'Rubbish!' Olivia folds her arms. 'I've never heard anything about that.'

'Well, what about...?' He gestures to me with his glass before catching my glare. 'Sorry.' He glances at Jennie. 'Sorry.'

'I think Jake was just thinking out loud... trying to figure out what happened eight years ago.'

Jake gives me a small smile in thanks.

'I don't think it's appropriate to be talking about all of that.' Olivia glances at Jennie, then stands briefly to pour herself another inch of white wine. 'Matt and Leah have a child together and they're both young.'

'Anyway, I digress.' Jake waves a hand. 'Some say that these men have been either pushed into the water or dragged to his lair where they've met their fate.'

'Well, which one is it?' Matt's shaking his head. 'You're making it up again, aren't you? I'm sure this isn't the same story you told us on Leah's thirtieth.'

I shoot Matt a look.

'I swear I'm not making it up,' says Jake, wide-eyed and innocent looking. 'I'm only going off what I read. I didn't follow it up with extensive research to corroborate the facts.'

The table falls silent. A breeze runs through the room, causing every flame to flicker. Everyone jumps as a solemn-looking Katherine walks into the room.

'Oh, for goodness' sake.' Olivia presses a hand against her chest. 'No more talk of gory nonsense.'

Katherine's expression is transformed as our eyes meet; her smile is wide, and it reaches her eyes.

'Happy night before the wedding!' She sits next to my dad, barely glancing at Jake. She picks up the bottle and shakes what little is left. 'Have we any more red wine?'

'I'll go and see,' I say quietly before Olivia has the chance to be offended.

She doesn't seem to notice me leave the table; she's still deep in conversation with Greg. In the kitchen, Teresa and Sandra are in the pantry, talking quietly.

'Wonder if it'll happen to her second...' is what I think the younger one just said.

God, they have no idea I'm here.

I clear my throat, and they spin around.

'Oh, gosh, sorry, Leah.' Teresa wipes her hands on her apron. 'Is there anything I can help with?'

What were you two just talking about?

'Red wine. We're almost out.'

She glances at the clock. We have been sitting at the table for only ten minutes. She probably thinks we're raging binge drinkers, downing wine like water.

'Of course.' She gives a polite smile. 'I'm so sorry. I'll bring two more out. I opened four to let them breathe. Let me know if I should open any more.'

'I think that should be fine.'

I go to leave the kitchen but pause.

'Have you heard anything from Olivia's original caterers? Are you from the same agency?'

'Yes,' says Sandra. 'Still no news.'

'That's ever so strange,' I say. 'Is that sort of thing common after taking so long with the planning?'

The two exchange a glance.

'Not really.' Teresa places two bottles on a tray. 'But the agency said they'll let us know on Monday. We don't want Olivia to worry.'

'Right, OK.'

I let her walk in front of me. Her neck twitches: she can feel me behind her. I don't know if she's actually hiding something, or my imagination is running away with me.

SIXTEEN

EIGHT YEARS AGO

Three hours until Callum's disappearance

We're sitting round the large dining table in the conservatory. Lit candles on the windowsill, table, and in the corners give the room a lovely cosy feel. Tania has, I think begrudgingly, done a great job.

Jake leans back and pushes his plate away.

'I'm so full,' he says. 'That mashed potato was the best I've ever tasted.'

'Secret recipe.' Callum looks so smug right now. 'Actually, it's just plenty of butter and cream and salt. All the bad stuff that makes everything taste delicious.' He laughs and tops up his red wine. 'I've made a cheesecake, if anyone wants dessert.'

He did actually make the cheesecake.

Everyone groans, and protests that they couldn't possibly fit in any more food. They'll change their minds in half an hour. It's been the same with every meal since we've been here.

'Are you OK, Leah?' Tania asks me quietly.

Whose idea was it to sit her next to me? These are the first words she has spoken to me since we sat down to eat.

'Yes, thanks,' I say. 'I'm just a bit tired. It's been a busy weekend. If I was at home now, I'd be horizontal on the sofa watching Netflix.' I add a laugh, but it sounds fake.

'I thought you were cross with me,' she says. 'About walking with Callum on the hike this afternoon.'

Wow, she really has some front.

'Not at all,' I say. 'Really. I'm not the jealous type. You can't be a jealous person if you're with Callum.'

'I know what you mean.'

I turn to glance at her; she's staring right at him.

'Do you like him?' I say, emboldened by the large glass of wine I had with dinner.

She blinks several times, reaches for her glass of water and takes a tiny sip.

'I guess. Not in that way, of course.'

'Matt told me you think he's full of himself.'

I glance at Callum. He obviously heard me: his eyes are wide, and his mouth is slightly open.

Tania's smooth cheeks have flushed.

'Gosh,' she says. 'I didn't think Matt would tell you that. Does he tell you all our private conversations? You should hear what Callum says about you.'

'Excuse me?'

Tania is saved by Callum tapping a knife on a glass.

Ding, ding, ding.

'And a toast.' Callum's standing now, pointing his glass towards me as I'm quietly fuming. 'To the birthday girl, Leah. Happy thirtieth birthday weekend, my darling!'

I raise my glass. 'Thank you, everyone.' I force a smile. 'And thank you so much to you all for spending this weekend with me. I'm grateful to your parents, Matt, for letting us stay in their lovely holiday home.'

'Cheers to that,' says Callum. 'Saved me a couple of grand.'

I notice a frosty glance exchanged between my brother and

Callum. I still haven't asked Jake what's going on because there's always someone else around. Unless he's making sure that's the case. I don't want to ask my husband. I won't get the truth from him, from what he's been like this weekend.

Why would Callum talk about me to Tania? Tiny betrayals are building up between us; I feel as though he's more of a stranger than she is.

Matt taps his glass with a fork.

'Now, it's time for games,' he says. 'Pictionary first. I've bought an easel for it and everything.'

'Ooh, an easel,' says Tania, giggling. 'You've really pushed the boat out.'

Matt throws her a questionable look.

'I love Pictionary!' I stand and grab my drink.

'I know you do.' Callum rushes to my side. 'That's why I asked Matt to organise it all.' He kisses me on the cheek. 'Anything for my princess.'

'Princess?' I hiss as we walk through to the lounge. He goes to hold my hand, but I whisk mine away. 'Why have you been slagging me off to everyone? And what's with all that weird stuff in the car?'

He stops suddenly; Tania walks around us.

'What stuff?'

'Under the spare tyre.'

'I have no idea what you're talking about.' He starts walking towards the living room. 'Is it still there?'

I shrug. 'I haven't moved it.'

I haven't looked inside the envelope, but if I go now, he will follow me. Why hasn't anyone left me alone since I got here? The only time I've had a moment's peace is when I woke this morning.

'Come on, Leah,' shouts Matt, standing near the large fireplace. 'Can't have the birthday girl missing out on her favourite game!'

Callum places his glass of wine on the coffee table that's between two large sofas. He claps his hands and rubs them together and stands next to the easel. How quickly his façade can change.

'OK, folks,' he says. 'Tonight, it's going to be boys versus girls. Come on, come on. Shift your arses. Boys on this sofa, girls on the other side.'

I sit in the middle of said sofa, and Tania leans her head close to mine.

'I was only joking before,' she says. 'Callum hasn't said anything mean about you.'

'OK.'

'Matt heard me say that.' She taps her right hand with her left. 'I've been suitably reprimanded. I was just a bit stung that Matt had told you what I'd said about your husband.'

What the hell is going on with everyone this weekend? Is it the sheer volume of alcohol everyone is getting through? Or is it my heightened emotional state, worrying about my mum, making me notice the small things that would usually pass me by?

'Leah,' says Callum. 'Earth to Leah.'

'Sorry.' I stand and grab the black marker that he's holding out to me. 'I was miles away.' I grab a card from the top of the pile and the timer is set.

* * *

Everyone has had too much to drink for the second night running and I want to make my excuses and take myself away from the noise. Ideally, to see what's inside Callum's coveted envelope upstairs. Would anyone notice if I were to slip away?

The others still have Post-it notes stuck to their heads. I deciphered mine (*Edward Scissorhands*) almost half an hour ago and it's pretty boring listening to them guessing their own after three hundred attempts.

I get up from the floor, trying to look casual.

'Just nipping to the loo.'

I glance at Callum; he's looking into his wine glass. Cheating, as usual.

I try to avoid all the creaks on the stairs – though it wouldn't be outside the realms to be using the ensuite – and the creak just outside our bedroom.

Inside, I drag my case from under the bed. Thankfully the envelope is still there. Callum mustn't have checked the boot of the car. I take it out from under my clothes and head into the bathroom, locking the door behind me.

I sit on the floor, take out the sheets of paper, shake out the photographs, selecting the one of Jake. It's what I thought it was. I turn the picture over to see if it's dated, but there's no writing at all. I turn the picture over because I don't want to see my brother like that and pick up the other one. Jake must know about this picture. It must be why he's so angry with Callum. I doubt Katherine knows about it, though.

I shove it back in the envelope and flip over the various paperwork. Most sheets are bank statements. Two are in a name I don't recognise; the other is in Callum's name. Deposits of five grand here, ten grand there. All within the past month or so. And there was me thinking his business was in trouble.

There's a footstep on the creaky floorboard outside the bedroom.

I stand after sliding the stuff under the bathmat, flush the toilet. Run the tap. In the mirror, smooth my hair. Face is flushed. Heart hammering.

A bang on the door.

'Leah!'

It's Callum. I knew it would be Callum.

'Won't be a sec,' I say lightly. 'Don't you know it's rude to—'

'I know you have my stuff in there with you. I need it back.'

'I've no idea what—'

'You're not stupid, Leah.' He's speaking ominously quiet. 'And neither am I. Open the door.'

I glance at the floor. It's not obvious the envelope is there.

I sweep open the door, chin up.

'What the hell are you talking about?' I say. 'You're pissed again.'

I push past him, head to the bedroom door. He rushes past me, blocking my exit.

'Let me leave, Callum.'

I try to push him to the side, but he grabs hold of my wrists, squeezing them tightly.

'Fuck off, Callum.' I twist, turn, yet his hold is strong. 'Get the hell off me.' I let out a guttural scream; he clamps a hand over my mouth.

With my free arm, I jab my elbow into his chest.

'What the hell, Leah?' He sounds winded. 'You're like some feral dog.'

I jab him again.

'Leah! Calm the fuck down.'

I stand still; the only movement is the pounding from my chest.

'That's my girl,' he says. Smug bastard. 'If I move my hand from your mouth, will you promise you won't scream?'

I nod, slowly, deliberate.

'I'm going to sit you on the bed and when I move my hand, I will tell you everything. OK?'

'Uh hmm.'

Fury is building in my chest. How fucking dare he?

If Jake were to walk in right now, I have no doubt he would kill Callum, or at the very least seriously harm him.

Callum pulls me towards the bed; he sits, and I have no choice but to follow.

'OK?' His eyes bore into mine.

I nod again.

He takes his hand slowly off my mouth.

My eyes are fixed on his. I press my lips shut.

I blink away the tears that threaten to fall; I don't want him to see me cry.

'Go on,' I say, monotone. 'Tell me where all that money in your account has come from and why you're behaving like some sort of criminal.'

He puts a hand over his face, rubs his eyes.

'I'm so sorry, Leah. I didn't want it to be like this. It was supposed...'

I stare straight ahead at the pink flowery wallpaper with tiny daisies. I rub his back, but inside my heart is racing. How could he physically hurt me? It came to him so easily. There's nothing stopping him from going further, is there? A line has been crossed. I never thought I'd be afraid of being alone with my own husband.

'There, there, Callum. Everything will be OK. I'm on your side.'

If anyone else were listening, I think they'd believe me too.

SEVENTEEN

NOW

Sixteen hours until the wedding

Matt is sleeping in the garden room tonight, even though we're not the most traditional of couples. I'm in our bedroom, though I probably won't get much sleep tonight. My wedding dress is hanging on the back of the wardrobe. It's nothing fancy – not like the one I wore for mine and Callum's wedding, but I love it. It's a vintage-style tea-length dress with translucent long lace sleeves in off-white. The hairdresser will be arriving at ten and she also does make-up, so I don't have to worry about making a mess of my face.

Noah is sleeping in the same room as my dad again. My son's having a wonderful weekend, but I feel terrible for not spending much time with him. I'm sure my dad's shattered looking after Noah, but he won't admit it. I want him to know that I really appreciate it. Perhaps I could take him away for a weekend, just him and me.

Although there's been nothing from the card writer since the text message sent to us all, I've been on edge worrying about it. Perhaps it was just a prank. I can't think of anyone who would do such a thing, though. Could it be Olivia after message-gate? It can't be Jennie; it wouldn't be in her nature to cause a stir like that, even if she was feeling sad that I'm moving on. And it's been years since Callum disappeared; it's not as though I jumped into another relationship. Unless she thought Matt and I were involved before Callum went missing. But the technology involved wouldn't be in her remit.

The caterers are staying in their huge campervan parked at the side of the house. They said it would be easier this way because of the early start involved in preparing the wedding breakfast and the actual breakfast. They have been extremely efficient, and they weren't lying when they said they would try to blend into the background.

There's a tap at the door before Matt walks in.

I quickly cover my eyes.

'We're not meant to see each other the night before,' I say with mock horror. 'It's bad luck.'

I feel him sit next to me.

'I think we've had enough bad luck this weekend, don't you?' He moves my hands from my face. 'And we've dealt with it pretty well so far.'

'We've barely seen each other, that's why.'

He leans close to kiss me briefly on the lips.

'We just sat next to each other at dinner,' he says. 'But I suppose we're used to seeing each other constantly. And that's why we'll appreciate tomorrow even more.'

'How's your mum?'

'Stressed. But to be honest, she'd be just as stressed if she had nothing to do.'

'I heard the caterers talking amongst themselves earlier.'

'They had the audacity to talk?'

'Ha.' I stick the tip of my tongue out at him. 'I think they were talking about the original couple who were meant to be here.'

'Ooh, wonder if there's been some catering espionage going on.'

'Hmm. Well, they've not actually done anything wrong, have they? And the food was delicious. Service was great and we've not had to wash up since they arrived. I'd call that a win. Wonder what happened to the original ones.'

I type in *accident* and *Windermere* into Safari on my phone but there are only results from the past few years; none that are recent.

Matt takes my phone away. 'I know you're trying to distract yourself right now.' He kisses my hand. 'Anyway,' he says, 'I just came in to say goodnight and sweet dreams and I'll see you in the morning.'

He kneels on the floor in front of me, cupping my face in his hands.

'I love you so much, Leah. I can't wait to be your husband.'

'Ditto.'

He laughs and gets to his feet.

'You're the least romantic and sentimental person I've ever met.'

'Yet, you still love me.' I attempt a cheeky grin. 'Night night, Matt.'

He leaves the room, but I remain on the bed. I don't think I'll get any sleep tonight. I go to the pillow end and put my feet up. I have three books in a pile next to me, but I haven't touched any of them.

I grab my phone and bring up Tania's Instagram. I don't tell Matt that I periodically scroll through her pictures to see what she's up to. It's like the five of us who were left that night eight years ago are linked. We experienced something that most people don't. There's a notification on the triangle in the top right corner of my screen; I tap it. It's a message request. Usually it's from strangers, scammers proclaiming to be US naval captains, or hero doctors working in Syria.

This one isn't. It's from Tania Strecker.

I'm sure that wasn't her surname before.

In this profile, there are several photos of her that aren't on the other one: Tania in a wedding dress, another of her with – who I assume to be – her blond-haired husband. They're not short of cash, judging by the convertible Mercedes they're sitting in in one of the few other pictures posted.

With a pounding heart, I open the message.

Leah, is that you?

Wasn't 100% given you don't post a lot.

Just got the weirdest text (not to mention the numerous messages from someone pretending to be Matt, but that's a whole other story).

It says one of us killed Callum. Any idea what that's about?

See you soon.

Tania x

She must've received the same text the rest of us were sent. Unless she's lying, and she's the one who sent them.

See you soon.

Is that just a turn of phrase or was there meaning behind that?

I tap out a quick reply.

Hey, Tania.

Yes, it's me Leah. We were sent the same message.

Are you free for a quick chat? I'd really appreciate you calling me to discuss as soon as you can.

Leah x

I add my phone number and wait for a few moments, but she's not online. Taking it offline and speaking to her would clarify that the person behind the message is actually Tania, given the profile is sparse.

I close my eyes for what feels like a couple of minutes, but when I open them, an hour has passed. It's only ten o'clock, but everyone must be exhausted because the house is totally silent. I swing my legs off the bed and head towards the bathroom to get changed for bed, when I notice a white slip of paper on the floor next to the door.

I dash to snatch it up.

I'm half-hoping it's a sweet little note from Matt, but he's never done that sort of thing before. With shaking hands, I open it.

I can't believe you're going through with it, Leah. You'd better keep an eye on little Noah tomorrow. Wouldn't want anything to happen to him. Can't wait to see you again. One more sleep.

Love, Callum.

I open the bedroom door.

There's no one on the landing. Whoever must've pushed it under my door is no doubt long gone. Why the hell did I fall asleep?

A shiver runs across my shoulders when I think of a stranger creeping into the house and up the stairs.

Noah!

I creep along the hallway, opening the door as quietly as I can to where Dad and Noah are fast asleep.

'Dad.' I try to say it as loudly as I can without waking Noah. 'Dad!'

He shoots straight into the sitting position.

'Leah?' He squints in the darkness. 'Is that you?'

I go inside and crouch next to his bed.

'Sorry to wake you.' I hand him the note. 'Someone has just posted this under my door. They've been in the house.'

He takes his glasses from the little table next to him and switches the small lamp on to read it.

'Can you stay awake for a while and keep an eye on Noah?'

'Of course, but where are you going?'

'I'm going to make sure all the windows and doors are locked.' I stand and gaze at my little boy sleeping with his arms above his head.

Dad gets up and starts to shuffle a chest of drawers closer to the door.

'I'll shift this up to block the door. The window's already locked.'

'Thanks, Dad.'

I leave the room and linger at the door until I hear the gentle thud of the furniture against the door. There's a smoke alarm right above, so hopefully nothing else terrible will happen.

I walk down the stairs, not trying to be quiet. If there's someone downstairs, I want them to know that someone is coming. The house is full. Whoever it is will be outnumbered if I have to shout to wake everyone up.

The snug is empty – I even check between the chair and the settee. It's the kitchen I'm most worried about as it backs onto the dense woodlands. I turn the light on straight away, scanning the room for any signs of movement or disarray. Just the soft *tick, tick, tick* of the clock. My heart thumps as I approach the pitch-black pantry. I slam the door open and switch on the light at the same time.

Nothing.

I turn the light off in the kitchen, and crouch down, moving towards the back window. I stand slowly, cupping my hands either side of my face to get a better look out into the darkness.

There's movement in the hedge to the right. But it's at such a short level, it must be an animal.

I head to the living room – a lamp has been left on. Olivia has done this since Noah was born, so it's not dark if Matt or I get up in the night with him, and I'm thankful for that right now. The room is still, save for the flashing clock on the ancient DVD player.

The curtains are drawn, and they reach the floor.

I have a vision of a man dressed in black hiding behind them, and I'm half-tempted to run upstairs and get my dad.

Deep breath.

I look around for something to use in defence. A mid-century Tiffany-style lamp will have to do. I unplug it loudly, looking at the fabric to notice any disturbances. A slight ruffle in the one on the right.

Oh fuck.

'I know you're in there.' I linger at the door. My stomach churns with nausea; I can feel my pulse in my ears. 'Come out now, before I pull the curtain away.' It shimmers again.

Come on, Leah. Just rip it open.

God, I think I'm going to be sick.

Come on.

I stride towards it and snap the curtain aside.

There's no one there, but the window is wide open.

Outside, the plants in the pot under the sill have been crushed but there's no sign of mud on the inside of the house. Is it a coincidence? Did one of us leave the window open? I pull it shut, lock it, and put the key in my pocket.

I check the rest of the room, then move into the dining room.

It's easier to tell if anything untoward is here because the room is basically empty. Just the table and chairs and candles long since blown out.

I head to the hall and slip on my walking boots.

Outside, the lake is shimmering with the light breeze. To the right, the lights are off in the campervan.

There's movement in the distance. Near the dense wood.

A figure. Dressed in black. I'm sure it is. Is it the same woman who was here the night before?

I blink again.

It was there. I'm certain.

I send a quick text to Matt – hoping he's still awake – before popping back inside for a torch and to grab the front door keys. I close and lock the door behind me before heading to the spot.

'Hello? Is anyone there?'

It can't be someone too scary if they keep running away from me.

'Tania? Is that you? I know you're there.'

I stoop slightly as I enter the forest path. It's been cleared since the last time we were here and made into an actual walking route, but the trees and shrubs seem to cave around me. It's so dark along here, I'm struggling to remember to breathe. Adrenaline is making me this brave, I'm sure of it. As is the desire to protect my family and to resolve all of this before tomorrow.

I start to jog, remembering that I'll soon be in the clearing near the ramshackle shack my brother took us to. I can't help thinking of the silly stories Jake told. I smile ruefully when I recall us thinking we'd found a drug stash. It was probably some hiker's stuff. Unless it was...

What if it's still there?

'Hello?'

I come to the clearing. I turn and shine the torch 180 degrees above and around me. The branches are still. There's no one here.

'Hello?'

I almost jump a foot in the air at the man's voice behind me. I flip round, almost blinding him with my torch, even though he's a good five metres away. He puts a hand up to shield his eyes. It's then I notice the cabin behind him. It's no longer derelict. It's had a total facelift.

'Can I help you?' he asks.

It's dark, but I can tell he's in his early forties, tall, greying dark hair that's shaved to a number two, dark eyes. He looks so familiar, yet I can't place him. He's wearing black jeans and an olive-green bomber jacket.

'Do you live here?'

He laughs, not unkindly.

'No,' he says.

'Oh,' I say, surprised by the lack of explanation.

A movement in the window, a shadow of a person behind a curtain.

He clocks my gaze.

'It's my wife,' he says quickly.

Is her name Tania? I want to ask, but he would think me crazier than I already appear to be.

Why has he offered that information so easily when he was so cagey just moments before?

'Have you been up to the big house?' I point my torch at Lakeside Cottage. 'Only I thought I saw someone from my window just now.'

He takes out a packet of cigarettes; I spot the sheen of the unopened plastic wrapper.

'Came out for a smoke,' he says, backing towards the steps to the house. 'It's a rental. For the weekend.'

'You haven't seen anyone else?'

'No, love. Sorry.' He stops still. 'Do you want me to walk you back to the big house? Heard some rumours around here. Might not be safe on your own.'

'I'm fine,' I say quickly. 'My husband's parents have owned the place for years, there's never been any trouble.'

'I'm not so sure about that.' He tilts his head to the side. 'I heard about a man going missing from here. Eight or nine years ago. One minute he was partying with his friends, the next' – he snaps his fingers – 'he's gone.'

I've never had a stranger talk to me about my husband's case without them realising it was me before. Though, I should stop calling him my husband in my head. He hasn't been my husband for one month and thirty-three days – or eight years, depending how you look at it.

'I reckon one of his mates bumped him off,' the man says. He points to the window. 'My wife followed it on the news at the time. She knows all about the case. True crime fan.' He laughs. 'I'm not surprised they keep it quiet around here, mind. Have you seen how much they ask for a night at that Lakeside Cottage on Airbnb?' He doesn't wait for me to reply. 'Three hundred and fifty quid! For one night. Not only that – there's a minimum two-night stay.'

I feel my body relax a little. A potential serial killer wouldn't make such boring small talk with their prey, would they?

'I'd better be heading back,' I say. 'I'm getting married tomorrow.'

His overfamiliarity is contagious.

'Congratulations.' He folds his arms – his biceps are huge. He looks like some kind of ex commando or something. 'I hope the weather turns for you.'

I tilt my head.

'For the better,' he says. 'Obviously.'

I narrow my eyes at him.

'Have we met before?' I say. 'Are you a friend of Matt's?'

He obviously isn't.

'No, no. We're here for the walking.'

A crash of a broken glass comes from inside.

'Nice to meet you, Leah.'

He almost spins on his heels and dashes inside, slamming the front door so hard it's like the whole place shudders.

I wait, expecting him to return. I don't know why I'm still standing here.

Two figures appear at the window; they're facing each other. The woman's gesticulating as though annoyed, but I can't hear shouting.

Could it be Tania inside? In the few photographs on her profile, her husband was tall, short-haired, but he was wearing sunglasses. Is my mind taking me there because I received a message from her?

I take a step backwards towards the opening.

He called me by my name, didn't he?

I almost sprint to the garden room, and bang on the glass door. Matt mustn't have been sleeping because he opens it after seconds.

'I...' I rest a hand on the door frame, breathless. I reach into my pocket for the note. 'Someone pushed this under my door. They said they might hurt Noah. Before that, I got a message from Tania on Instagram. I was going to come and talk to you about it, but I closed my eyes for a second... Did you get the same one?' I turn, pointing to the dark entrance to the path. 'I saw her, I'm sure I did. I chased after her, but it was a man. Do you think it was her husband?'

Matt's mouth is slightly open, his brows furrowed.

'Take a breath, Leah,' he says. 'Come in here.'

'We can't stay here.' I go to walk. 'Dad's watching Noah, but we have to be in the house. It might not be safe.'

He shoves on his trainers, not waiting to tie the laces and follows me to the house and into the living room. I give him the note and watch his face as he takes in the words.

'Bloody hell.' He rubs his eyes. 'Is it the same handwriting as the card?'

'I think so.' My breath is calming, but my body is trembling.

He takes his phone from his pocket, presses 999, walks to the window and pulls across a curtain to look outside as he talks to the operator. He reads out the note, describes what's been happening, before his voice lowers.

He turns, glances at me.

What was that look? What is he telling the person on the other end of the line?

He finishes the call. Slides his phone into his back pocket.

'Are they sending someone?' I say, pleading. 'Are they going to patrol the area, guard the house?'

'Yes,' he says steadily. 'Someone will be coming to the house.' He takes me by the hand, guides me to the settee. 'You're shaking, Leah.'

'Did you get the same message on Instagram?' I say, and he's staring at me quizzically. 'I know it's a lot. And I'm not making any sense. But it must be her.'

'Who, Leah?'

'Please don't look at me like that, Matt.' I swipe my hands from his grasp. 'I'm not making it up. There was someone out there. Check your phone.'

He sighs and I want to scream, shake him and tell him I'm not going crazy.

'Where am I looking?' he asks.

'Look in your message requests on Instagram.'

I look over his shoulder.

'There are loads,' he says. 'I never check them on... Oh.'

There it is. The same profile photo. The same message.

'Is this a real profile?' he says, tapping the picture. 'There aren't a lot of photos.'

'I don't know. I gave her my number, told her to call me.'

'Yes, yes. Good idea.' He returns to the message. 'What does she mean about me texting her, though?'

'You've not heard that before? She hasn't rung you?'

'Of course not.' He closes the app, flings his phone on the seat next to him. 'This is just madness. Who would go to the bother of ruining our wedding like this?'

'Tania,' I say simply. 'That's obviously a fake profile. She probably isn't married at all. She's trying to cause trouble by insinuating you and her are messaging.'

He shakes his head.

'I can't see it,' he says. 'She's had years to try to cause more trouble. Why start again?'

'I don't know,' I say. 'But we're going to find out.'

EIGHTEEN

EIGHT YEARS AGO

Two hours before Callum's disappearance

Callum and I have been downstairs for almost an hour since the incident in the bedroom. He keeps glancing at me, giving me a warm smile. Checking that I won't *become hysterical* again. This time, I smile warmly back, as though everything is fine.

I pull my sleeves further over my wrists because they're still red.

Callum notices the gesture. Mouths *I love you*.

'Me too,' I whisper.

He gets up, heads to the kitchen with his empty glass to get another. It must be his fifth or sixth whisky.

'Gosh I can't see properly,' says Tania, slipping her phone into her pocket. 'I think it's a migraine. It always happens when I have too much screentime and not enough sleep.'

Matt hasn't heard her. He, Katherine and Jake are sitting in a circle on the floor with Post-it notes on their foreheads. It's painful watching them repeatedly fail at guessing who they are. I can't believe they're still playing that game.

'Do you have any medication?' I say. 'Do you want me to get it for you?'

She has one eye closed and reaches out a hand.

'If you help me to the kitchen,' she says. 'I'll get them.'

I stand and take her hand as Callum returns.

'What's going on?' he asks. 'Has she had a stroke or something?'

'Migraine,' says Tania, wincing. 'It's so painful.'

'Right, right,' he says, wandering off to the three on the floor.

Hand in hand, Tania and I walk to the kitchen.

'Thanks for helping me, Leah,' she says. 'Matt's so pissed now. He barely pays me any attention when he's drunk.'

'That's not often, though?'

'No. I guess not. I can't help feeling jealous, though,' she says. 'Even when he's only talking to Katherine.'

'Katherine's lovely!'

'Sorry,' she says apologetically. 'I know. Sorry. I can't help myself sometimes. Katherine seems older than her years, if you know what I mean.'

'I do.'

We've reached the kitchen.

'God, can you turn the main light off, please,' she says, covering her eyes. 'The light is stabbing my head.' I flick the switch, and she visibly relaxes. She points to the corner. 'In that cupboard near the sink.'

Inside is a green first aid container the size of a shoe box. I fetch it down and inside are boxes and tubes of pills: sleeping tablets, paracetamol, Imodium, codeine, Migraleve.

'Bloody hell,' I say. 'It's like a pharmacy in here.'

'I know,' she says, reaching for the silver box labelled 'Pink'. 'It's great, isn't it? If you mix the codeine with the antihistamine, it totally makes you zone out for at least two hours.'

'Shit, Tania! Is this why you've been so chilled out this evening?'

'Only a little. But the tiredness has given me a migraine.'

'Should you be having more pills?'

'It's fine. Last time was just before dinner so I'll be OK.'

I take a clean glass from the drainer, fill it with water and pass it to her. She shoves two of the pink pills into her mouth and swallows them down, only having a sip of water to chase them down.

'This isn't your first rodeo,' I say.

'Sometimes I don't have water to hand.' She links an arm through mine. 'They take about half an hour to kick in. Would you take me upstairs, please?'

'Of course.'

Callum's standing in the hallway as I guide Tania up the stairs.

'She's going for a lie down,' I say.

'I'll be back down,' says Tania. 'Don't want you to think I'm a party pooper.'

He raises his glass, says, 'I'll be waiting with bated breath,' and returns to the sitting room.

It's like he's waiting for me to tell someone his secret; he doesn't know if he can trust me. If I put a step wrong, he'll silence me. I know that for sure.

'Does he always follow you around like that?' Tania asks as we reach the landing.

'No.' I push open her and Matt's door and guide her towards the huge bed in the centre of the huge primary suite. 'He feels bad for the text messages I read on his phone.' I watch to see if her expression shifts. 'From a woman with the initials TS.'

'That's weird,' she says. 'They're my initials.'

I sit on the end of the bed as she lies on top of the covers.

'I know.'

She sticks her hand in the glass of water on the bedside

cabinet for a few seconds before taking it out and resting it on her forehead.

'Oh, that water's nice and cold,' she says.

'So they're not from you?' I say.

She lifts her head slightly. 'Hell, no! I don't have Callum's number.' She flops back down on her pillow. She closes her eyes, breathes in slowly, exhales. 'I don't think Callum can stand Matt, you know. The way he talked about him yesterday when we were on that ghastly walk.'

'Ghastly? I thought you got on well with Callum.'

'He brought vodka in a hip flask. We had a few shots. I love everyone when I've had vodka.'

'I see. What gave you the impression that he hates Matt? They've been friends since they were kids.'

'Yeah. Says it all. They're like siblings. Like me and my sisters. They loathe me.' She sits up a little. 'I think the tablets are kicking in now. I'll just lie here for a little bit, then I'll be back down.'

'I'll leave you to it.' I stand. 'I'll see you down there.'

I get back downstairs to find Callum sitting in the chair Tania vacated a few minutes ago. He's staring into a glass of whisky, swirling it about, but not drinking any.

A hand rests on my arm, and I jump, startled.

'Hey. Sorry.' It's Matt.

Callum doesn't even look up. It's like he's only semi-conscious.

'Come into the kitchen,' says Matt. 'I'll make us some supper. The others have already scoffed some leftovers. I got those Heinz Toast Toppers you like. Remember we used to buy them from the Poundstretcher around the corner from that shitty house we rented in second year?'

'No way! The cheese and ham ones?'

I hadn't realised how hungry I am – it's been hours since dinner, and events since had dulled my appetite until now.

Matt pulls out a chair for me at the kitchen table.

'Why, thank you, kind sir.'

I try to perch on the chair delicately, but of course I land like a sack of bricks. Matt doesn't notice.

'Thanks for taking Tania up,' he says.

'You sound as surprised as I was that she asked me,' I say. 'I think the high-strength painkillers, and everything else she's taken today helped with that.'

'Hmm.'

He ignites the grill and takes out a fresh loaf, placing it on a chunky wooden chopping board to cut it into thick slices. He lays four slices on the pan and sticks it under the grill. It's nice to watch something so mundane after the drama of the past few hours. It helps calm my mind. Process all of what Callum has told me.

'Have you noticed anything weird going on between Tania and Callum?' he asks.

'No.' I'm not going to mention the text messages. I don't think they're from her. And their cosy conversation this afternoon was obviously lubricated by Callum's salubrious intentions. I don't want to ponder why he'd want to get Tania drunk. 'I can sense there's something not quite right, though. With Callum, I mean. You're his best friend – he tells you everything.' What does Matt know? Does he know about the photo of my brother?

'I sense that too.' He picks up the knife again. 'It's like he's changed over these past few months. Years even.' His eyes glaze for a moment before he stabs the knife into the chopping board. 'But even back then there was a shift in him that I couldn't put my finger on. And yet he still has a mother who dotes on him and a wife at his side.' He focuses his gaze on me. 'I wish you were happy, Leah.'

'I...' How am I supposed to argue the contrary? This

weekend has been miserable, despite Matt's best intentions. It feels like in a few short hours my life has gone to shit.

'You've not had the best birthday, have you?' says Matt. 'I'm sorry it went a bit pear-shaped.'

'It's not been that bad.' I'm trying to sound cheerful. 'I really appreciate your parents letting us have the house for the weekend.'

'My mum loves you,' he says. 'You can do no wrong in her eyes. She always thought you and I would get together.'

'Really?' I shift in my seat; heat rises up my neck, across my chest. 'You're just saying that to be nice.' It's not as though Olivia and I have spent any meaningful time together. I glance at the door, but Callum's not lingering in the hall. 'I can't stop thinking about my mum. I feel awful abandoning her when she's just received the diagnosis. I can't wait to go and see her. Put this weekend—' I stop myself before I sound ungrateful.

'She wouldn't want you missing out.' Matt pulls out the grill pan to turn the bread. 'Plus, they've caught it early. That's what your brother was saying before. She'll be fine, Leah.'

'I hope so. I know she can be a bit too involved in my life, but it's only because she cares.'

'Has Callum calmed down now? I don't mean to be nosy but that argument you had upstairs earlier sounded a bit heated. What happened?' He raises a palm. 'I didn't listen in, I promise.'

'Nothing, really.' *Everything, actually.* 'His business, mainly.' My go-to phrase of this weekend.

I stand to take two plates from the cupboard.

'I'm guessing,' he says, 'by you pretending to be distracted with plates that you don't want to talk about it.'

I lay them on the table, and I've no choice to sit because he's already put out cutlery and glasses of water. He takes out the toast, slathers it with butter and tops each slice with a thick layer of cheese and ham deliciousness. My mouth is watering just looking at it. He places it back under the grill and watches until it bubbles.

'It's so great to see you again, Matt,' I say. 'It's always so easy being with you.'

'Ha!' he says good-naturedly. 'Are you suggesting I'm a simpleton?'

'Not at all.'

I want to tell him that he's the opposite to Callum; there's no hidden agenda with Matt, no duplicity. But I don't want serious conversation right now. I need to keep it light, especially as Callum is stewing in the living room. Any hushed voices, he'd come running in.

'Here you go.' Matt slides two slices onto my place. 'Toast a la carte.'

'Merci beaucoup!' A loud crunch as I bite into it. 'Oh my God it's better than I remember.'

I could sit here forever with Matt, and not have to deal with Callum.

'We *were* best friends.' He places his remaining toast on his plate.

'What?'

'Sorry.' He wipes his mouth with a piece of kitchen towel. 'You said before we started eating that he'd have told me every-thing because we're best friends. But the truth of it is that Callum and I don't really talk to each other that much anymore.'

I push my plate away. 'Callum's not mentioned anything. Did you have a falling out?'

'Not about one specific thing.' He runs his finger along the edge of the plate. 'Since I've been with Tania, I suppose. I haven't been there for him at all times of the day and night.'

'I thought Tania didn't mind Callum coming round. I thought he was round at yours just the other week.'

He shakes his head.

'Leah, he hasn't been over to mine for almost two months. When I send him a check-in text or some crappy meme, he leaves me on read for days before a short crappy reply. I thought *you* would know what's going on with him.'

I stand, pick up our plates and place them on the kitchen counter. I don't want Matt to see the confusion on my face.

'So where has he been going?'

'I've no idea,' he says. 'That's why I was asking you.'

I look at my reflection in the kitchen window. How different things are now. I wish I could turn the clock back and —And what? Not marry Callum? Leave and never see either Matt or Callum again?

'So here's where you two are hiding without me.' Callum sloppily leans against the doorframe, looking decidedly more pissed than he did just half an hour ago. 'Going over your sad little uni memories like time has stood still.' His movements are loose, but his words are precise.

'What are you on about, mate?' Matt asks, gently, as though he's talking to a child.

'You think that because you two went to university and I didn't, then I'm some thicko you talk down to.'

'Don't be ridiculous!' Matt shoots back. I can feel his knees going up and down underneath the table. 'Where has all of this come from? It certainly isn't from me!'

'You, swanning about this place as though you own it, you privileged wanker.' Callum's forehead is dotted with sweat; his nostrils are flared. 'Trying to make everyone else feel as though they're not good enough. I've seen the way you and Tania have been giggling in the corner, laughing at the rest of us – the *small* people, the *plebs*.'

Matt taps a finger to his temple. 'It's all in your head, mate. What have you been taking? It's messing with your mind.'

'I've taken nothing.' He holds up his glass. 'This is just apple juice. My mind has never been clearer.'

'I beg to disagree.'

'I don't give a shit about what you think, you—'

I slam my hands on the table, pushing the chair back as I stand.

'Enough! What's happened to you two? You're talking as though you hate each other!'

Callum raises a palm.

'Whatever. Calm down, Leah.'

'Saying *calm down* is never going to help a situation,' says Matt.

'I'm past caring,' I say evenly. 'You two can sort your own boring shit out. I haven't got time for it all. I'm going.' I walk towards the door. 'Happy fucking birthday, Leah.'

I'm almost at the staircase when Callum rushes towards me. He embraces me in a hug.

'I'm sorry, I'm sorry,' he whispers in my ear. 'I love you.'

I take a step back.

'OK.' Another step. 'I'm going to freshen up. Maybe have a shower. It's been a long day.'

'You'll be back down, won't you? It's only eight o'clock.'

'Of course.'

It's not as though I'm eager to spend the night in bed with my husband.

'Leah?'

I pause halfway up the stairs and turn to face him. His big brown eyes looking up at me as though he hadn't just been shouting at his friend only a minute ago.

'I do love you,' he says.

'Thanks,' I mumble and resume climbing the stairs.

I feel numb. Like my mind is outside my body and this isn't really my life. What the hell am I doing here? I've just turned thirty years old, and I should be travelling the world, experiencing things for the first time. Not locked in a perpetual circus of Matt and Callum's squabbles; my husband keeping huge secrets. But no. I've been with Callum since I was nineteen years old. Ten years that feel an eternity because most of my close friends from school don't even live in the same area anymore.

When I was nineteen, anything seemed possible. Now it seems as though nothing is, and I'm trapped in a life I didn't sign up for.

NINETEEN

NOW

Thirteen hours until the wedding

I'm lying in bed after checking all windows and doors three times over and making sure that Dad and Noah are safe, even though Matt and Jake are in the living room and the police said they'd station a patrol car close to the house until morning. When I close my eyes, I can still see the woman lurking in the shadows. Was she the wife of that man at the cabin? Am I reading too much into notions that have a simple explanation? Was it even a woman? Whoever it was, they were wearing a dark blue jacket with fluorescent stripes on the arms. It was just like the one Callum was wearing the night he disappeared. Did they wear it on purpose to taunt me? Or am I seeing things – imagining it all because I feel guilty that I'm alive and he's not? Perhaps the person who is messing with me has nothing to do with what happened to Callum.

I think back to that night after Matt called the police; they were there within minutes. I thought that was quite unusual for a missing man in his thirties. Don't they usually ask the circumstances? Perhaps Matt hadn't stated that Callum had left in a bad mood, and after arguing with multiple people. Or perhaps he had. Perhaps that was why: they thought he was a danger to himself after Matt had found Callum's jumper and phone. Or maybe it was because Olivia had gone to school with the local Chief Inspector.

We hadn't told the police about arguments that night. Different quarrels were had. My brother being blackmailed, which Katherine definitely knows something about; Matt being angry about Callum's treatment of me; Tania being... Being what? Did anything happen between her and Callum? I wasn't sure at the time, and I'm not sure now.

The police never suspected Matt of doing anything to harm Callum, but a lot of people did. How did he find Callum's clothes so quickly? they said. He was jealous of his friend's success, they said. Before the truth started to filter through.

I couldn't believe that Callum had kept all of that from me about my dad's investment. What a coward.

It was shortly before the first newspaper article came out that my dad told me. I had stayed at Lakeside Cottage with Matt and Jennie for three days after Callum's disappearance before finally going home to an empty house. I slept in the spare bedroom because our bedroom felt thick with his presence and I wasn't sure if it was because he was dead and it was his spirit (I know, but I wasn't thinking straight at the time) or because there was so much of his stuff in there. Much more than mine because he always had double the amount of clothes than I did.

I went round to Mum and Dad's every day for a month when Mum was recovering after treatment and also because I didn't want to be rattling around the house on my own. Two weeks after, when Mum was feeling a lot better, I answered the door to Dad, wondering why he'd come alone. They barely did anything apart after her diagnosis. He sat me down at the dining table and I thought back to the time when I was sixteen with him and Mum. I immediately suspected bad news.

He made us a cup of tea, but he didn't put out a plate of biscuits like he usually did. He'd brought his leather satchel with him and took out a plastic wallet of papers.

'I didn't want to have to tell you this,' he said. 'But do you remember that investment I made into Callum's business?'

'No?'

'Didn't he tell you? You know I don't like to talk money to my children, but I thought *he* might have told you.'

Goosebumps prickled my arms.

'How much did you give him, Dad?'

'It was to help you out, too, you see. He was so excited about this new idea. Said you had your heart set on it, but to keep it a secret as it was going to be a surprise for you.'

'Dad, what are you talking about?'

'The café round the corner from here. You've always wanted to run a café, haven't you?'

'Maybe,' I said. 'But it was just an idle dream. It's hard to make money in the food business.'

'He even showed me round it. The owner gave us a tour of the back and upstairs.'

'What?' I gripped the seat of the chair. 'When was this?'

'Around a month before he went missing. He said he wanted to buy it for your birthday, but he couldn't fund all the deposit himself.'

'How much did you give him, Dad?'

He took out a piece of paper and laid it in front of me.

'It looks so official, doesn't it?' he said. 'But when I went round to the place last week, the owner said it was still for sale. Callum hadn't even put in an offer. The man said he hadn't seen him since the day he and I viewed it.'

My stomach churned; my mind clouded.

'Please, Dad. How much?'

'Fifty thousand pounds,' he said. 'He said he'd pay it back when another business he was selling would be settled. And I didn't mind because it was for you. You'd have ended up with that money as your inheritance anyway. And this way, you'd get it early.'

'Oh, God.'

I stood and paced the room.

Picked up the piece of paper.

Agreement between Callum Critchley and William Moretti... The sum of fifty thousand pounds... 12a High Street... to be repaid in full within six months...

'Oh, Dad.'

'I'm not bringing it to you to make you feel bad, love.' He stood and put his hand on my shoulder. 'I was showing it to you before I take it to the police.'

'What?' I sat back down. 'Yes, of course.'

'Because this is motive for him to run away, isn't it?'

'Yes. Yes, it is.'

How could I not have known? On the statements I found in Callum's envelope that night I didn't see my dad's name. Perhaps I overlooked it, not expecting to see it. And I doubt Callum had only one account.

What else had he kept from me?

'I'm so sorry, Dad. I had no idea.'

'I know you didn't.'

'I can sell my car. That's got to be worth at least twenty grand. I can get myself a little runaround. I'll find a way to pay you back, Dad.'

'What if he comes back?' he said. 'I won't be the only one he's conned out of money. I was talking to Matt's dad when we were at the house. I know it didn't seem like the right time, but he brought it up first. He said he'd invested in a property in the south of France with Callum. Said it all seemed legit. They'd taken a trip there, apparently. But it was only after he went missing that they realised it had all been a sham.'

'Property?' It was getting worse. 'I thought Greg had taken Callum and Matt on a golfing holiday.'

Dad scooped up the papers and returned them to the folder.

'I'm sorry to have to bring this up on top of your worries. I know Greg went to the police yesterday. He thinks it's important – a reason why Callum would want to vanish.'

'It's OK, Dad. I get it. Do you want me to come with you?'

'I think it would be a good idea...'

It felt like the blood had left my brain.

'Do you think they'd suspect I knew about it all? That I was in on it?'

'That's why it's a good idea for you to come, love. Do you share a bank account with him? I'm sorry for asking you this. I doubt they'd think you were privy to this, given that you're still around.'

'We have a joint account for the mortgage and all the other bills, but we each have our own for personal spending.'

'Do you know where he keeps the statements?'

'In his office, I assume.'

We both headed out into the outdoor cabin, but there were no statements. He certainly covered his tracks, should anyone go snooping amongst his things.

'He must've switched to online statements,' I said, after checking the last file in the cabinet. 'I don't know where his laptop is.'

'Did he take it to Windermere?'

'I can't remember. If it is, it'll still be in the car.'

Dad headed out the office and onto my drive to peek through the car windows.

'You'll have to open the boot,' he said.

I popped inside for the keys, pressed the fob and Dad opened it up.

'There's nothing in here,' he said. 'Completely empty. Is that usual? I've never known a car to have absolutely nothing inside.'

I stood next to him to look.

'There's usually a couple of blankets. Some bottles of water. I don't know how long it's been like this. Callum sorted our bags. I dumped mine on the passenger seat on my way home. It's not that big of a deal, is it?'

I felt awful for lying to Dad. I knew full well that the car boot would be empty.

Dad peered closely at the boot's carpet.

'What are those marks there?'

He pointed to several dark circles against the light grey interior.

'You don't think he was involved with some dodgy people?'

I didn't reply.

'It might be blood.' Dad took a few pictures on his phone. 'Don't touch anything, love. I'll show the police the photographs when I take in my paperwork.'

Bless my dad. The police weren't interested in Dad's photographs, but they pretended to be. Gave him an email address to send them to; took photocopies of the agreement Dad and Callum had signed. They were very sympathetic to Dad losing his money, but after several weeks of silence from them, we realised there was nothing they were going to do about it.

Thankfully, the house was in my name only. Something Callum said about Capital Gains because he owned several other rentals I later found out he'd already sold. But it took only four months to sell the house to release the money I needed to pay Dad back. It was too big for only me anyway.

Dad is still convinced that Callum is either sunning it up in Mexico, his money long since spent, or he was bumped off by the Manchester Mafia. There probably isn't such a thing as the

Manchester Mafia, but Dad often looks behind as he's walking, thinking someone's following him.

The truth is that Callum would never have gotten involved with loan sharks. I should've realised he was spinning me a yarn, too. Callum's not sunning himself anywhere. He wouldn't have left his mum. He wouldn't have left me. Not without him sending word after a year or so.

I wouldn't have wanted to hear from him anyway.

He's dead to me.

And now, since one month and thirty-three days ago, he's dead to everyone else.

I won't have to wait long to find out who's behind it all.

Tomorrow, I will have to face them. And I'm ready for it.

TWENTY

EIGHT YEARS AGO

One hour before Callum's disappearance

I'm staring at the bedroom ceiling. Without meaning to, I must've slept for a little while. I glance at my watch to see it's only nine o'clock.

There's a tap on the door.

'Hey, sis.' Jake walks in and sits at the end of the bed. 'How's your headache?'

'My headache?'

'Callum said you weren't feeling well.'

'Right.' *Good little wifey, resting her delicate little head.* But what does it matter any more? 'I'm fine. Had a micro sleep.'

'Ah, a good old power nap.'

'I'll head downstairs in a minute.'

'Tania's recovered and making up for time lost with a margarita.'

He doesn't pair his words with a smile. I push myself up to a sitting position.

'What is it, Jake? Are you all right? You've been pretty quiet this weekend.' I'm trying not to picture him sitting in a chair with a tall blonde woman in only a bra and knickers sitting astride him. 'And, considering there was tequila last night, it's well out of character. What's up?'

'I didn't want to bring this up tonight, but considering Katherine and I are going away for a few weeks... And I had to tell her what Callum—'

'You're going away? I didn't think you could get term time off.'

He looks down at his hands; his fingers are linked and he's pressing his thumbs together.

'I've been signed off with stress.'

I reach over to him, squeeze his knee.

'Oh gosh, Jake. Why didn't you tell me?'

'I didn't want to burden you. You seem so sad all the time. I didn't want to add to your worries on top of what's happening with Mum.'

He lifts his gaze and fixes it on mine. He seems to be searching for something in my eyes, and I can't bear the scrutiny. I dart my eyes to the side.

'I'm not sad all the time.'

I can't tell him the truth about Callum's criminal behaviour; I can't involve him in any of this. By the sound of things, Jake's having a hard enough time as it is. We've both been hiding our worries. I can't believe it's taken me so long to realise my little brother hasn't been himself. And here he is now, worried about *me*.

Tears spring to my eyes. I want to tell him everything – for him to tell *me* everything. His care for me right now is overwhelming; my heart feels like it's expanding, warmth spreading across my chest.

I must be tired. My emotions are always magnified when I'm tired.

'You've been withdrawn all weekend. I thought you'd be able to totally chill,' he says. 'I'm concerned about you.'

'Don't worry about me. I'm a big girl.' I shuffle closer to him, wiping my eyes with my sleeve, hoping he doesn't register the tears. 'You can tell me what the problem is, Jake. Please. I'll only worry if you don't.' I give him a wry smile. 'I'll blow it up in my mind so you've only days to live.' His expression remains the same. 'You're not dying, are you?'

He nudges my shoulder with his.

'Everyone's dying. But I'm not dying any time soon. And it's not something to joke about when Mum is...' He glances at the ceiling before looking me dead in the eye. 'Callum's been black-mailing me.'

'What?'

It takes a moment for the words to sink in. I had been torn whether to mention the photograph to Jake, but it seems he already knows all about it. But I don't want him to know that. Callum had dismissed it as nothing. What an absolute coward.

'He has been for months.'

'I can't believe it.' I pace the area between the bed and the window. 'Blackmailing you about what? Something that happened before you met Katherine?' I can't let on that I've seen the photograph – he'd be mortified.

'What? No.' He takes in a breath and when he exhales, it's clear his whole body is shaking. 'I met this woman on a night out with him and Matt. Callum paid for a lap dance at one of these clubs. It wasn't seedy or anything. She didn't take *all* her clothes off. There was nothing in it, of course. I love Katherine. She's the best person I know. She hates any form of sex work. Especially the men – because it's mostly men, she says – who pay for it. Callum took several photos of me while it was going on. We all took turns; it wasn't just me.'

'Are you sure Callum isn't just pulling your leg? I mean, I know he can be a bit much, but he'd never be so terrible to friends and family. Especially if you all took part.' I would have thought this myself only a short while ago, but now I know my husband is capable of pretty much anything, and why else would he have the photo of Jake in his envelope?

Jake shrugs, but he's close to tears; his cheeks are red, and his hands are shaking. 'I'm just telling you what happened and what's happening now. Katherine can't find out about this. She'd leave me, I know she would.'

'How much did he ask you for?'

His gaze drops to his hands.

'Fifty thousand pounds.'

'Oh my God, Jake. You haven't paid him anything, have you?'

Not only did Callum lie to me about the picture, he lied about the amounts he was taking from people. Five grand, he said. Ten grand. But fifty thousand pounds?

'I could only manage to get hold of four grand,' says Jake. 'I had to sell my moped. The one I go to Mod meets on. Katherine thinks I've lost the plot, selling that. I don't know what I'm going to do if I can't get him the rest of the money.'

I wrap my arms around him.

'Oh, Jake. You should've come to me straight away. I'm so sorry that you've been dealing with this all on your own. Don't give him another penny. God, I can't believe my own husband has done this to you.'

Jake shrugs off my hands.

'It's not like he's going to tell you, is it?' He stands and wipes his face with the sleeve of his jumper. 'If he mentions any of this shit to Katherine' – he walks towards the door – 'I swear I'll fucking kill him.'

That's the second time in two days Jake has said that, and I'm beginning to think he means it.

TWENTY-ONE
NOW

Five hours until the wedding

Unsurprisingly, I didn't get much sleep last night. Most of my dreams during what sleep I *did* get, were that I was searching for Noah. I waited until after seven a.m. before I opened Dad and Noah's bedroom door to check on them. They were both fast asleep.

Now, it's almost eight and I need to start getting ready. There's a pit of butterflies in my stomach and I know they'll be here until this day is over.

After showering and dressing in a T-shirt and some joggers, I head downstairs. Jennie is sitting at the kitchen table, sipping a black coffee.

'You're here early,' I say. 'Who let you in?'

'I found the key under the mat.'

'Really? I didn't know they kept one there.'

'Teresa made a pot of coffee.' She takes a sip. 'It's nice and hot.'

I wonder if Olivia knows that Jennie just let herself in. I

can't imagine she'd be happy about it; she's never mentioned a key being under a mat. I'm not even sure there is a mat at the front door. One of the caterers probably let her in and Jennie doesn't want to get her into trouble.

Footsteps down the stairs and Katherine wafts into the kitchen wearing a long silky robe and her hair in massive curlers.

'Leah!' She rushes over to me and wraps her arms around my waist. 'It's your wedding day!' She goes to the fridge and pulls out a bottle of champagne and a carton of orange juice. 'I'm making us some mimosas to get the celebrations started.'

'It's barely past eight!'

'I won't make them strong. Will you be having one, Jennie?'

'What is it?'

'It's Buck's Fizz,' I say. 'Same thing.'

'I don't mind if I do,' she says with a small smile. 'There are worse ways to start the day.' She glances at Sandra in the utility room where she's chopping vegetables. 'We won't be stepping on her toes, will we?'

'Sandra!' shouts Katherine. 'Would you like a mimosa?'

She turns and smiles.

'Not for me, thanks. Have a million things to do before twelve.' She comes into the kitchen wiping her hands on her apron. 'Congratulations, Leah! Not long now until *I do*. How are you feeling?'

'Excited. But also apprehensive. This weekend has been a strange one.'

'You're not still worrying about that card, are you?' Katherine pops the cork, and Jennie visibly startles. 'It's probably some disgruntled neighbour. Pissed off about us ruining their peace. It's always something mundane.'

She's obviously put the text messages out of her mind. I take out the note from last night, waiting until she's topped up the glasses with orange juice before silently handing it to her, my

back to Jennie. I don't want her to worry that someone is imper-
sonating her son.

'When did you get this?' asks Katherine.

'Shh. It was posted under my door last night.'

'Someone was in the house?'

I nod.

'Matt called the police last night – they came round and we
showed them the notes. There was a police car outside the
house until seven when Matt went out to talk to them. And just
a minute ago,' I add, 'Jennie said that she let herself in with a
key under the mat.'

'Is there a mat?'

'I don't know. I don't tend to notice things like that.'

'You don't think...' She flicks her head in the direction of
Jennie.

'What are you two whispering about?' Jennie asks. 'My
hearing's not as good as it used to be.'

Katherine spins around and hands Jennie a glass.

'We were just debating the orange to wine ratio.'

'I hope it's eighty-twenty.' Jennie takes the glass. 'In favour
of champagne.' She takes a sip. 'And I'm not far wrong. Well
done, that girl.'

'I wondered why Jake and Matt were sleeping in the living
room,' says Katherine, guiding me into the hall. 'I thought you
wanted to stick with the traditional not-seeing-each-other
thing, so I suggested they leave when I woke early, but Matt
was having none of it. Said he wouldn't forgive himself if
anything happened to you or Noah and he was in another
building.'

'There was no way he wasn't going to be under the same
roof as his own child,' I say, 'after receiving a letter like that.
And I'm done with tradition. It's not as though it's cancelled
any bad luck so far, is it? I didn't see Callum a whole weekend
before our wedding and look where that got us.'

I glance behind, but thankfully Jennie doesn't seem to have heard.

Katherine presses her lips into a line. She can see I'm obviously upset.

'We're going to stick together, OK?' she says. 'I know this letter and the texts have riled you—'

'Have they not upset you?'

'Of course, but we're only here for a few more hours. Everything will be fine. Nothing bad has actually happened, has it? Apart from a few messages here and there.'

'But someone was in the house, Katherine. If it's someone with connections to Callum, then...'

I know I should stop talking about Callum, but everything's conspiring against me to remember. Perhaps that's what the letter writer intended.

'Ladies.' Jennie is standing at the kitchen door. 'Are either of you secret smokers? Only I do love a little cigarette with white wine. It really hits the spot.' She walks towards the front door wearing no shoes. 'I'm sure I saw a packet and a lighter hidden behind one of the plant pots.'

Katherine folds her arms as she watches Jennie exit the front door.

'Hmm,' she says. 'Do you think she's putting that on?'

'Putting what on?'

'Oh, come on, Leah. I'm not buying that confused old lady act she's putting on.'

'But she's eighty-four.'

'Sharp as a tack, she is. I know it. I was talking to her last night at dinner.'

'It's probably the mimosa. I doubt she's used to drinking at eight o'clock in the morning.'

Katherine downs half of it.

'Neither am I,' she says. 'Now the decision is, to continue in earnest and risk a slump, or to low-level carry on.'

I place my untouched glass on the kitchen counter.

'I'm going to stick to coffee. I need to stay alert.'

'What did the police say, by the way? When Matt phoned them.'

'They're going to have a patrol car again along the road up there. Make sure their presence is noted in the area. But they said there's nothing they can do unless something actually happens.'

'Even if it's a child?'

'What can they do? Give us our own security? There are thousands of stalking victims out there. You know that.'

'I know. But it's so hard. Do you have one of those key trackers? Perhaps we could attach it to Noah, so we know where he is at all times.'

'I don't. Maybe we should start microchipping children like dogs.'

'Ha!'

'I'm only half-joking.'

'Right,' Katherine says after gulping the rest of the drink, 'I'm going to make myself a weak one and take it upstairs. If you need any help watching Noah, I'm there.'

'It's OK. He and Dad are walking me down the aisle. But an extra pair of eyes won't do any harm if anything unexpected happens.'

'Of course. There'll be plenty of people keeping an eye on him, too. Don't worry, Leah. Nothing's going to happen to him.'

I grab a mug of coffee from the kitchen, and peek into the living room. The supposed security that is Matt and Jake is sleeping like a couple of sedated guard dogs. It's still only early, I guess. Perhaps they were awake until the early hours, judging by the whisky bottle next to Jake's resting place. At least there's only an eighth missing from it.

I close the door gently before heading outside. Jennie is nowhere to be seen, but I can smell tobacco. It seems she found what she was looking for. I walk to the lake, the gravel crunching under my slippers. There's no one in sight. The water is still.

Perhaps everything will go to plan.

After all, luck is what you make it.

TWENTY-TWO
EIGHT YEARS AGO

Thirty minutes until Callum's disappearance

I'm stirring hot chocolate in a pan on the hob, and I can hear Callum's voice from here. Why the hell did I come back down-stairs? Has he always been this loud? I'd have no doubt heard him from the bedroom.

'And you,' he booms, though I've no idea who he's talking to, 'can fuck off as well. Call yourself a best mate?' That'll be to Matt, then. 'You're embarrassing yourself, fawning over Leah. Can anyone else see that?'

Heat rises from my neck to my scalp and it's not because I'm standing next to the cooker. I wish he'd stop. I'll have to live with the consequences of what he's saying. It's just mortifying and embarrassing that he's saying things about me. He's making things up, now. He just doesn't care.

'And you, Tania. God, I feel sorry for you. You're actually not that bad.' He's pacing the wooden floor. Poor Tania. Bet she wishes she'd stayed upstairs, too. 'Why are you crying? It's not as though I'm saying anything bad about you, is it? I know most people can't bear to be around you, but I never said anything awful, did I? Not like Matt. He hasn't stopped banging on about how you're so needy, how crap you are in bed – that drought you're having has nothing to do with *you*, has it? He can't stand to be in the same room as you, let alone the same bed.'

'What the hell, Callum?' yells Matt. 'I have never once said anything like that to you. Those words wouldn't even come out of my mouth. I've never used the word drought in regard to sex in my life. Tania, wait.'

Footsteps, and sniffing, the slam of the downstairs bathroom door.

Poor Tania. This has probably been one of the worst week-ends she's ever had. God knows why she's still here – I'd have left on the first night if I were her. Hell, I should've done anyway.

'Now look what you've done.' This is the angriest I've ever heard Matt. 'Is it your mission this weekend to piss the whole world off?'

I turn off the hob and almost jump when Katherine appears at my side.

'Sorry,' she whispers. 'I sneaked out of there. I didn't want Callum to fix his sights on me. He's really going for it tonight. I've never seen him like this before. I don't think whisky agrees with him. My dad used to get like this on the drink when he lost a big trial.'

'Callum's been super stressed these past couple of weeks. I feel awful that he's taking it out on everyone. He's so drunk he won't even remember in the morning.' I can't mention anything about Jake, about Callum's widespread extortion. She wouldn't just take my word for it, she'd dig deeper – reveal Jake's darkest secret that would destroy their relationship.

'Maybe we should film him,' she says. 'He probably won't believe it when we tell him.' She folds her arms. I glance at her, expecting a wicked smile, but her lips are fixed in a line.

I picture in my mind a video of my husband ranting incoherently to my family and friends, his face flushed, words slurred. What if it went viral? Strangers would watch and ask: *Why is someone married to a man like that?*

My family must think that already.

Who, exactly, am I trying to kid? Has he always been this way and I've not seen it for myself until now? Poor Jake, trying to protect me for weeks, keeping it to himself when I could've been there for him.

'To be honest,' I say to Katherine, 'I don't think I can see myself with him for—'

She peers over my shoulder. 'Ooh is that hot chocolate? What's the flask for?'

Perhaps she's used to my brushing aside and excusing Callum's behaviour that she expects nothing else.

I take in a deep, calming breath, my eyes brimming with tears again.

'I'm making it up for later.' Like my brother did before when he was explaining what Callum has been doing to him, I try to hide the tremble in my voice and turn to pour the hot drink into the flask. I surprise myself by not spilling a drop. 'I'm planning on hiding out in the snug until Callum calms down.'

'Good plan,' she says, grabbing a bottle of Prosecco from the fridge and two glasses from the cupboard. 'I'll sneak this in.'

'Excellent.' I screw the lid on the flask. 'I know how to handle Callum when he's like this, though I'm hoping I won't have to. I'll wait a few minutes before I join you.'

She puts her arms around me in a warm hug.

'You know,' she says, 'you don't have to stay with him. I know this amazing family lawyer. Shall I give you her card?' She drops her arms. 'She's expensive, but worth it.'

'I don't think I see a future with him anymore,' I say. 'Not after this weekend. His behaviour has been terrible. But I don't think I can afford a shit-hot lawyer.' I press my lips together. I shouldn't be talking about money. 'I mean, not thousands of pounds. I don't have any to spare. It's all tied up in my business account and the house.'

'What Callum has is half yours.'

'I suppose. But wouldn't it be mean to use his own money to divorce him?'

She folds her arms and tilts her head to the side.

'Oh, Leah.' She briefly touches my hand. 'I'll call you about it when I get home from our holiday.'

We both flinch at the sound of a glass smashing in the living room.

'I'll see you in a minute,' I say quickly. 'You go and crack open the fizz.'

She nods, and dashes out of the kitchen.

I close my eyes. I feel as though I'm lying to Katherine by omission.

How has this become my life?

* * *

Katherine and I have almost finished the bottle between us, and I've nipped upstairs to put on my comfy pyjamas, but as I take them from under my pillow, there's a creak of the floorboard just outside the door. I pause my breathing. I don't know why I'm afraid. It's not as though Callum would hurt me again. I stand, stride to the door, and swipe it open.

'Tania?' She's carrying a tumbler of whisky and ice. 'Are you all right? Should you be drinking that if you've just had a migraine?'

'Can I talk to you?' She holds up the drink. 'It takes my mind off the headache.'

'Is your head any better?' I say. 'I was surprised to see you out of bed.'

I stand aside to let her in. There are no chairs to sit on; she perches on the end of the bed and pats for me to sit next to her.

'A lot better.' She sips the drink. 'Thanks to this.'

'What did you want to talk about?'

She clears her throat, straightens her posture. It feels awkward, sitting next to her like this. She was a lot more approachable when she was half-sedated.

'Callum.' She glances at the ceiling. 'You must've heard what he was saying about me. You were in the kitchen, weren't you?'

'I'm sorry. I can't control what he says.'

'I know. Have you always been that way?'

'What way?'

'So meek.'

'I...' I sigh, feeling myself crumble a little. 'Not usually. I don't know why I behave that way around him. This weekend has certainly given me something to think about.' My heart is racing. I stand and go to the window, leaning my back on the sill. 'It's been getting gradually worse, I suppose. It's easier when he's out of the house. Then I don't have to tread on eggshells in my own home because yet another one of his ventures has fallen apart, while my own is taking off. He's been a nightmare to live with, and now everyone else has witnessed it. I'm sorry I didn't stick up for you.'

'Oh, I'm fine. They were just crocodile tears down there. I can take care of myself. It was a way of leaving the room.' She pauses. 'Look. I'm worried about you.'

'You're not the first person to say that.'

'Callum's behaviour tonight shocked me. How can someone be so unpredictable? I don't know how you put up with it. Really, I don't. You know Callum thinks there's something going on between you and his best mate? And Matt talks about you like you're the perfect woman. Then there's Callum's huge chip that he carries round on his shoulder. Jesus.'

'I'm not to blame for my husband's behaviour.'

'I didn't say you were.'

The slam of the front door almost shakes the whole house. Tania rushes to the window.

'It's Callum.'

I reach over to turn off the bedside lamp and look through the window.

Callum's wearing his dark blue North Face hiking jacket with fluorescent stripes on the arms; he's shining a torch ahead of him as he walks to the right of the lake.

'Where the hell is he going?' asks Tania.

'I've no idea.'

'I hope he gets lost.' She says it distractedly. 'And I hope he *stays* lost.'

She strides out of the room, leaving the door open, and goes down the stairs. A moment later, the front door opens again, but I can't see who it is from here.

I draw the curtains.

I just want this night to be over with and I want to go home.

TWENTY-THREE

NOW

Twenty minutes until the wedding

In half an hour, it will be over, and we'll be married. Matt, Olivia, and Katherine have reassured me that nothing can happen to Noah when we are all together. They made it seem unreasonable to think of calling it off: we've been here all weekend – what's another hour? A ten-minute service after months of planning. I just want it over with and to get away from here, but whoever is behind this knew where to find me. If nothing happens today, they'll know where to find me tomorrow, the day after. For the rest of my life.

Who hates me this much to ruin my wedding, my life, and threaten my child? I've been so focused on Tania, and I know I *thought* I saw her last night, but what if it isn't her at all? I picture Katherine wandering down the side of the house the first night we arrived here, just minutes before we spotted the wedding card. Have I done something so awful to her that she'd orchestrate something like this in revenge? She's certainly intelligent enough. But why? Did Jake believe I was privy to Callum blackmailing him?

I hate that I've been reminded of Callum so much this weekend when it was meant to be about Matt and me. Our relationship is worlds away from mine and Callum's. What began as amazing – we said we were each other's soulmate – descended into coldness, violence and deceit.

I don't believe in soulmates anymore.

Matt and I started as friends; he's my best friend and I want him in my life forever.

It was five years ago that our relationship changed. It was Matt's birthday, and he was single after a several short-term relationships. I'd texted him to see what he was doing that night, expecting him to say he was going to the pub with his mates, but he said he was home alone. I turned up with wine for me and beers for him and a silly helium balloon I'd spotted in the corner shop.

To see his face, it was as though I'd shown up with the keys to a Lamborghini.

'No one's ever bought me one of those before,' he said, taking hold of the string. 'I've always wanted one.'

He led the way to his kitchen, which was all black because that used to be his signature decorating style.

'Are you joking?' I said. 'Because I can take it home with me. I've never had one before, either.'

'Ha!' He tied it to the back of a stool under the kitchen island. 'Don't tell me Callum never bought you a bouquet of balloons.'

My face straightened.

'No,' I said. 'To be honest, can we have a night when we don't talk about Callum?' I perched on one of the stools, unscrewed my wine. 'It's been three years. I'm sick of thinking about him, let alone talking about him.'

He stared at me for a few seconds before smiling.

'Of course.' He spun round, reached into a cupboard and took out two glasses. 'If I can share the wine?'

'Of course,' I echoed. 'You're a wine guy, now, then?'

He sat on the stool next to me and poured generously.

'There are so many things you don't know about me.' He shrugged. 'But mostly you know everything.'

I tilted my head, met his gaze.

'So, what don't I know about you?'

And that was how we carried on for the rest of the evening. Talking as though we had never met, but with the familiarity, the safety of knowing each other so well.

My skin tingles at the thought of that perfect night. I can't wait to marry Matt – to be a family. My small, happy, perfect family.

My bedroom is now a makeshift beauty parlour and it's times like these that I miss my mum. She loved having her make-up, hair and nails done; she rarely did it for herself. It's one of the treats she liked when she was undergoing treatment.

Two months before she died, I took her to a lovely hotel nestled in the Yorkshire Dales. The masseuse had to work gently on her as she bruised so easily. It was hard not to cry when I saw the different shades on her arms. 'I know,' she said. 'It looks as though I've been in a car accident. But I only slipped a bit in the bath.' She gave a small smile, yet she said it without sadness. Later, after I had gotten changed for dinner, I found her in the swimming pool with the lights dim. It had a glass roof, and Mum was lying starfish, floating in the middle of the water. I sat on a lounger, watching her peacefully looking at the stars, not wanting to interrupt her, until she noticed me sitting there.

'Love! You should've told me you were waiting! Am I running late?'

'Not at all, Mum,' I said. 'You take your time. If we're too late for dinner, then I'll drive us to McDonald's.'

'Do you know,' she said, climbing up the metal steps, 'I think I might prefer that. Ooh, a quarter pounder with cheese, large fries, an apple pie with a McFlurry on the side.' She giggled. 'I know. My eyes are always bigger than my belly.'

'You can have all of that,' I said. 'And some chicken nuggets as well.'

I stood and wrapped a fluffy white towel around her shoulders.

'Now you're talking. You go cancel the restaurant, while I get changed.' She kissed me on the cheek; I didn't wipe away the cold water that ran down my face.

'Don't cry, love,' says a voice, now, close to my ear. 'I've spent half an hour on your eyes.'

Dove (*like the bird, not the soap*), the make-up artist slash hairdresser, narrows her eyes as she scrutinises my face. She takes a cotton bud and dabs under my eye.

'There. All better.'

There's a knock at the door, and Dove shouts: 'Anyone but the groom may enter.'

This isn't her first rodeo.

'Ah, Dad. You look so smart.'

He's wearing a three-piece navy suit, a bright white shirt and a pale blue tie.

'I don't get the chance to dress up, these days.' He glances at Noah who's on the bed with a selection of books. 'Morning, Noah!'

Noah replies with a little wave. I'm not going to change him into his page-boy suit until the very last minute in case he spills anything down it.

Dove moves aside as Dad stands before me.

He takes hold of my hands.

'Happy Wedding Day, love!'

'Just got to pop downstairs for a glass of water,' says Dove. 'I'll be back in five.'

'You look stunning, Leah,' says Dad, once she's left the room. 'So beautiful.'

He sits on the bed, close to me on the chair.

'You look just like your mother did when I met her.'

'Thanks, Dad.'

'Though she wasn't wearing a fluffy white robe when she was working at the library.'

He reaches over and plucks a tissue from the stash of items Dove brought on her put-up table.

'I'm so proud of you, Leah.' He dabs his eyes, points to the hanky square in his jacket. 'I've been told I can't use that one.' He laughs. 'It's not the first time I've shed a tear this morning.'

'It's meant to be a happy day, Dad.' I reach over to rub his arm. 'Though the way things have gone, it's been a weird few days.'

'Have you had anything else? No phone calls or messages?'

'No, nothing like that.'

'I've been thinking about that letter you got last night. You don't think someone actually came inside the house, do you? Perhaps they posted it through the main door and someone else posted it under yours. I've asked everyone but Olivia and Greg, so it's possible.'

'It won't matter after this afternoon.' I stand to take the plastic cover off my dress. 'In thirty minutes, I'll be married. The car's picking us up at four this afternoon to take us to the airport. That's basically straight after the wedding breakfast. And until then, we'll be surrounded by people. It's not as though we're alone in some remote location.'

'True. And the police are aware.'

'Did you speak to them, too?'

'I called in the early hours of the morning. Olivia has a contact in the local constabulary. I think she contacted him as well.'

I sit back down and relax a little.

'Thanks, Dad. It's just really scary, you know. Thinking someone wants to do Noah and me harm.'

I'm about to add, *Especially as I haven't done anything wrong*, but that wouldn't be true. I shouldn't have got together with Callum, I shouldn't have put my head in the sand when he was out at all hours – "business meetings" that were probably him trying to con people out of money. I shouldn't have—

Dove returns to the room, noticeably not carrying a glass of water.

'Most of the day guests have arrived,' she says. 'Matt's about to head to the celebrant.' She takes the dress from the hanger and hands it to me. 'So we'd better get you dressed.'

'Erm.'

'It's just an expression. Just head into the ensuite, or we could leave if you want total privacy.'

'It's OK.' I take Noah's outfit from the wardrobe. 'Dad, would you do the honour of dressing your favourite grandson.'

He takes it from me. 'Indeed.' He smiles again, his eyes shining with pride.

I hang my lovely dress on the back of the bathroom door and shake off my robe. I chose it alone. I had already done the whole rigmarole of champagne and Mum and friends the first time around. It wouldn't have felt right without Mum being here.

I slide the dress off the hanger and slip it on.

I look in the mirror. With my hair up like this, in delicate pin curls, with two tendrils framing my face; my make-up done with a smoky eye, I look like someone else. I feel like someone else. There's something about becoming a mother that changes something so deep. It's like both Noah's DNA and mine course through me and has made me a new person. Someone who is fiercely protective, someone who would fight for him, do anything for him. It's like I was waiting all my life to be his mother. That it was always meant to turn out this way. And it's not all by luck.

I take a deep breath and open the bathroom door.

TWENTY-FOUR

EIGHT YEARS AGO

Three hours after Callum's disappearance

I can't stop pacing the living room, glancing out the window into darkness every two minutes where the moonlight is reflected on the cold shimmering lake in the distance, reminding me that it's gone midnight and Callum has been gone for hours. If we'd gone ahead with my plan to have my birthday party at ours, then none of this would have happened. I should have ignored Matt's suggestion of holding it here – that the place was free and convenient for everyone.

Jake's sitting in the corner, sipping on whisky, warming himself by the log fire. Katherine is on the floor near his feet.

'I don't know why you're so worried, Leah,' says Jake. 'It's not as though Callum can't look after himself.'

'He's right,' says Matt. 'He's been here loads of times.' He glances at Tania at his side as he stands. 'Are you going to be OK for a sec?'

She nods, still staring out the window. She's barely said a word since Matt called me downstairs, saying Callum still hadn't come back.

He leads me into the hallway.

'What is it?' I whisper, because even though the wood-cladded walls are thick, sound travels through the gaps. 'Do you think something bad has happened to Callum?'

He glances at his watch. 'Shit, it's been almost three hours. Do you think we should call the police? We could tell them he's been acting strange. That he might be a danger to himself... try to do something stupid? He was on about swimming in the lake the other night, wasn't he?'

'I didn't hear him say that.'

I look at my phone for the millionth time. My messages to Callum are still unread:

> Are you OK?

> Don't ignore me, Callum.

> I've tried calling you seven times, why aren't you answering?

> Callum? Are you getting these messages?

> It's not funny, now. Everyone is worried.

I type out another.

> We're going to call the police. If you've gone somewhere to cool down, just let us know before we get the authorities involved.

I stare at the phone as yet another message remains unread.

'Don't you have "Find My Phone" for Callum's mobile?' Matt asks.

'I would've used that ages ago if I had.'

I go back into the living room, straight to the window.

'Do you think he's gone into the water?' asks Tania, standing next to me.

'I don't know.' I frame my face with my hands to get a better view of the lake in the darkness. 'He knows how cold it is. It'd be silly of him to go out there on his own.' I turn and rest the bottom of my back on the window frame. 'Do you think he's doing this out of spite? Or do you think someone's hurt him?'

'He was talking shit to everyone,' she says, 'wasn't he? I wouldn't be surprised if either were true.'

'Really?'

'Jake went out shortly after Callum left in a huff, then came back about ten minutes later. Said he couldn't see him,' she says. 'Matt went outside briefly, too, after your brother came back. I went out to find him, but by the time I came back everyone was here. Except Callum, of course. And that's when Matt came up to tell you that he was missing.'

'I'm going out to search for him,' says Matt from the hall. 'It's been too long.' He puts on his walking jacket, heavy boots and a neon green hat. He takes a torch out of his pocket. 'Jake, you stay here. Make sure everyone stays safe.'

'Yeah, thanks, Matt,' says Katherine. 'Don't know what we'd do without a big, strong man in the house.' She folds her arms and rolls her eyes.

'Sorry, Katherine. I didn't mean it to sound like that.'

'Well, I would feel better with him here,' says Tania. 'What if there's a killer on the loose? Perhaps they're going to bop us off one by one.'

'Bop us off?' Katherine rubs both temples. 'For God's sake, Tania. We're not in some horror movie.'

'Did you hear that?' Tania grips hold of Katherine's arm, but Katherine shakes it off. 'No, I'm serious. There was a bang coming from the kitchen.'

'I haven't got time for this,' says Matt. 'I've got my phone.

There's a good signal round here. If I'm not back in an hour, give me a call.'

'An hour?' says Tania. 'Callum won't have gone far.'

'He's been gone almost three hours,' I say.

Matt leaves the house, ignoring the remark. If he listened to everyone then he'd never leave. It doesn't help that everyone has been drinking for most of the evening.

Jake rests a hand on my shoulder.

'Come and sit down,' he says. 'You've been hovering at the window for ages.'

'I can't. What if Callum's done something stupid?'

He cocks his head to one side. 'He's always doing something stupid, Leah. You, more than anyone, are aware of that.'

'But...'

'He'll be fine. He always lands on his feet. It wouldn't surprise me if he's hiding in that rundown cabin, sulking, making us worry about him.'

A shiver runs through me.

'But... But it's cold out there. What if he's harmed himself? He was behaving strangely – he wasn't himself at all.'

'I doubt he'd harm himself. He's got too much of an ego for that.'

'Shall we go and check? He's been gone for ages and it's cold out there.'

'It's May. I know it's not a pleasant spring evening, but he won't freeze. Wasn't he wearing that massive coat? The one that cost over two hundred quid.' He narrows his eyes. 'That's what he was telling everyone, anyway.'

'I've no idea. He might be in the boathouse. Something might've happened... an accident. Maybe the kayak fell on top of him. They're heavier than they look.'

'Matt said he'd already checked in there,' says Tania.

I head to the hall and open the front door. There's no sign of Matt in the distance.

'I'm going to look again.' I already have my boots on, and I grab any coat from the rack. I think it's Katherine's. 'Are you coming with me?' I reach into a pocket and there's already a torch in there. Katherine is always prepared for anything. 'I said, are you coming with me?'

Jake shakes his head; back into the room from wherever he was in his mind. 'What? Oh. Yes, yes.' He places his glass on the carpet. 'I'll just get my trainers and gloves on.'

'Gloves?'

I head out in front of Jake. Matt's parents have owned this place since she – Olivia – inherited it from her mother. She's always saying that she used to go playing in the forest when she was only five years old, it was *that* safe. But how can she know every nook and crevice? She let Matt do the same, apparently, but I think that's bullshit. Matt's not the strongest swimmer – he hates the water. He won't be the first to volunteer to search for Callum in the lake.

I'm almost at the boathouse. The wooden door looks like it's the original. It's not locked and is open only three inches wide. The padlock's lying on the floor.

'That's weird,' says Jake behind me. 'Wasn't that locked this morning?'

'I've no idea.'

'Yeah. Matt showed us his dad's new kayak thing. They keep the key...' He bends down to move a boulder that seems lighter than it looks. 'It was here this morning.'

'This morning was a long time ago,' I say. 'Or at least it feels like it was.'

Jake pulls the door fully open.

I lift the torch and shine the light along the walls.

'Wait.' Jake takes hold of my arm and guides it until the light reaches a smear on the wall. 'Is that blood?' He walks towards the stain.

'It's probably paint...' I stay near the door, near the light of the moon. 'Come back out, Jake.'

'We've only just got here.'

He takes off a glove and reaches over to touch the wall.

'Stop!' I shout. 'What are you doing? If it *is* blood, we shouldn't go anywhere near it.'

I feel sick just thinking it might be a possibility.

He steps back and the heel of his foot sends a bucket noisily onto its side.

'Jesus! You said it probably wasn't!' He rights the bucket then shines the torch along the wall with the stain. 'It was there the other day when Matt and I came looking for his dad's weed. But look. All that stuff has been messed up.' Two of the wetsuits are on the floor; they look almost lifelike – like whoever was wearing them has just evaporated. Jake shines the torch in my face. 'Callum and Matt haven't been on the best terms this weekend, have they? Do you think things got physical?'

'Hey!' I shield my eyes, and he lowers the light.

'Sorry.'

'I don't know. You haven't done anything to—'

'No, I've not hurt him. Not that I'd tell you if I had. That bastard deserves the worst happening to him. But I'm not going to start shouting that from the rooftops, am I?'

'Matt wouldn't have hurt Callum,' I say, trying to dispel the image of my brother murdering my husband from my mind. 'He's not violent at all.'

'You don't know what people are capable of when they're driven to the edge. Matt might have really hurt him. You know what his parents are like. They let him get away with anything. They have friends in high places, remember.'

'What exactly have you been drinking, Jake? Your imagination is going wild.'

'I don't understand why yours isn't.' He gestures to the door with his torch hand and heads back to the door, careful not to step in anything that looks like liquid. 'At least we're each other's alibis if something untoward has happened in there.'

'What?'

'Come on, Leah. Callum's pissed everyone off.'

'I know.'

'Katherine's defending this bloke accused of murder. I happened to have a peek into one of the files.' He catches my expression. 'Well, she shouldn't have left it out. Anyway, I don't know how she does it, defending scumbags like that. Of course he did it. Most of them did it. Police don't just set people up, not in real life. Maybe Callum's upset the wrong person.'

'I think we should go back inside.' I take the torch out of his hands, and he offers no resistance because he's drunk. I don't know how he's managing to walk straight, and I can't believe the stuff he's coming out with. I turn around and he's still in the same spot. This place seems so spooky at night, especially with Callum out here somewhere. God, what if we were to find his body? I'm working myself up, and my brother seems to have zoned out. 'Jake?'

He's looking into the distance. 'Can you see that?'

The water is calm, and there's no one sneaking around near the trees as far as I can tell. It feels as though someone's watching us. It's eerily quiet. Where the hell is Callum?

'I can't see anything unusual,' I offer.

I keep walking. I reach the front of the house and he's still standing there.

'Jake! Come on. The last thing we need is someone else getting lost.'

He thrusts his hands into his pockets and stomps towards me.

'It's really creepy out here when it's so quiet,' he says, walking past me and in the front door. 'I think you're right. I've just got this really weird feeling that's something's off.'

Inside, I sit on the Monk's bench in the hall to take off my boots.

'You've been ages,' says Katherine, gripping both sides of the living-room doorway. Her cheeks are flushed, and her mascara is smudged under her eyes. 'Where were you?'

'We checked out the boatshed, then Jake thought he saw something – I couldn't see it personally, but it's weirdly quiet out there.'

'It'd just be like Callum to spoil the weekend on purpose,' says Jake, kicking his shoes off. He sways as he bends to straighten them on the floor. 'He gets away with things no one else would. I can't even...'

'What?' I say. 'Two minutes ago, you were worried that he'd been in a fight.'

'A fight?' Katherine places a hand on her forehead. 'God, I'm boiling. I think I'm coming down with something. I'm so tired.'

'Yes. Jake thought he saw blood in the boathouse, but then he realised it had been there yesterday. The door was unlocked.'

I take a deep, calming breath and rest the back of my head on the wood of the bench. This is absolute chaos. Everyone's drunk. Not thinking straight. How the hell am I—

The door blasts open.

Matt's standing at the door.

He's carrying a piece of clothing and a mobile phone.

I leap up and reach for it, but Matt turns away from me.

'We shouldn't touch them,' he says. 'I'm wearing gloves. Get me a carrier bag to put these in.'

'It's Callum's jumper.' I say. 'And is that...? Callum doesn't go anywhere without his phone.'

'I know.' Matt places the bundle on the bin liner Katherine has got from the kitchen and laid out on the floor. 'This is Callum's stuff. He's not going to get very far without his phone.'

'Unless...'

'Yes.' Matt doesn't finish my sentence, but we're all thinking it.

Unless Callum's gone into the lake.

TWENTY-FIVE

NOW

The wedding

My legs are shaking, and I cling to Dad's arm as we walk down the stairs; my other hand is holding Noah's tightly.

'Is Matt definitely there?' I say, voicing many of the worries I've had in the past five minutes. 'Is Katherine definitely at the front so she can watch Noah while we say our vows?'

Dad laughs lightly, hiding the apprehension I know he feels.

'Matt is definitely there, and so is Katherine *and* Jake. Don't worry, Leah. We're all going to keep a tight watch on Noah.'

'Are you sure? Do you want to go out and have a look to make sure before we leave the house?'

'Everything's fine,' he says. 'Stop worrying.' We reach the bottom of the stairs, and he takes me by the hand. 'You look so beautiful, Leah. And you're looking very smart, Noah.' My son beams under his grandad's gaze. 'And I have to ask this,' Dad says quietly into my ear, 'but are you sure you want to go through with this?' He winks. 'It might be a bit awkward saying no, mind, what with you and Matt taking your son on honey-moon this afternoon, but I felt it my duty to ask.'

'Yes, I'm sure.' I shake out my hands, releasing Noah for a small moment before gripping his hand again. 'I've known Matt longer than I haven't known him.'

'You'll be fine.' Dad takes a step ahead and holds out his hand. 'Are you ready?'

The music's playing outside.

'I'm ready.' I reach out a hand and take my dad's. 'Let's get this...' I was going to say *get this over with*, but immediately feel a pang of guilt towards Matt, towards Olivia, and everyone else who has worked so hard to make this day special. '...show on the road. Sorry about the cliché.'

Dad shrugs as I link my arm through his. Noah's clutching a velvet bag with our rings inside and he's putting all his concentration into not dropping it. I'm so glad my anxiety hasn't rubbed off on him.

'I'm all about the clichés, love. I think I've said about twenty already today. All's well that ends well.'

'Don't count your chickens.'

I straighten my face as we head out into the sunshine. Don't want to look like I've been on the champagne all day like Katherine.

'What a lovely day,' says Dad. 'I knew the clouds would part for you.'

'A proper Jesus, I am.'

Dad pauses.

'Are you having a moment?'

'Dad, I'm fine.'

I stop myself from looking at the forest opening, across the lake, behind the shrubs. Unless it was a six-person operation, no one can ambush Noah nor me in front of thirty people.

But who's that man there in the sunglasses? I've never seen him before. I didn't consider that this mystery person could hide in plain sight as a guest; it's the perfect disguise.

The man's smiling. He lifts his sunglasses onto his head.

Oh. It's Matt's friend from work. Anthony.

Smile, Leah. Everything's fine.

I fix my gaze ahead as Matt turns around. His eyes light up when he sees me, his smile beaming. After all this tension around the letter, the card, the messages to Greg, seeing Matt ahead of me waiting, makes it all worthwhile.

Noah's walking in front of me now and I feel a warmth in my whole body knowing my family surrounds me.

'Ooh, you look lovely, Leah,' whispers Jennie as I pass, and I'm glad, now, that she's here. It feels right, and I'm grateful that she's happy for me.

I reach Matt and hand my bouquet to Katherine, who's wiping away a tear.

She kisses me on the cheek and whispers, 'Good luck.'

'Thank you.' I pass Noah's hand onto hers and he sits between her and Jake.

I take hold of Matt's hands.

This is it. The day we become a proper family.

But what if it all goes wrong like it did with Callum?

No, stop it, Leah.

It's romantic; it's beautiful. I smile at Matt.

'Good afternoon,' says Penny, the wedding celebrant. 'And good afternoon on behalf of Leah and Matt.'

Matt squeezes my hands, and my trembling subsides a little. I look into his eyes, and I almost forget everyone around us. This, I realise now, is a moment I've waited for, for most of my life. He's my family; we will always be family.

'Good afternoon, ladies and gentlemen. My name is Penny Simpson, and it gives me the greatest pleasure to be here today, to celebrate the marriage of Leah and Matthew, marking a moment for a beautiful family of three.'

I hear several people sniffing, and I glance over the guests, expecting smiling faces dabbing away happy tears, but Olivia and Greg are frowning. So is Jake. He's peering over at the barn behind us. He points, seemingly freezing for a moment.

'Smoke!' he yells. 'There's smoke coming from the corner.'

As soon as he says it, I can smell it. Grey plumes float across and they're becoming thicker.

'Noah!' I shout over at the bubbling panic of worried voices. 'Come here, love.'

He shuffles to the end of the row of chairs and reaches a hand out to mine.

An almighty bang comes from the outbuilding.

There's more smoke. It's everywhere.

I can't see. It's stinging my eyes.

'Noah!' I yell. I can barely see my hands in front of me. 'Noah, follow my voice. Come here, love.' I'm blindly throwing my hands around, desperately in search of my little boy. 'Noah!' My voice is getting hoarse. The smoke seems to be clogging my airways.

A hand grabs the top of my arm yanking me away from the house, towards the lake. As we near the water, I realise it's Matt.

I cough, spluttering foul fumes from my throat, my lungs.

'Where's Noah?' I shout. 'Where is he? He was just with Katherine!'

'It's OK.' Matt's voice is wobbly. He's trying to stay calm. 'Noah!' he yells, his voice carrying further than mine. 'Who's got Noah?'

Our guests are as stunned as we are, one by one emerging from the cloud of grey smoke. Dad staggers out of the fog, gripping a chair from the back row.

'I can't find Noah,' he gasps.

I grab one of the chairs – Dad looks as though he's about to collapse – and guide him to sit down at the water's edge.

'Wait there,' I say.

Katherine and Jake aren't amongst the people sitting on the grass outside the cottage.

'Matt,' I shout as he runs to the right. 'I'll take the left. Shout me when you find him.'

'Noah!' I get down on all fours, looking under chairs. 'Noah! Come here, love. Now's not the time for hide and seek.'

'Leah! Leah!' It's my brother's voice.

'Jake! I can't find Noah.'

He takes me by the hand as we finally reach each other.

'Katherine's hurt,' he says, his voice full of panic and worry. 'She fell and tripped. Cracked her head on the corner of a chair. I've already rung for an ambulance.'

'I... I'm sorry, Jake. I need to find Noah.'

Oh God. Noah's not with Katherine. Olivia might have him.

I stand, surveying the area. The breeze is slowly blowing away some of the mist. Chairs in disarray. Katherine lying on the ground, one arm stretched in front of the other.

I race to her, crouching on the gravel.

'Katherine, can you hear me?' I know it's awful and it seems as though I don't care about her. 'Where's Noah? Did you let go of Noah or did someone take him.'

'Leah,' Jakes says, distraught. 'She can't hear you. She's unconscious.'

I tap her face gently, noting a streak of blood running down her cheek. 'I'm so sorry, Katherine. Can you hear me?'

Her body starts shaking, before several small coughs come from her chest. Finally, she opens her mouth and takes in some air. Her eyes flicker.

'Katherine, it's Leah. Did someone take Noah from you?'

The fingers on her outstretched arm wriggle. She blinks faster.

She lifts her head sharply; tries to sit up.

'Noah,' she says quietly. 'Noah was with me. He had hold of my hand. I said I wouldn't let go.'

I look to Jake. 'Noah's been taken. Did you see anyone you didn't recognise, or someone who looked out of place.'

'I saw nothing, Leah.' The tears are making tracks through the dust on his face. 'Literally couldn't see anything. What the hell is going on?'

'Stay with Katherine. I need to find Noah.'

Oh, God, please don't let Noah have been taken. He could be anywhere. It could be a...

No. There's no way this is a coincidence.

Someone planted a smoke bomb or threw a smoke grenade – as incomprehensible as it sounds.

'Noah!' I can't shout it any louder. 'Noah, please.'

Matt is checking the garden room – his voice a loud echo through the murmurs of confusion. Olivia and Greg are scrambling through the barn, even though that's where the blast came from.

Matt runs from the garden and grabs me by the elbow.

'He's probably in the house.' He almost drags me to the front door. 'He was probably thirsty. The smoke. It's probably gone to his chest, panicking and looking for help.'

'Yes, you're right. The smoke. He's looking for me at the house.'

My mind isn't concentrating on words. I need to find my son.

He's my world. If I lose Noah, I can't survive.

'Noah!' Matt's voice echoes against the high ceiling of the hall.

I rush into the living room, pulling the cushions from the sofa, knowing there's no way he'd fit in between them. I pull apart the curtains, just as I did last night. There'd been someone in the house. I shouldn't have dismissed the idea so quickly. We should've left. Gone back home.

'Noah!' My voice is high; my throat is burning. 'Noah, please come out. You aren't in any trouble.'

Outside, there are yells of *Noah, Noah. Where are you, Noah?*

I check inside the cupboards of the dresser, the sideboard.

Nothing.

Next, the dining room, but the place is so bare, after a look under the table, he's not in here. In the kitchen, Teresa and Sandra are checking inside the cupboards. News travels fast when there's a child missing.

'Have you seen him?'

'I'm so sorry.' Sandra's eyes are wide – she's obviously hasn't if she's still looking. 'Have you checked outside in the back garden?'

'No, no.' I yank the back door handle. 'He might be out here, exploring. Call the police,' I yell over my shoulder. 'They said they'd be close by.' I stand in the middle of the garden, circling. Where the hell can he be? He's so little. He never goes off on his own. 'Noah!' I crouch down to his level, scanning the shrubs. 'You can have an ice cream if you come out now! You've won at hide and seek!'

It's wishful thinking, isn't it? To think that over the course of two days, he's suddenly changed to a child confident enough to just wander off on his own and hide in some scary thick bushes.

Tears fall from my eyes as I wade into the thick sharp shrubs. My dress is getting ripped to shreds but I don't care. 'Noah!' I wipe the tears from my face, and they're mixed with blood. I must've caught my cheek on a thorn, but I feel no pain. 'Please, Noah! Where are you?'

My little boy is somewhere that I'm not. Somewhere I don't know.

What if someone's hurting him? I can't let my mind go into dark places. I need to find him.

'Noah!' My voice is getting raspier. 'Noah!'

There are sirens in the distance. One, two, three police cars.

'Leah!' Someone's standing in the back garden. 'Leah, are you in there?'

I turn around and part the greenery, stepping over piles of twigs and leaves.

'Katherine!' I'm trying to read her expression. Frowning, crying. Still with a bloody streak down her face. A thousand questions but I only say, 'Have you found him?'

She shakes her head, takes my hand.

'Are you OK?' I say. 'You were unconscious only a few minutes ago.'

'I'm fine, fine. Olivia and Greg have looked all over the house,' she says, leading me through to the kitchen. 'All the rooms and cupboards upstairs, all the ensuites. Jake's just checking inside the cars of the day guests.'

'But how come you're OK, now?' I let go of her hand. 'Were you just stunned before?' I shake my thoughts away. *Jake's checking inside cars.* 'Good idea.' I race towards the front door. 'He loves cars. He'll want to see inside the posh cars he's never seen.'

As I say it, I know it's ridiculous. He wouldn't go off on his own and open a stranger's car – or even a car belonging to someone he knows. And he's not strong enough to pull a car door open in the first place.

I run to where the cars are parked on the gravel near the entrance gate – there are at least ten. Jake's banging on the window of a black BMW.

'Noah!' he shouts. 'Come out, Noah! Everyone's looking for you.'

I peer into the front and back of a small silver car, standing on tiptoes to see in the footwells. I go to the boot, pound on the metal with a fist.

'Did you get stuck in there, Noah?' I look around me, shout at whoever's nearest. 'He might be trapped somewhere and not able to breathe. Everyone, please, open your cars and your boots.'

I know the chances are slim, but anything's worth a shot. I look at each person as they unlock their cars, and my hopes are dashed by every sombre expression.

He's not here. He's not in the house, in the cars, in the barn.

'We need to keep looking,' I yell, as they appear to pause. 'We need to search over there, up there.' I point to the trees, the main road above. 'Please, don't stop looking for him.'

* * *

Five minutes later, three police cars speed down the steep driveway, skidding to a stop near the gate. A police officer climbs out of the first; five uniformed officers follow as he walks towards us.

'Leah Moretti?'

'Yes.' I rush to him. 'My son has been taken. There was an explosion in the barn. A smoke bomb or something. We couldn't see anything. People bumping into everyone, chairs and... Someone has been threatening to take him – someone pretending to be my dead husband.' I look behind for Katherine; she's walking towards me. 'Do you have my phone? I need a picture of Noah.'

She shakes her head and reaches into her bag that's across her body.

'I have some on mine,' she says. 'I've been taking them all weekend.'

So have I, I want to say, but I've been so caught up in all of this mess. I wasn't paying enough attention. Too wrapped up in the wedding to notice my own son being snatched from right in front of me.

'OK,' he says. 'Shall we go inside? I'll be able to hear you better in the house.'

The wind has picked up; the shouting from my family and friends travels on the breeze.

'Yes, yes.'

I start walking.

'I'm PC Harry Fern,' he says. 'We have officers scanning the area. Did you hear a vehicle near the house?'

I shake my head. 'I didn't hear anything but screaming and shouting. I couldn't see.'

In the distance, Matt is wading through bushes; he's seen the police officers' arrival and jogs over. His suit's covered in dirt; the bottom of his trousers is wet to his knees.

'He's gone.' Matt's eyes are red, his cheeks flushed. 'I can't believe it. He just vanished. And the explosion. Someone caused a distraction. We had Noah close to us. He was just here.'

Matt opens the front door to the cottage but lingers outside.

'Shall I wait out here? I need to make sure Noah can see me.'

The police officer takes off his hat as he steps into the house.

'It won't be for long,' he says. 'I just need some details from you and then you can search again.' He glances at me. 'Or stay here and wait for his return. It's entirely up to you.'

We file into the house, heading to the main living room.

It's happening all over again. In the same place, in the same room. The day after my birthday. Police searching the house, searching the grounds. Though not with as much urgency as they're doing now. Because we're near water; and Noah's only little. If he's not in the house, he could be in the lake, just like...

This isn't about Callum, right now.

Or is it?

I go to my bag, which is lying on the sideboard, and take out the card and the note, handing them over to the police officer.

'That' – I point to the note – 'was slid under my bedroom

door last night. I called the police and they said they'd have a patrol car in the area.'

'And the house was full?' he asks.

I nod.

'And no one saw anyone come in or go out? No one heard a stranger walk up the stairs?'

'No.'

'Hmm. That's very odd.'

Why is he making me feel as though I'm making all of this up?

'I thought someone might have posted it through the letter-box,' I say, my heartrate rising again, 'and then one of the family members might've pushed it under my door. But when I asked them, they said they'd never seen it before.'

'And you asked all the family, all the guests staying here?'

'I didn't ask Greg.'

Why are we just chatting like this when my son is somewhere out there? He might be on his own, lost. We might just be jumping to conclusions that someone has taken him. Perhaps he's in the water.

The officer is examining the note.

'Would you say the handwriting is the same in both?' he asks.

I turn around to check he's talking to me.

'I thought it was.'

'Do you recognise the writing as your ex-husband's?'

'I haven't seen it in a long time, but yes it looks a lot like it.'

'But surely there were things left in your house? Old birthday cards, anniversary cards?'

'I...'

I can't tell him that I burned most of them. I didn't want them to catch me unaware if I found them in the future and felt his presence around me like some ghost. But he's still managed to do just that, hasn't he?

'What's this got to do with the search?' asks Matt, at last.

'I'm just trying to decipher what we're dealing with. To make sure your son hasn't just gone wandering, though we are still exploring the area.'

'Why are we wasting time with such useless questions?' Matt asks.

'I'm not just spouting nonsense. We're trying to help. We've only just arrived on the scene.'

'Right.'

No matter how much we press that we should be out there, this man will keep asking questions. And the sooner I answer them, the sooner I can go back outside.

'I received a card two days ago from someone pretending to be my dead husband,' I say. 'He went missing from this house eight years ago.' He's writing in his notebook. 'Whoever it was said they'd be here today. It wasn't threatening at first – alarming, yes. But then we received –' I stop myself in time. I can't disclose the texts accusing us of murder. 'I received a letter under my door, saying they were going to harm my son. We told the call handler this when we phoned the police in the early hours.

The officer turns to Matt again.

'It's highly unusual for a predator to happen upon a remote location such as this—'

Why is he addressing Matt when I'm the one talking? Treating me as though I'm some hysterical woman. But my son has gone missing. How else am I going to be? We shouldn't have stayed here. We should've gone home. I shouldn't have been placated by well-meaning people who wanted to believe that nothing bad would ever happen here again. Lightning doesn't strike twice.

But it does.

'It's hardly remote,' says Matt. 'There's a main road up there.'

'It's hardly a main road,' the officer says lightly. Is he trying to calm us down with his tone? It's certainly not working with me. 'And unless you knew it was here, the house is quite private.'

'What about that cabin through the woods?' I say. 'There was a couple staying there last night.'

'The officers will be searching the whole area. I promise you.'

'Do you think they have something to do with it?' I ask.

'Without talking to them,' he says. 'I don't know.'

'Well, what are you waiting for?' asks Matt, standing. 'We've told you everything we know. I must get back out there – I need to keep looking for him.'

'It's best someone stays here, though,' says PC Harry Fern. 'Someone familiar to greet him when he gets back.'

'He's not a teenager who'll just wander back through the front door when he's hungry. He's a little boy. He needs his mummy now!'

'I know that, Leah.' He picks up his iPad. 'It's for the best, though.'

If something awful has happened to Noah, I want to be the first to see him. He's my son. Good or bad I need to be the first one there. He needs me; he's part of me.

I hear yelling outside.

I jolt up from the chair, run to the window.

'Have they found him?'

Another police officer outside, dressed in combat trousers, a black T-shirt and a high-viz vest, is laying a map on Olivia and Greg's patio table.

'They're organising a co-ordinated search until a leading detective gets here,' the officer says, 'to make sure they cover everywhere. Not just the obvious places. And of course the cabin along the way.'

'This house, too,' says Matt, 'is advertised on Airbnb. Will that make a difference? Given that the house's layout is in the public domain?'

'I can't be certain on anything at this time.'

The living room door opens. It's Jennie. I haven't seen her since I walked down the aisle.

'Can I get anyone a cup of tea?' she asks.

'Not for me, thank you very much,' says PC Fern. 'I'll just pop outside. Won't be a moment.'

I lean into Matt, finally letting myself burst into sobs. My whole body is shaking.

'Oh, darling.' Jennie stands next to me, rests a gentle hand on my arm. 'There, there. It's awful, isn't it, lovey?'

Of course it's awful.

I nod; she hands me a tissue.

'He'll be OK,' she says. 'I can feel it in my bones.'

She said that about Callum. She was wrong.

'I know I said that about my son,' she says, reading my mind, 'but this is different. No one could harm such a lovely little boy.'

I sob even harder when I think of the types of people who would harm such a lovely little boy. I want to scratch the images from my mind.

'It's like history repeating itself.' She looks around the room as I wipe my face. 'Same house, same time of year. But at least it's daylight. The search will be easier. It was terrible, then. I often thought that if it had been daylight then we would've had a chance to find my Callum.'

I want to scream at her and tell her to shut up about bloody Callum, but he's her son. Imagine if we don't find Noah and someone said that to me in ten years' time.

'I can't just stand here,' I say. 'We have to find him. We need to find him now, today, tonight. If we don't find him in the first twenty-four hours...'

'Come on.' Matt takes hold of my hand. 'We're not bloody staying in this house while our son is out there somewhere with God knows who.'

TWENTY-SIX

Noah has been missing for almost three hours. I'm no longer in my wedding dress, but in this morning's clothes that were draped across the bedroom chair. Anything but the white dress, and something that would enable me to help with the search.

I feel as though I'm outside my body, which is now ploughing through tall grass, my arms sweeping left and right to clear a path. I dread every swipe. What if I find him? I know I said I wanted to be the one, but the reality is much starker, bleaker, and heartbreaking.

I once read about a little French boy who went missing fifteen years ago. He wasn't much older than Noah, and his family have only recently found his remains not far from where he went missing. The agony they must be feeling. They still don't know what happened to him, his remains were—

No. I mustn't think of it.

I can't let myself go there. While we don't know, there is hope. Ignorance that's not so much blissful, but optimistic.

'I'll find you, Noah,' I say aloud. 'I have to find you.'

Katherine is a few paces behind, and we have been silent for almost thirty minutes because there's nothing to say. We don't want to voice the various possibilities.

'What's that?' she asks.

I pause, turn around. She's looking across the water.

'Did Noah have his football with him?'

'No,' I say. 'But it was outside the house. No one has seen it since this morning.'

I squint into the distance. A black and yellow dot, bouncing along with the ripples of the water, about a hundred metres away along the bank.

Wordlessly we break into a run, following the water's edge. The mud is dry, but these stupid trainers are useless, and I worry my legs will fail me.

Katherine blows on the whistle, one of many handed out by the search and rescue team. She waves with both arms, and points, trying to catch the attention of the officers on the boat. They're close to the bobbing object, but they don't seem to have spotted it.

Katherine catches me up, blowing the piercing whistle in between breaths as we run, gaining momentum the closer we get.

'It looks like his ball.' I'm so breathless, the path's incline is so steep. Finally, we come to a drop.

At last. The people in the boat have seen us.

The black and yellow ball is caught in the reeds. It has his name written on it from when he took it to playschool. He scribbled some extra circles next to my writing, in the attempt to write his surname and age. His lovely little hands, and perfect little fingers.

I can't bear this.

If anyone has hurt him, I don't know what I'll do.

The static from the radios they speak into carries across the wind.

We're almost there. The ground is getting harder to walk

on; we're so close to the water my trainers are beginning to stick in the mud.

'Is it Noah's?' I shout.

Ten metres away. A man is casting a fishing net.

'No,' I shout. 'Wait for me. I have to see it first.'

What if my little boy is next to the ball? What if he's still clinging to it in the cold, cold water?

I slow when close to the edge.

It's a black and yellow ball.

They're pulling the rod into the boat.

'Is it his?' I shout again.

They glance at each other. A man sombrely nods.

I brave a glance into the water. I can't see my baby like this, still, lifeless. The police officer was right. I'm not strong enough for this.

The boat coasts towards the place the ball was bobbing.

'Is Noah there?' Katherine's arms are around my waist. 'Is Noah there?'

A woman in diving gear tumbles gracefully backwards into the water.

It's an agonising five minutes when she finally resurfaces.

She shakes her head exaggeratedly.

Thumbs down to the boat.

I collapse onto the muddy ground.

'Does that mean he's not there?' I say.

'I think so.' Katherine lands next to me. 'I think so.'

'I need to go back to the house.'

She puts her arm around my shoulders and pulls me close.

'I know,' she says. 'Let's get you back. We can wait there.'

TWENTY-SEVEN

Olivia has sent the day wedding guests home, but Teresa and Sandra remain. They've laid out sandwiches and hot drinks on a large table outside the house for the officers and volunteers who are searching for my son. Finally, Olivia has heard from the original caterers who have apparently been taken ill but that's the least of our worries right now. There are far more important things to be thinking about.

Matt is out searching with Greg because he can't just sit around, waiting. Finding the ball this afternoon was all it took to make me realise I do not want to be the one to find my little boy if only his body remains. I can't believe I'm thinking like this. I pull his duvet close to my chest. Whenever we travel, he has to have his covers from home. It smells of him. His shampoo, his sleep, the smell of his scalp that he still has from when he was only a few days old.

I can't bear this.

I really can't.

I want something to knock me out so I can wake up when he's back and everything will return to normal.

But I can't do that. I'd be letting him down. I can't just check out when things become unbearable.

Outside, the sun is setting, and I don't want anyone to be the first to say it. I can see their pensive expressions when they – Olivia, Katherine, Dad – look to the sky at the helicopters that now shine spotlights on the ground in the fading light.

'Are you OK, Dad?'

He's sitting at the window on the footstool, but the skin on his face is grey.

'It's all my fault,' he says. 'If I'd have been looking after him, he wouldn't have been taken.'

'You were walking me down the aisle, Dad. It's not your fault. It's no one's fault except the person who took him. I'm his mother. I should never have let him go. If it's anyone's fault, it's mine.'

Unless it's the light making his skin look like that.

'Dad?'

Still holding Noah's quilt, I get up from the sofa and kneel at his side.

'I'm just feeling a bit funny,' he says, 'that's all.'

Sweat is beaded on his forehead, down the side of his face.

'Dad?'

He puts a hand on his chest.

'I... I... I can't breathe, Leah. I... I'm sorry.'

I jolt up from the floor, rush into the hall. It's faster with a landline – they can trace where you are more quickly.

It answers after two rings.

'Ambulance, please. I think my dad's having a heart attack.'

After confirming the address, I drop the handset into the cradle.

In the living room, Dad's on the floor; Jennie's laying his head on the carpet.

'What happened?' I kneel next to him. 'Dad, are you OK?'

His eyes are closed. Jennie's a picture of calm. How can she be so calm? 'Is he breathing?'

'Yes, he's breathing.' She takes hold of his wrist, looks at her watch. 'Pulse seventy-five.' She places his arm on the ground. 'Has he had a heart attack before?'

'No.'

Unless he's kept it from me. But he wouldn't keep something like that from me.

'Is he on any medication?'

'I don't think so.'

'Go check his bags.'

I put my hand on Dad's shoulder.

'I can't leave him. What if...?'

'If he has heart medication, he needs to take it.'

I spring up, run up the stairs.

'What's happening, Leah?' Olivia's standing at the kitchen door holding a glass of water.

'We think Dad's having a heart attack. I've called an ambulance.'

The bedroom door whacks the chest of drawers as I press it open, almost slamming me as it ricochets. Dad's little brown leather suitcase is next to his bed and I almost cry at the sweetness of it.

Inside, there's a zip lock bag, but the only medication inside is paracetamol, Gaviscon, Rennie, and Ramipril. He told me he's on that for lowering his blood pressure. I take the bag downstairs, handing it to Jennie.

'Dad?'

He's still breathing, but his eyes are firmly shut.

'Dad?' I look up to Jennie. 'Shouldn't we keep him awake?'

'I tried, love. I tried.'

Olivia appears at the living-room door.

'The ambulance is almost here. They had one on standby with the searching of the lake. I'll show them through.'

Moments later, two paramedics are inside.

I stand back as they try to rouse Dad. Take his vital signs.

A technician rushes in, pushing a gurney, and I watch helplessly as they lift Dad on. They place a mask over his face.

'Is one of you coming?' the woman asks.

'My son is missing.' The tears stream down my face. 'I can't leave the area while my son is missing.'

This is an actual living nightmare.

'I'll go with him.' Jennie picks up her handbag and Dad's medication. 'I'll give you a ring when we know more.'

I follow outside and Matt's running towards us from the road.

'Have you found Noah?' he yells. 'Is he OK?'

I rush into his arms as Dad's lifted into the ambulance.

'It's Dad. He's having a heart attack.'

'Oh my God.'

The doors are slammed shut and the ambulance siren sounds as it navigates up the drive.

'What if I lose them both in one day?' I bury my face in Matt's once-white shirt. 'I can't bear it. I can't believe this is happening.'

He puts his hand on my head, protecting me from the breeze from the lake that's getting stronger. 'He's going to the right place.'

I pull away from him and he takes a tissue from his pocket to wipe my face.

'What happened?' he asks.

'He went grey, said he felt funny. He had loads of indigestion remedies in his bag. He probably didn't realise it might've been a heart problem.'

'We can't diagnose him. It might be something completely different. Peter – a bloke at our office – said he thought he was dying once, but it was a panic attack. It might be that.'

'I guess.'

'He's so close to Noah. He'll be in shock like the rest of us.'

Matt takes out his phone.

'Do you want to give me Jennie's number,' he says. 'I can ask her to update me. Just in case.'

In case of what, I don't ask.

I take out my phone with a sinking feeling.

'I don't think I have her number.' My heart rate rises. 'I can't believe I let her go with Dad not having her number.'

'Don't worry, don't worry.' Matt puts his arm around my shoulders and guides me back into the house. 'I'll give the hospital a ring in an hour or so.'

'We might've found Noah by then.' My voice sounds more optimistic than I feel. 'Maybe?'

'I'm praying we do, and I'm not sure I actually believe in God.'

'We need all the help we can get.'

We're in the living room again. I hate this room. It holds too many bad memories. What were we thinking, coming back here?

TWENTY-EIGHT

The police have expanded the search, and we're seeing most of it through *Sky News*. They had cameras and a reporter in the area within an hour of Noah going missing. It makes me think of the children they've covered before, and the outcome was so devastating. I shouldn't be watching it; I know I shouldn't. But even just looking at the screen is making me feel as though I'm part of the search.

Some of the reporting teams have arrived and they're filming at the cordon across the lake. It's quite grim, really. I'm sitting so close to the television I can see details in the reeds. It's like I am looking from here. They pan across to the village. Posters are being taped to lampposts. How have they managed to get them printed so quickly? My heart warms when I think of all the people – mostly strangers – who are coming together to try to find my little boy. Whoever has taken him can't have made it too far away. There were only thirty seconds tops since we discovered Noah was missing. There were no boats on the lake near the house, no cars came to and from the driveway.

They're interviewing a woman I recognise from the corner shop. Noah and I went in there yesterday afternoon with Dad for him to choose an ice cream. Dad lifted him up so he could look in the deep freeze. Held him like Superman. He had picked up three, like a grabber machine in an arcade, but I made him choose only one. Why hadn't I let him have all three? He's only little for such a short while. If he comes back to me, I will make sure he feels special all the time. He can have whatever he wants.

There I go again, wishful thinking.

His little face – in a photo taken last week when we went to the park – is in the top right corner of the television screen. I lift a hand to stroke his little face.

'Hang in there, my love. We're going to find you.'

My phone is constantly beeping with messages of support from people I barely know. The ones with children no doubt thinking, *I'm glad it's not me.* They'll be hugging their little ones closer. I imagine they think it's my fault. Who lets a three-year-old just run around by themselves? You can't trust anyone these days. And more sinister thoughts of: *I wonder if one of the parents had anything to do with it?* Because nine times out of ten it is someone close to the victim.

I can't think of Noah as a victim.

I think my heart is physically breaking, it hurts so much.

I look across at Matt.

'Could you ring the hospital again? They might know more, now.'

'I rang them ten minutes ago,' he says gently. 'It was too soon to have any information.'

'That's a good sign, isn't it?' I say hopefully. 'If it were the worst news, they'd have asked us to come in.'

That's what happened with Mum. Even though the doctors said she had three months. In the end, it was two. I felt like I'd been robbed. Even though we had said all the things we had wanted to say. Did she know? She always said she didn't want us to see her pass away. Wanted us to remember her with a light in her eyes.

'Yes,' he says. 'It's a good sign.'

Matt doesn't sound convinced. I know he's trying to make me feel better. If everything wasn't happening at once, he wouldn't feel the need to fill me with false hope, but he knows I can only take so much heartbreak.

I glance at the clock.

'Will you call in thirty minutes?'

A focus. A countdown. Anything could happen in thirty minutes. Noah might be home in thirty minutes. Perhaps he's fallen asleep somewhere. He had a broken night's sleep last night, so it's possible.

Possible, but not probable.

My phone beeps again.

It's from a number, not a contact.

It could be Jennie – she could've got my number from Dad's phone.

It's not.

> Come with me and your son lives. Meet me by the blue boathouse at the entrance to the marina and come alone. If you tell anyone, you will never see your son again. All my love, Callum x

TWENTY-NINE

Matt hasn't noticed that I'm stunned; I'm still facing the television. The blue boathouse is only five minutes' walk away. Surely the police would've found them if they were in there.

I tap out a reply.

> Please don't hurt Noah.

A red exclamation mark appears above the words *Message not delivered.*

The phone has been switched off, or the SIM discarded.

I stand slowly.

I expect Matt to ask me what's wrong, but no one is acting normal right now. I'm about to meet the person who claims to know everything about that night, and I don't want Matt to hear what they have to say.

And if I can get to the boathouse with no one stopping or following me, then I might get my son back.

Or it could be a cruel joke.

There might be no one in the boathouse.

Then I can tell the police. They could trace the number. See who's behind it, although I've already given them the number that the messages to Greg came from, and they've not mentioned anything about that.

The sound of a helicopter comes from above the house, and from the television. People are going to see me.

Unless I go through the back, through the trees and bushes that the police have already searched. Go up to the road and back down again.

I turn to Matt, hold up my phone, and say, 'I'm going out to get a better signal at the road up there.'

'Hmm.'

He's engrossed in both his phone and the television, gorging on what information he can get.

If you tell anyone, you will never see your son again.

The hall is empty, so is the kitchen. Everyone must be searching.

I grab a hoodie off the back of one of the chairs, put it on and pull up the hood.

There's no one in the back garden, either.

I look up to the path I need to take. It's steep, but there are a few rocks and trees to help my ascent. If anyone sees me with this hood up, I'll look suspicious. Garner more attention than if I was just a mother searching everywhere for her son. I flip it off.

A surge of adrenaline boosts my steps up the hill. The passing cars seem to whoosh in front of me, but they're still metres ahead.

'Hey!'

A shout in the distance.

I pause. Hide behind a tree. My heart is pounding so hard.

I get out my phone and turn off my location services. No one can find me. I can't have Noah's safety put at risk. Even though I have no idea what I'm walking into. Several faces come to mind. Tania. Still in love with Matt and hates that we're together. Katherine or Jake for thinking I was partly to blame for Callum blackmailing him. Olivia, Greg. Do they believe I wanted to tear their marriage apart – that it was really me messaging him? Matt. No, it can't be Matt. He's the one person I can count on, surely.

I have to face this, or these thoughts will never stop.

I can finally put an end to the nightmares. To the feeling that someone is constantly watching me.

Just one more push to road level. I grab the trunk of a small tree and heave myself up. There's a gap in the traffic. On this side, there's no pavement. Luckily, I'm wearing sweatpants. I could be a jogger. Nothing to see.

I break into a light run; the boathouse is only minutes away, but there are police and people everywhere. What would I say if they were to stop me?

I cross over onto the pavement.

Two police officers are deep in conversation in front of the path I need to take.

I'll have to approach it from the other end.

I pull up my hood. There's a group of teenagers walking towards me; their bantering has caught the officers' attention, and they call them over.

The lads walk over willingly and my heart warms again at the willingness of strangers to help find my child.

I cross again as I come to the gravel road that leads to the marina. The place is quiet. It's already been searched.

My heart is racing, my body is trembling as I approach the blue wooden boathouse.

I pause as an engine starts close by. It's another search boat a hundred metres further down.

The name plaque on the door has fallen from one of its nails and the wood is rotten, with only a few strands of paint remaining. There's a fluorescent sticker next to the window, which I presume means it has already been searched. The door handle is hanging off; I just have to pull it open, but first I listen at the door.

Silence.

If Noah was inside, there'd be no way he'd be able to stay quiet, especially if he heard my voice.

'Noah?' I say it into the gap in the door. 'Noah, it's me: Mummy.'

I half-expect him to come barging out, delighted to see me after almost six hours of not.

'Shh.' Hisses a voice. 'Get inside.'

My hand shakes as I grip the edge of the door. It drags on the ground and judders as I force it open.

It's dark inside. I see no one; the corners are shrouded in darkness.

My instinct is to run away, get help. Call for the police.

My phone is in my hand, ready to dial 999.

'Whoever you are, let my son go. Why the hell are you doing this? What have I ever done to you?'

My voice sounds a hundred times braver than I feel.

A crunch, a footstep on the floor.

A trouser leg lit by the dim light from the small window.

He steps into view, and I almost collapse to the floor. My knees give way. I grip on the wall, a splinter digging into my palm, but it stings for only a second.

He looks so much thinner than I've ever seen him. His head's shaved. There's about a week's worth of beard on his face. He's wearing combat trousers; a walking jacket. He could easily be a hiker – we see hundreds a day around here.

'Callum.'

He takes another step. Tilts his head to the side. Takes his hands out of his pockets and clasps them in front.

'You look like you've seen a ghost, Leah.' He walks slowly

towards me. 'I thought you'd be happy to see me after all this time.'

'I thought you were dead.'

'Yes.' His eyes are dark, a wicked smile on his face. 'I bet you did.'

THIRTY

EIGHT YEARS AGO

Three hours until Callum's disappearance

There's a footstep on the creaky floorboard outside the bedroom.

I slide the stuff under the bathmat. Stand. Flush the toilet. Run the tap. In the mirror, smooth my hair. Face is flushed. Heart hammering.

A bang on the door.

'Leah!'

It's Callum. I knew it would be Callum.

'Won't be a sec,' I say lightly. 'Don't you know it's rude to—'

'I know you have my stuff in there with you. I need it back.'

'I've no idea what—'

'You're not stupid, Leah.' He's speaking ominously quiet. 'And neither am I. Open the door.'

I glance at the floor. It's not obvious the envelope is there.

I sweep open the door, chin up.

'What the hell are you talking about?' I say. 'You're pissed again.'

I push past him, head to the bedroom door. He rushes past me, blocking my exit.

'Let me leave, Callum.'

I try to push him to the side, but he grabs hold of my wrists, squeezing them tightly.

'Fuck off, Callum.' I twist, turn, yet his hold is strong. 'Get the hell off me.' I let out a guttural scream; he clamps a hand over my mouth.

With my free arm, I jab my elbow into his chest.

'What the hell, Leah?' He sounds winded. 'You're like some feral dog.'

I jab him again.

'Leah! Calm the fuck down.'

I stand still; the only movement is the pounding from my chest.

'That's my girl,' he says. Smug bastard. 'If I move my hand from your mouth, will you promise you won't scream?'

I nod, slowly, deliberate.

'I'm going to sit you on the bed and when I move my hand, I will tell you everything. OK?'

'Uh hmm.'

Fury is building in my chest. How fucking dare he?

If Jake were to walk in right now, I have no doubt he would kill Callum, or at the very least seriously harm him.

Callum pulls me towards the bed; he sits, and I have no choice but to follow.

'OK?' His eyes bore into mine.

I nod again.

He takes his hand slowly off my mouth.

My eyes are fixed on his. I press my lips shut.

I blink away the tears that threaten to fall; I don't want him to see me cry.

'Go on,' I say, monotone. 'Tell me where all that money in

your account has come from and why you're behaving like some sort of criminal.'

He puts a hand over his face, rubs his eyes.

'I'm so sorry, Leah. I didn't want it to be like this. It was supposed...'

I stare straight ahead at the pink flowery wallpaper with tiny daisies. I rub his back.

'There, there, Callum. Everything will be OK. I'm on your side.'

If anyone else were listening, I think they'd believe me too.

'I'm in a spot of bother,' he says. 'Bit of an understatement, actually.'

'Are you talking about the photographs you have of my brother?' I try to keep my voice calm, but it's hard. I want to lash at him with all the fury that's been building over this weekend.

It takes a moment for him to register my words.

'Oh, that,' he says dismissively. 'God, no. That's nothing.' He sighs wistfully. 'I don't know what it's like to have a sibling. It's only ever been my mum and me. Her and me against the world. That's what she used to say all the time.' He shakes his head, back into the present. 'I'm going away, Leah. Tonight, as it happens. I'll swim across the width of the lake. I can do it easily – I've been practising in the evenings. I have a boat on the other side, tucked up somewhere no one will find. Just until everything blows over. It's only money, isn't it? Five grand here, ten grand there. People will stop worrying about that once I've gone. That's what people say when someone dies and they inherit, isn't it? *I'd rather have him back than have the money.*'

'How many people did you take money from, Callum?'

'Oh, I've lost count. People can be so gullible when they believe they'll make double of what they invest. It serves them right for being stupid, doesn't it? There's no such thing as easy money. Well, not to them anyway.' He lets out a dry laugh. 'I've withdrawn it all now, though. It's safe.'

My heart is hammering. For all this time I was thinking of leaving Callum and now he's laid out his plan to just flit off into the night without me. And he's conned countless people in the process.

'What?' is all I can say. 'What?'

He pats me on the leg.

'Chill, Leah. It's going to be fine. I'll let you know where I am, and then you can join me.'

'Chill? You weren't even going to tell me all of this, were you? You were going to have me think you'd disappeared.'

'It was for the best you knew nothing about it. Now, you're going to have to pretend you know nothing.'

'This is ridiculous.'

'You know how hard it's been trying to be perfect for you, Leah? The pressure that's put me under. Everyone thinks I'm a joke.'

The rage is boiling inside me. Always the bloody victim. This man will never change. Who else has he stolen money from? Whose lives has he ruined? Leaving a trail of destruction, only to flee and cause havoc somewhere else.

I press my hands together. Stabilise my breathing.

'They don't think you're a joke,' I say steadily.

'Everyone thinks I'm a fuck up. I know they do. And now I'm about to prove it.' He pauses, tilts his head, smiles. 'And you won't tell a soul – at least not tonight. I'll tell them you're crazy – that you're making things up.' He strokes the side of my face. 'I love you, Leah. I'm sorry for getting so cross before. Everything will be OK. Trust me.' He leans to kiss my cheek, and I have to ball up my fists to not shirk from his touch. 'I promise you.' He places a finger on my lips. 'And all you have to do is keep your pretty little mouth shut. Deal?'

I nod, again.

I don't want to be here.

Or rather, I don't want Callum to be here.
I don't want to be anywhere near him anymore.

THIRTY-ONE

NOW

'Where's Noah, Callum?'

I was never physically afraid of Callum until that night eight years ago. He's a virtual stranger to me now and could be capable of anything.

'Is that all you have to say after so long?' he asks. 'I thought this would be a happy reunion.'

'Noah's all that matters to me.'

'I wouldn't let Matt hear you say that.' There's a smirk on his face. 'How is snivelling Matt?'

'Where is he, Callum?' I take out my phone. 'If you don't tell me now, I'm calling the police.'

He whips the phone out of my hands.

'Ha.' He slips it into his jacket pocket. 'Too slow.'

I step towards him. The urge to retrieve it is strong, but I don't know this person. Is he armed? Would he hurt me now? What has he been through since he's been gone?

'Please, just tell me where he is.'

He raises a palm. Calm down.

'Relax,' he says. 'The kid's fine.'

'Relax?' I shriek so loud and piercingly he winces. 'How am I meant to relax when my son has been snatched?'

'Snatched.' He rolls his eyes. 'Stop being so dramatic. Did you like my little party trick?' He holds up a balled fist, then flicks open his hand. 'Puff! Gone like magic. Smoke and mirrors.'

'Were you there at my wedding?'

'Ah, you see, I had a special little helper. She's been helping me for years.'

'Was it Tania?'

My breathing quickens, I feel as though I might hyperventilate.

'There's only one woman you can count on in life, Leah,' he says.

'Why are you doing this, Callum? Why, after so many years? I thought you were dead.'

'Yes.' He steps closer, runs a finger down the side of my face. 'Yes, you did.'

'It wasn't an unreasonable assumption, Callum. It's been years!'

'And then, THEN! I hear that you don't feel guilty anymore. Fuck, you played the grieving widow, for how long? A year, tops? before you got together with Matt.' He begins pacing the floor. 'A child, yes. I knew you wanted a child. I let you have that. I thought, *Go Leah, have a kid with the rich guy and that's you sorted for life*. It will help you get over the grief and the guilt of killing me. But no. You go ahead and arrange a wedding! At the same place I disappeared from! You're some piece of work, Leah. And everyone thinks you're this beautiful little victim. How wrong they are.' He barks a manic laugh – his eyes are wild. 'I started small, I know that. The taxis and the takeaways at two in the morning. It was too subtle.'

'That was you?'

He laughs again. But it's like I'm not actually in the same building – he's not hearing what I'm saying.

'I know I joked about you getting together with Matt for his money,' he says, continuing his rant, 'but I didn't think you'd actually go through with it.'

'What the hell are you talking about?'

'Don't say you've never thought about it. Matt's parents are millionaires. I wouldn't be surprised if Matt's not far behind.'

'I don't think about money.'

'That's what people who have money say. Imagine never worrying about paying the gas bill or your rent. Oh, my bad. You don't have to.'

'You've been keeping tabs on me.'

'Of course I have! You didn't think I'd leave and just forget about what you did to me.'

I think I'm going to be sick; my stomach is churning, my head feels light, as though I'm about to faint.

'How does that make me look?' His eyes narrow. The man is insane. 'Did you think you would get away with it?'

'Has your money run out, Callum?' I feel my way down the wooden wall and collapse onto an upturned cable reel. 'Is that why you're doing this?'

'You owe me, Leah. You've been living a lie for almost ten years. There's no way you're in love with Matt. I could blow your whole life apart.'

'I've always loved Matt. We have a child together. We're a family.'

'Two hundred thousand and you'll never see me again.'

He inches close but I push him back by the shoulders.

'I don't believe you.' I stand closer to the door. 'If I give you money now, you'll never stop.'

He steps nearer. I could slip my hand into his pocket, reach for my phone.

'Tell me where Noah is,' I say firmly, 'and I won't go to the police.'

'Oh, you won't, will you? Maybe I should tell them a few things.' He turns, paces the length of the boathouse. Spins, walks back. 'How fucking dare you!'

He tilts his head to the side again. 'I could get you into a lot of trouble, Leah. I know what you did.'

'I didn't do anything. You're a born bullshitter. A narcissist.'

I can't stop myself. I know I shouldn't be talking like this to the man who knows where my son is.

'You tried to kill me, Leah. And you're not going to get away with it.'

'Don't be so ridiculous, Callum.'

'Deny it all you like, but I know what you did. You thought I'd drown, didn't you? I'm sorry to disappoint you, but I woke up eight hours later to the sound of people shouting my name.'

'What?'

'You thought I was at the bottom of the lake, didn't you? You sound so disappointed. You thought you'd murdered me, and yet here you are, basking in your new life.'

'I didn't try to kill you. Why do you keep saying that?'

'No one has fooled me more than you have. And you played the long game, too. I was quite rich when we got together, wasn't I?'

'Stop judging me by your standards. Not everyone lacks morals like you.' I hold out my hand. 'Give me my phone back.'

He laughs, hollow.

'As if. Do you think I'm stupid?'

'What have you done with Noah?'

'Calm down, calm down. He's somewhere safe.' He glances behind him nervously.

'Is he outside?'

'I'll let you know in good time.'

'Police are everywhere. You're not going to get away with this.'

'How can they arrest me when I don't exist? I'm legally dead. I could disappear again, and no one will look for me. I can do whatever I want and not face the consequences.'

'It's what you've done all your life, Callum. As if the authorities will hold up the declaration when you're right here.'

The door behind me flies open.

It's Matt.

'Holy shit.' Matt pauses at the doorway. 'I thought it was your voice. What the fuck?' He walks slowly towards Callum, taking in his friend's slighter frame, the lighter hair. 'I can't believe it. I can't believe you're alive. Where have you been?'

'Around. Scotland, France. Have myself a new name. Amazing what a waster of a father can get for you at the right price. I can't believe you moved in on my wife. Actually, strike that. I *can* believe it.'

'She's not your wife.'

'*She* is right here!' I step between the two of them. 'Matt, phone the police.'

'You don't want to be hasty,' says Callum. 'I don't know how much you heard just then, but Leah here is only marrying you for your money.'

'As if he's going to believe you,' I say. 'A proven con artist.'

'I don't believe him. It's OK, Leah.' Matt rests a hand on my shoulder. 'It really is OK. I know what he's saying isn't true.'

His gaze is so intense, it's like he's conveying a hundred words.

'We're going to be OK,' he says. 'We just need to find Noah.'

'Hey!' There's banging on the back of the boathouse. A dog barking. 'Hey!' It's a woman's voice. 'The little boy is out here.'

I scramble out of the shed, leaving Matt and Callum inside, and dart round to the back.

There's a small white Fiat 500 parked there. Has that car always been there? Standing next to it is a woman in her late sixties with a dog that's sniffing around it. She's pulling on the door handle.

'I saw you heading over here,' she says, 'and my dog went mad when we came near the car. It's locked, though. I heard on the news and thought me and Ziggy would come out to help.' She yells to police officers in the distance. 'He's in here. We found the little boy! He's in here. We need help, quickly!'

I race to the car to see Noah, lying motionlessly on the back seat.

'Stand back.' I bend to pick up a rock. 'I'm going to break the glass.'

THIRTY-TWO

'Wait!' Matt's next to me. 'Smash it from the driver's side, so the glass doesn't cut Noah.'

I break the glass with three sharp hits against the window. I cover my hand with my sleeve to reach in and unlock the door. I clamber into the back, and pick up Noah under his arms, resting his warmness against my chest, breathing in his hair. I stroke his smooth cheek with the back of my hand.

I feel it.

I feel him breathing against me.

Thank you, God.

I turn him around and let his head drop into the crook of my arm.

'Noah, love? Can you hear me?'

Matt has unlocked the passenger door, he crouches next to me, phone in his hand.

'The lady's calling an ambulance.' He stands, wiping a speck of blood from his cheek.

'Whose blood is that?'

'Let's get Noah out of the car, Leah,' he says. 'Come on. We don't know if Callum has harmed him.'

'He's OK,' I say, willing it to be true. 'He's just sleeping.' Tears run down my face. 'That's all. He's still warm, Matt.'

'Get out the car, Leah. Please,' he coaxes. 'We need to make sure he's all right. Then you can hold him again, I promise.'

I shuffle out of the car, pulling Noah closer to me. I don't want to let him go. 'He's my little boy.'

'It's going to be OK, Leah. But we have to check. Get him the help he needs, if he's not. Yes?'

I look down at my sleeping boy. His eyelashes so perfect, his lips slightly parted. But his cheeks are so pale.

I nod slowly.

Matt gently prises Noah from my arms and lays him on the jacket he's put down on the ground.

I kneel on the floor, taking hold of Noah's hand.

'Can you hear me, Noah?' The tears won't stop falling; they drop onto Noah's little waistcoat. 'What's that?' I point to brownish stains on his shirt. 'Is it blood? What has Callum done to him?'

'I don't know.' Matt's trying to sound calm, but I hear the panic in his voice. 'Noah, can you hear us, love?'

Noah takes in a deep breath. Sighs loudly as he exhales.

His eyelids start to flutter, before he finally opens them.

He fixes his gaze on my face; it takes him a moment to focus.

'Mummy,' he says sleepily. 'You found me.'

'Yes, I found you, baby.'

I look up, around, and my gaze lands on the beautiful woman who I will be eternally grateful to. She gives me a warm smile in return.

Matt bends to kiss Noah on the cheek.

'I'm so glad you're OK, little man.'

'Daddy.' Noah tries to sit, but it's too much effort for him. 'You got mud on your face.'

Matt laughs. His tears streak through the dirt as he wipes his face with the back of his hand.

I hear the sound of footsteps running towards us.

It's PC Harry Fern.

'Is he OK?' He kneels down. 'You OK there, Noah?'

'Yeah.'

Noah's eyes keep closing; he's so tired.

'The ambulance isn't far off,' says the officer. 'Did Noah say anything about who took him?'

'It was Callum. My ex-husband. He's alive.'

'What?'

'He was in there.'

I point to the boathouse.

PC Fern stands and calls out to three officers walking towards us on the gravel path.

Matt stands as they head towards the ramshackle building.

'Wait,' he shouts. 'Can I have a word, officer?'

I kiss my little boy's cheeks as I try to listen to what Matt is saying.

'He came at me,' he says. 'I just pushed him back, defended myself. He'd taken my son.'

'What's happened, Matt?' The policeman's tone is sombre.

'I pushed him... Callum. He hit his head on a metal rung. I don't think he's conscious... or breathing. I didn't mean to...'

The officer rushes into the building as three policemen guard the entrance.

Moments later, Harry Fern radios for another ambulance as Matt returns to where we're sitting.

'What did you do, Matt?'

He's pale; sweat is dripping down his temples.

'I think Callum's dead.' Tears gather in his eyes. 'He lunged at me, and I couldn't just stand there and let him go for me – or leave and come for you. I pushed him and...' He rests his head in his hand. 'I think I've just killed my best friend.'

'You mean...?'

The colour has drained from Matt's face.

'Callum's dead.'

I thought he had died years before but seeing him only minutes ago erased that from my mind. A part of me wants to see him – to look at him for one last time: a ghost that's been exorcised. This is an awful nightmare that's never ending.

Snap out of it, Leah.

I take hold of Matt's free hand and squeeze it.

'You were trying to protect us, Matt. The police will see that.'

'But how am I going to live with that?'

I look down at Noah; eyes flicker open, his lips give a small smile.

'You will live with it. You've got to. For your son, for me.'

I look at my beautiful child. I'm so grateful he's back with me. No one is going to take him away from me again.

* * *

The ambulance finally arrives; it crunches down the small road, coming to a stop. Two paramedics race to Noah's side.

'Who do we have here, then?' asks the woman, crouching on the floor.

'Noah,' he says, bless him.

'Would you like to take a trip in an ambulance?'

As she's talking to him, the man is taking his pulse.

'Yes!' says Noah, rousing a little more. 'With Mummy. Not that other man.'

'And Daddy?' says Matt, smiling as the paramedic scoops Noah into her arms.

'Yeah. Daddy can come.'

We follow him into the back of the ambulance as they lay him on a stretcher. He looks so little.

'What happened, Noah?' the woman asks. 'Did something happen to you to make you so sleepy?'

'Hot chocolate,' he says. 'Man gave me hot chocolate.'

THIRTY-THREE

Noah's sitting up in his bed on the children's ward. The doctor said he was given a mild sedative, which will be out of his system in a few hours. They're keeping him in overnight for observation, then we can finally get him home.

'Would it be all right,' I say to one of the nurses, 'if I take Noah up to see my dad? He's on a ward on the next floor up?'

She gives a warm smile.

'One sec.' She leaves for a moment before coming back with a wheelchair. 'Do you want to have a ride in this, Noah?'

Noah whips off his cover, slides off the bed and jumps in.

'Well, aren't you getting stronger by the minute?' she says. 'I'll see you shortly.' I take hold of the handles, and she adds, 'Not too long, OK?'

'OK.' I smile. 'Thank you.'

I push him out of the ward and down the long corridor. He stands to press the button that lets us out and we head towards the lift.

'Are you OK?' I ask as I press the button. It opens straight away, and I wheel him inside. He's been asked a thousand times if he's OK, but I don't want him hiding things from me. He hates seeing people upset. I crouch down before him. 'Did that man hurt you?'

'No, Mummy. But I lost my football.'

'We'll have to get you a new one. You can choose one when we get home. You can have three, if you like.'

The lift dings and the doors open.

'It's OK, Mummy. Only want one.'

'You're a good boy, Noah.'

'You're a good girl, Mummy.'

I'm not so sure about that one.

'Your grandad has missed you so much.'

I break into a light jog.

'Weeee!' Noah giggles. 'Grandad, you see me?'

We turn into the ward. Dad has a bed by the window.

His face beams when he sees Noah.

'My lad!' he says. 'Are you getting the same fancy treatment I'm getting?'

Noah scrambles out of the wheelchair and climbs up onto Dad's bed.

'Yeah,' he says.

'What have you had to eat so far?' Dad asks Noah.

'Toast,' says Noah. 'And orange squash.'

'Ooh,' he says. 'I love a bit of toast. I wish I'd had toast, but I'm on a special diet.' Dad rolls his eyes. 'I've got soup for my lunch, and salad for my tea. Hmm,' he adds drily, 'can't wait.'

Dad had a mild heart attack, but you'd never guess it from looking at him now the colour's back in his cheeks. That, combined with him putting on his best face to Noah, makes it seem as though nothing happened.

At least the doctors will keep a good eye on him in here.

Dad reaches over to the cabinet next to him.

'Wheel that table over here, will you, love?' he says to me. 'Katherine bought me these puzzle books. Noah, do you fancy drawing me a picture? Then I can look at it and think of you when you're not here.'

'Yeah.' Noah swivels to face the table and grabs a pen. 'Gonna draw you playing football.'

'That's a fella.' Dad nods his head towards the window; I walk around to the other side. 'Any news from Matt?'

I take out my phone.

'Callum was declared dead just over an hour ago. I can't believe it. They've taken Matt's statement; he'll be here soon. I'm so glad you're OK. You said Katherine bought you some puzzle books?'

Dad nods.

'What happened to Jennie?'

He narrows his eyes. 'She had a strange turn,' he says. 'She said she'd done something truly horrible and that she hopes we forgive her.'

I reach over for Dad's hand. 'It was Jennie who was helping Callum.'

'How did we not see that?' Dad asks.

Jennie who's been playing the grieving mother, when she was the one helping her son out for years. *There's only one woman you can count on in life, Leah.* She was probably the contact on his phone. Telling Callum that she would do anything for him – that he was a shadow of himself because of me. And the things he's told her since he left – that I'm a murderer. No wonder she played the role so well. My God, she was good at it. I can't believe I thought it was Tania who was stalking us – for years I had believed it.

'It's a lot to process, Dad.'

'It is. And I have nothing but time in here to think about it.' He glances at the ceiling. 'Thank the Lord I live to see a lot more of you and Noah. I'll never joke about *that* again. Your mum will have to wait a lot longer, touch wood.'

I lean over to kiss his cheek. 'Amen to that. I'll get Noah back to his bed. Hopefully, Matt will be back soon.'

'Will you two come back for a visit later?'

'Yes,' I say. 'Of course we will!'

Noah climbs back into his wheelchair.

'S'you later, Grandad!' he says, gripping onto the handles.

'See you later, Dad.' I turn the chair one-eighty and make to leave before Dad shouts my name.

'I'm so proud of you, you know,' he says, his eyes glistening. 'My beautiful brave girl.'

THIRTY-FOUR

ONE YEAR LATER

We're at the register office, but Matt still wanted to wait for me at the altar, which is actually just a desk. Our only guests are Noah, Olivia and Greg, Katherine and Jake, and my dad who's standing next to me.

'Third time lucky, eh?' he says straightening his tie.

'Yes, very funny, Dad.' He's so much stronger after twelve months of both recuperation and gentle exercise. 'Let's get this over with, shall we?'

'What are you like?' he says. 'Nothing will spoil this one.'

'Well, now you've gone and said it.'

Dad pushes open the heavy mahogany doors and we walk into what looks like a court room, where Matt and our little boy are waiting. I can't believe our son looks so grown-up in his suit. He's starting school this year, so I have to learn to let him go. It'll be hard, even when I know he'll be relatively safe.

But I don't have to worry about Callum any longer. He's no longer a noose around my neck – a threat to my family.

Because what I started all those years ago, Matt finished for me.

THIRTY-FIVE
EIGHT YEARS AGO

Thirty minutes before Callum's disappearance

I was stirring hot chocolate in a pan on the hob, and I could hear Callum's voice from the kitchen.

'And, Matt, you can fuck off as well. Call yourself a best mate. You're embarrassing yourself, fawning over Leah. Can anyone else see that?'

An excuse to leave the house. An excuse that will cover me missing for over an hour.

Shouting, shouting, attacking people.

Footsteps, and sniffing.

'Now look what you've done.' Matt was furious. The angriest I'd ever heard him. 'Is it your mission this weekend to piss the whole world off?'

I turned off the hob. Katherine appeared at my side.

'Sorry,' she whispered. 'I sneaked out of there... What the hell has gotten into him?' She peered over my shoulder. 'Ooh is that hot chocolate?'

I said he was stressed; she said we should film Callum. Show him the evidence in case he didn't remember it in the morning.

But he wasn't drunk. There was nothing but apple juice in his glass all evening.

'What's the flask for?' said Katherine.

'I'm making it up for later.' I turned to pour the hot chocolate into it. 'I'm planning on hiding out in the snug until Callum calms down.'

I hated lying to her.

'Good plan,' she said, grabbing a bottle of Prosecco from the fridge and two glasses from the cupboard. 'I'll sneak this in.'

'Excellent.' I screwed the lid on the flask. 'I know how to handle Callum when he's like this, though I'm hoping I won't have to. I'll wait a few minutes before I join you.'

She put her arms around me in a warm hug.

I can't remember what she said after that. I think about it all the time, but right now I can't remember. Only fragments of the conversation come back to me.

I closed my eyes.

Was I really going to do this?

I unscrewed the lid to the flask and opened the kitchen drawer, took out the crushed sleeping tablets in the wrap of tinfoil. Poured them into the hot drink. Got a knife and stirred quickly. Replaced the lid.

He appeared at the kitchen door. Cheeks red from his ranting at people who didn't deserve it.

'Are you going up to bed, now?' he said, as though he hadn't just been shouting in the other room. 'I can't go without saying a proper goodbye.'

I let him hug me, returned his kiss.

And after, I passed him the silver flask.

They never did find that flask.

I hadn't thought of that, then.

'What's this?' he said.

'Hot chocolate. It'll warm you up before you make the

swim. I read online just now that it's good to get heat and carbo-hydrates inside you before you get into the cold water. I'll put it in your coat pocket on my way upstairs.'

What was I thinking would happen to him? That he'd down the drink, then be swimming when tiredness overcame him, and he had no choice but to stop? To sink to the bottom of the lake without resistance?

'That's so nice of you,' he said. 'I love you so much, Leah.'

'I love you too.' I didn't meet his gaze. 'Take care of yourself, Callum.'

A LETTER FROM ELISABETH CARPENTER

Dear Reader,

I want to say a huge thank you for choosing to read *The First Husband*. I hope you enjoyed it and, if you did, I would be very grateful if you could write a review. I'd love to hear what you think, and it makes such a difference helping new readers to discover one of my books for the first time.

I love hearing from my readers – you can get in touch with me through social media or my website. I make sure to reply to every message!

If you want to keep up to date with all my latest releases, just sign up at the following link. Your email address will never be shared, and you can unsubscribe at any time.

www.bookouture.com/elisabeth-carpenter

Very best wishes,

Elisabeth

elisabethcarpenter.co.uk

 facebook.com/ElisabethCarpenterAuthor
x.com/LibbyCPT

ACKNOWLEDGEMENTS

Thank you so much to my brilliant agent, Caroline Hardman. Thank you to Joanna Swainson and Lucy Malone at Hardman & Swainson.

Thank you to my wonderful editor, Ruth Tross, for the notes and suggestions that helped transform this book. Thank you to Susannah Hamilton for brainstorming with me to get maximum twists and turns! Thank you to Jenny Hutton and Janette Currie for the fantastic notes and suggestions. Thank you to Liz Hurst for the wonderful proofreading. Thank you to the brilliant team at Bookouture – you are all amazing!

Thank you to my family and friends for your constant support.

Thank you to my readers – I hope you enjoy this one!

PUBLISHING TEAM

Turning a manuscript into a book requires the efforts of many people. The publishing team at Bookouture would like to acknowledge everyone who contributed to this publication.

Audio
Alba Proko
Sinead O'Connor
Melissa Tran

Commercial
Lauren Morrissette
Hannah Richmond
Imogen Allport

Cover design
The Brewster Project

Data and analysis
Mark Alder
Mohamed Bussuri

Editorial
Ruth Tross
Imogen Allport